LOVE

OVER

GOLD

John G Markowski & Gavin WJ Young

Copyright © 2023 by John Markowski and Gavin WJ Young

All rights reserved. The rights of John Markowski and Gavin WJ Young as the sole authors of this novel must be recognised and adhered to by copyright law. To be identified as the authors of this work has been asserted by them following sections 77 and 78 of the Copyright, Designs and Patents Act, 1988. Commercial copying, hiring, lending, and selling are prohibited and will constitute an infringement of copyright. This book or any proportion thereof may not be reproduced or used in any manner whatsoever without the publisher's express written permission except for the use of brief quotations in a book review or scholarly journal.

First Printing: 2023

ISBN: 9798872128908

Mark2

www.loveovergold.co.uk

Original Cover Artwork: Andrew Weir

Cover Artwork: Brian Pedley

Cover Design: GL Young

Printed in the UK by Amazon.com

Authors' Note

The events within this novel are based on fact, however, we have unashamedly used wide swathes of artistic licence to fill in the gaps. This said, we have endeavoured to portray every character with due respect and have tried to do as much research as we could to make the people, settings and events more authentic. In the parts of the book set in WWII, we decided to keep the names and roles of people as we believed them to be, however in the parts set in the late 70s and early 80s we changed all of the names, to defer any attention from those involved in the happenings who are still alive upon publishing. Overall, it is worth noting that the entire story is seen through the eyes of our very charming, yes, but also very opinionated narrator, who offers his slant throughout the whole tale.

Italian, German, Polish & Russian Words Used In The Story

amore mio - my love (Italian)
ankavagista - nickname for NKVD officers (see: **En-Ka-Va-De**); pronounced: *aankavajista* (Polish)
babcha - Grandmother (Polish)
bajki - fairytales; pronounced: *bayki* (Polish)
bambinos - babies (Italian)
Boża - God, the equivalent of Oh Dear God; pronounced: *bosja, with a soft 'j'* (Polish)
cholera jasna - equivalent of holy shit or God-dammit; pronounced: *holera yasna* (Polish)
Diabła - Devil; pronounced: *diabwa* (Polish)
En-Ka-Va-De - phonetic version of NKVD, which stands for The People's Commissariat for Internal Affairs, the Soviet police force in charge of prisons and prison camps (Russian)
Fangshuss - coup de gráce; literally: catch shot (German)
gotówka - cash (Polish)
Gott - God (German)
grayznaya krysa - dirty/grisly rat; pronounced: *grezne krussia* (Russian)
kieleszka - shot glass, singular; pronounced: *keelishki* (Polish)
kieleszki - shot glass, plural; pronounced: *keelishka* (Polish)
kiełbasa - sausage; pronounced: *kewbassa* (Polish)
kochanie - sweetheart; pronounced: *with a soft 'ch'* (Polish)
komoda - sideboard (Polish)
Kriegsmarine - German navy (German)
Lwów - Eastern city of the Republic of Poland, 1918-1939; now the Ukrainian city of Lviv; pronounced: *Vulvova/Vloff* by Poles)

mamu - mother (Polish)
matka - mother (Polish)
Matka Boża - equivalent of Our Lady; pronounced: *matka bosja, with a soft 'j'* (Polish)
moj drogi - my dear/precious; pronounced: *moy drogi* (Polish)
natürlich - naturally/sure (German)
na zdrowie - cheers; pronounced: *nazdarovya* (Polish)
piccolino - little one (Italian)
proszę - please; pronounced: *porsche* (Polish)
Russki - Russian (Polish; slang)
ser - cheese (Polish)
scurva sin -
sobaka - dog (Polish, Russian, Slovak)
staruszka - old woman; pronounced: *starushka* (Polish)
Strauchritter - bush knight; (German)
suka - bitch (Russian)
sukinsyn - son of a bitch (Russian)
świnia - pig; pronounced: *svinia* (Polish)
szafka - cabinet; pronounced: *shafka* (Polish)
tak - sure/yes (Polish)
Ulica - street; pronounced: *ulitza* (Polish)
Wiśniówka - cherry vodka; pronounced: *vishnoovka* (Polish)
zatknis - shut up (Russian)

Introduction

I'll tell you a story, a true story, of the journey that led my uncle to the largest salvage haul in history, and the uncanny set of circumstances that connects my family to the treasure.

The tale will have us weaving back and forth through time, from the cobbled streets of Lwów, in pre-war Poland, to a decompression chamber off the coast of Peru in the 70s, from a World War II naval convoy on the icy waters of the Barents Sea, to a rickety office on a windswept dock in 80's Netherlands, from the cruel reality of a Siberian gulag in wartime to the peacetime promise of a new life in Italy.

Even for me, being so close to the events that led to my family's fortune, it is an astonishing adventure. And a riveting one too, because all the way, threading itself through with the unmistakable glint of hope and desire, ambition and love, there is *gold*.

John G. Markowski, December 2023

Chapter 1
Streets of Lwów

1939 Lwów, Poland

Josef was running frantically down the hotch-potch cobble streets of Lwów, clutching his gun to his chest, zig-zagging and weaving through the network of alleys and lanes, keeping his head low as he could, not making eye contact with anyone, looking left to right, sometimes even behind him without breaking his pace. He knew the archway to every square of tenement flats and the passage that went through to every road, always aware of which arcade he could run through, which alley he could slip down, should he spot the Russians.

He had fled as soon as he had seen the Reds marching down the main street of the city the evening before, the glint of bayonets and high-step of marching soldiers, flags furling and white horses lifting their hooves proudly - an elegant and frightening sight. Pushing away from the crowds, all of them standing in a haze, numb and uncertain of what this parade meant for them, he took off in the opposite direction. Even as he had run, getting as far away from the clatter of hooves and the stomp of boots echoing through the streets as he could, he had known, for his part, that it was the beginning of the end.

There had been no announcement, no declaration of war. Were they liberators or invaders? As far as Josef was concerned they were enemies. Even though people were desperate to play down the rumours of Russians killing Poles behind their borders, Josef knew full well the truth of it all. He worked at the railway station, that crossroads of information, where news arrived before it even hit the papers - real news, from real people, not edited fluff in propaganda sheets. He had heard of tension in Ukrainian-ruled Kiev from Professor Krasinski, who travelled frequently to and from the University there, where he lectured in economics.

Perpetually wool-clad, with walking stick in hand, never a hair out of place on his perfectly groomed beard, the sophisticated man had often commented on how Josef seemed to be more interested in his viewpoints than his own students and, on occasion, would let the bright young man in on the goings-on politically. Of late, there had been no good news. Over the last few weeks, the professor had been getting increasingly agitated and began to look dishevelled, which was almost as unsettling as the news he brought of Poles having gone missing in Kiev. For no apparent reason. They were just gone.

Two days ago the professor had all but said goodbye to Josef, telling him, shaking so much that his cane tapped on the wooden decking, that one of the other Polish lecturers had disappeared amidst whispers of Russian spies in the University, spiriting people away, and that he feared he was next.

"They are not just rumours, Josef, you need to get out, go," were the last words the professor had said to Josef, as he clutched Josef's arms, eyes filled with intensity, before walking briskly away with his head down, as though he had thought he was being watched.

And it was not just the old man, concerning information had come from the bellhop too. Everyone on the trains ignored the lad, carrying on speaking as though he was transparent. It was not as though he could hang around and listen to a whole conversation, but he was always quick to pick up on the snippets of information he had overheard about passengers and their lives, giving them to Josef in exchange for some halva, chocolate if the information was particularly good and Josef could use it to his advantage. Say, finding out that a regular wealthy passenger, like the accountant from Krakow, liked krupnik, so that he could be sure to place the honey vodka in the gentleman's carriage. This was how Josef would win himself the approval of the station master - which is precisely why he had managed to work his way up to be the master's protégé. That week the bellhop had tipped Josef off about several passengers exchanging rumours of Poles being killed in Russia. People were frightened, and some said that they were getting as far away from the Commies as they could.

And the night train manager, whom everyone disliked for his tendency to take one by the ear like a child under the headmaster's grip if he thought they were being insolent, had also told him outright, completely out of character, with none of his customary disregard, "Save yourself. When the Russians get here you'll be first to go. All of you young men, of fighting age, are in danger."

Standing there with the other onlookers, as the Russians brazenly marched into the city, Josef's usual confidence had diminished with each hoof-fall of the proud horses as they approached. Now it did not seem so brave to walk around like all the other young men who fashioned themselves to be soldiers, should the Germans try to take Lwów, with a gun openly displayed, sticking out the front of his trousers. It just seemed stupid. He knew right away that he would have to stash it, and that was why he had not stayed to watch the parade.

With the onlookers distracted, occupied by the parade pompously working its way to the heart of the city, on the streets beside this spectacle, quietly, cunningly, precisely, street by street, the NKVD were fanning out, spreading like a plague through the inner city suburbs. An entirely separate unit to the Russian army, the NKVD were the judge, the jury and the executioner all in one. Stalin's version of the Gestapo. The untouchables. A law unto themselves.

When Josef went south, he almost ran headlong into the ranks of black-clad troops of secret police, still tightly bound in their ordered squadrons, sets of six being sent off at each junction. Josef then watched in horror as they began immediately to knock on doors and, once opened, to force their way in.

As the evening progressed so did the invasion of the NKVD. Whichever way he turned he could not find a safe haven. In every direction, he would see more of those sinister men in black, and Josef had gradually begun to realise that his options were running out. The Russians must have entered the city from different directions, he thought. They were everywhere - a dark plague engulfing Lwów.

The stifling presence of secret police intensified with each hour. Yet somehow during the night, in his frustration and confusion, Josef would end up behind their lines, to find rows of houses with open doors, contents scattered across the street, dogs barking, wives crying on their knees, children calling for their fathers, for their elder brothers and sisters. The door of his friend's house, where he had hoped to take refuge, was open too.

Sidling up to the doorway of the tiny two-room apartment, he strained his neck round to look inside. Clothes were strewn all over the furniture, most of which had been toppled or broken. Crockery and ornaments were smashed on the floor. It was not enough that the Russians had to take the men, they had looted whatever else they could get their hands on too. There, in the midst of the mess, knelt the grandmother by the window, with a cross in her hands, lips pursed in resentment, anger and loss, quiet tears running down her cheeks.

Josef entered carefully, not wanting to shock the old woman as she rocked back and forth, murmuring a rosary almost inaudibly. He winced as he stood on the remains of a vodka bottle, the hint of cherry hitting his nose, yet she prayed on, lost in her despair. He was about to step over to comfort her when he saw what it was that she was staring at. There in the wall were the tell-tale signs of gunfire. The plaster shattered and a messy hole in the brickwork, and below that, a terrible smear of red. Josef's mind reeled, screaming at the unwanted image that forced its way into his thoughts: his brave friend putting up a fight, being knocked down below the window ledge and shot before he could stand, only to slump down to the floor, dead. What chance had he stood? A teenager with a gun against trained soldiers.

It was only then that Josef realised the screaming was not in his head but rather the kettle that was whistling, almost to the point of exploding. His body one step ahead of his shell-shocked mind, he went over automatically and shakingly took it off the stove, using the first item of strewn clothing he could pick up, only then to look at what he was holding. His friend's flat cap. The same one he always wore, jauntily tipped to one side to match his lopsided grin. Clutching it to his chest, the hat covering the gun he held tight there with his other hand, Josef turned and leaned against the table. Taking a moment, he looked at the cap in his hand, turning it over. His eyebrow rose and his head tilted in strange wonder, before he flipped the cap onto his head and glanced over once more at the grandmother.

She still had not acknowledged him or seemed to have registered that he was even there. Gingerly, Josef approached her and knelt in front of her, looking up at her face, eyes distant behind a veil of misery. Looking then at her twisted old hand, hanging limply at her side, he took it up, like a dying bird, and softly stroked it. He could not imagine that it would be any real consolation, yet, as he did so, she came to, and looked him in the eyes. In that moment she could have been any grandmother, and he, any grandchild.

"Where did they take Tomasz?" he asked, quietly, gently squeezing her hand. When she did not respond he asked, "Was Tomasz shot? Where is he?"

The trauma of what she had witnessed came back to her, the pupils of her eyes dilating for a second, her hand clutching his, before just as quickly relaxing, as recognition hit her, "*Josef?*"

"Yes, Babcha, it's me, Josef. Have they taken Tomasz?"

She simply replied, "He's in the hands of God now." Then, abruptly, she stood unsteadily, Josef helping her up. She shuffled over to the adjoining bedroom, leading him by the hand, and pointed at Tomasz's bed. As kids, he and Josef had slept top and tail there many a time. With the familiar sternness of a Polish elder in her eyes and voice, the old woman said, "You need to rest."

Seeing the anxiety in Josef's own eyes she said, "They won't be coming back here. They have already taken what they want. You need to rest. You are going to need all of your strength."

He realised then, what a state he must have looked and how tired he felt, it was all that he could do not to collapse. The relief of not having to run washed over him. Exhausted, he lay down on the bed, and the grandmother pulled Tomasz's blanket over him with aching tenderness. Within moments, the picture of the old woman standing over him with cross still in hand faded, and all he heard as he drifted off was the sound of her shuffling out of the room, mumbling a prayer under her breath as she closed the door.

The sound of a whistle woke Josef. Half asleep, his first thought was that he had drifted off in the staff room at work. For a moment, the world was normal, until he began to come to and remember that he was at Tomasz's house. Another whistle blast and a command in Russian from outside and suddenly he was wide awake.

Right then, the doorknob turned with a squeak and as the door opened, in that split moment, Josef thought, *No way out. I'm done for!* He went for his gun but, to his dismay, his fingers fumbled and he dropped it with a clatter to the floor. Still scrabbling to pick it up he lifted his head to see that it was not the Russians but Tomasz's grandmother at the door, heaving a world-weary sigh.

She held out her wrinkled beetroot-stained hand, and said plainly, "Give it to me."

Josef fought against the steadfast gaze in her eyes and was about to object when she said, "If they catch you with that, you are as good as dead. The Russki are going house to house now telling everyone to hand over their weapons…"

Josef cut her off, saying defiantly, "They take my gun, what have I got? They *will* come for me. But this way, I've got a fighting chance. Even if they still get me, at least I can shoot one of them."

With a pause her face hardened with zeal, as she said with a vengeful glint in her eye, "No. *Two* of them. One for you and one for Tomasz," and with that she said, "Now go. Back door."

The old woman hugged him, then lightly pushed him away and, putting her hands to his cheeks, she kissed him and said,

"Godspeed. Michael speed your way." From the broad pocket of her apron, she took out a parcel wrapped in a light blue napkin, saying, "Kiełbasa i ser." He put the sausage and cheese sandwich in his coat pocket with a grateful nod.

They both got a shock as the back door burst open and a dark-eyed girl in boy's trousers came breathlessly in. She could not have been older than nine but spoke with a vaunty conviction, "Don't go via Uska or Jana, or the church square. The Russki are there, they are setting up in the church. There's this short, fat guy in a long coat giving all the orders. I heard him say 'Ulica Uska' and 'Ulica Jana' - his men went that way."

Josef put his hand to his lip, biting it, figuring, "Okay, so if they're between Jana and Uska, I could go through the market…"

But the girl said, "No, Adash…you know, *Barty*, he said they are there too. Go by the high street. There's no one there."

"What?" baulked Josef. "That can't be right."

"They are not going into the shops, only into flats and apartments," the girl offered confidently.

Josef needed no more encouragement, he bent slightly and stroked her hair and pinched her nose. "The Reds will never get you, will they? Look after Stefan, huh. Teach him that coin trick I showed you."

"You said never to give away my secrets."

"You're right. That's what you must tell Stefan too." Then he straightened up, tucked his shirt in, tilted his friend's flat cap, gave a proud nod toward the grandmother, and made for the back door.

Chapter 2

Decompression

1975 Pacific Ocean

In decompression chambers, people had little to do but talk. For days on end, as their bodies were brought back to equilibrium, several divers would be cooped up in a small space, with not much else to do other than read the few dogeared books, play cards or have a long game of chess. One would not find a three-piece suite or reclining chairs in there. It would be basic. Bunk beds. Table. Chairs. An intercom for contact with the outside world. A deck of cards to help pass the time. So what else would one have to do? A crew living on top of each other in a pressurised tube, five metres wide and ten metres long. For days, weeks even.

A captive audience.

That was how Eddie saw it. Like having five cons in a prison cell. They were not going anywhere. All he had to do was start talking and without even the need to coax they would be speaking about the next job. Chances were, he figured, in that cell you might just have the right people with the right skill sets for just that job.

It was Eddie's skill as an engineer that put him in that claustrophobic little room full of eager ears, but it was his resonance as a storyteller that had the whole crew waiting to hear what scenario he would come out with next. Because he was a talker, Eddie. More than that, he had a panache. He was a showman.

That was the thing about Eddie: he knew how to fill a space. He was Mr Personality Plus. You only had to have Eddie in a room and the magic would begin to happen. He was just such a likeable character - everybody got on with him.

One of Eddie's particular gifts was the devilish knack for walking into a room and immediately sizing everyone up. He was an opportunist who was able to work a room, any room. A story here, a joke there, greasing his audience up, getting them involved, listening to their language, gauging responses, pushing buttons to get the right connections, all so that he could work out how he could best use them; for mutual advantage, of course - that was always his selling point: every player would be a winner with one of his schemes. In the end, everyone would be up.

Any decompression chamber was not just a room full of divers. Diving was secondary. Sure, it was part of the job, but it was the crew members' skill sets that they were employed for. They were qualified people in their fields - a sub-sea decommissioning specialist, a gas engineer, a risk analyst, a survey technician, an infrastructure engineer - many of them recruited from mining, engineering or construction industries and some with multiple tasks to execute on a dive: a pilot was also a cutter and welder, medic even.

It was a very tough industry. Not just in the 70's - it was a tough industry full stop. It was hard out there and they were hard men. In the expanse of the Pacific, for instance, things could get pretty dicey. The sea has a mind of its own, changeable and tempestuous, it is a force to be reckoned with. Add to that the fact that these men were often working in freezing conditions, in the far north, off the coasts of the Shetland Islands, Norway and Iceland - rapidly changing weather conditions meaning they had to be vigilant at all times. Everything needed to be lashed and tightened correctly: no loose straps, not a single nut unchecked, every gauge tested and retested. All it took was one discrepancy overlooked, one flaw missed, one mistake and the job could be compromised. Something that could be easily fixed on the surface became more and more difficult the deeper you went. At 4- 5- 600 feet down the smallest task becomes arduous. Dangerous even.

Just like the others in the chamber, Eddie had a competency that was vital for the work carried out by oil rigs. However, for a long while, his focus, once in the decompression chamber, switched to selling his idea for an impossible salvage job that only a certain crew might be able to undertake. It had never been done before and there was only a slim chance that it could even be done then. The catch, the thing that drove him to keep pushing for the right team, was what lay on the seabed, waiting to be found.

All Eddie needed was a team of men who, like him, were resolute, would do what it took to get that loot regardless of the odds. What he was after, when all was said and done, was a band of treasure hunters.

The real deal.

That said, he was not going to be able to sell those kinds of characters thin air; there had to be substance to his offer. Yet what Eddie had to propose was solid gold, and he knew it, only he was not about to put that out there. Not until he was in the right room, with the right people who could get the salvage done, retrieve the goods.

So he would cast out his line, to see who took the bait and then reel them in to find out what they were worth. For the most part, he threw them back again. So many jobs, where there had been one person here, two there, who had the right knowledge and skills, but never the full complement. And that was the clinch because what Eddie had in mind was not a one-man job, it required a whole team, and every player had to be at the top of their game.

Each contract had the same set of workers with the same credentials, people who could do the work required of them, however that did not make them the appropriate people for what Eddie had in mind. This was never going to be about skills alone. For the salvage job that Eddie had thought through, it was going to take an extraordinary combination of divers. What he was also looking for was the right chemistry between the crew members. Nothing like this had ever been accomplished and it was going to take a group of pioneers to get it done. People who could be up against the wall and still pull it out of the bag. When the going gets tough and all that.

Holding out for the ideal crew, it would not do for Eddie to put the whole offer out there until he was fairly sure that he was with the people he was after. Then, and only then, would he lay out a scenario that resembled what he had in mind. This was a test in its own right. Describe a nigh-on unreachable salvage and watch to see who would rise to the occasion, who would see the opportunity for what it was, who would get creative, gutsy. All it took was for one man to back off, to say that it could not be done, and often the whole prospective team would follow suit, and Eddie would hold back on revealing his full deal and wait for the next job, to try one more time.

Sitting once again in a decompression chamber like any other, this time out in the Pacific, off the coast of Peru, Eddie found himself surrounded by yet another crew, some of them familiar, others new to him, except that this time, something was different.

As he had plied his personal trade in stories, teasing out information and noting the competence of that crew, eureka, the dots began to connect and the picture he had been after began to take form. He might just have hit upon the team he had been looking for. If that turned out to be the case, the next trick would be to get them to see it for themselves. Any good card player could tell you that you needed to hold back on the reveal. Ask a leading question, get them chatting, drop in a hook and a hint, and then eventually he would come out with it, no hesitation. Clean.

But not yet.

His reluctance to go ahead and reveal his plan lay not only in the desire to find a good team to work with. The fact was, the job he had in mind was no ordinary project. There was an element of uncertainty to it that even the most seasoned of divers would be unaccustomed to. This particular job required finding the kind of men who would be willing to work in the roughest conditions out on the Barents Sea, going the deepest anyone had ever gone, and that was risky in itself. The added element of danger, the one which required extraordinary men, was that they would have to work behind the veil of the Iron Curtain.

Chapter 3

Wrong Turn

1939 Lwów, Poland

So far Josef had done well, apart from one narrow scrape when leaving the apartment block, he had managed to elude the NKVD completely, but inevitably, the Russians had made their way to the high street stores, and were now turning them over, harassing and interrogating shopkeepers and staff as they moved through the shopping centre of the city.

Forced to backtrack a little, he was now walking as calmly as he could across the street to head into the delicatessen, on the corner of Ulica Ruska and Ulica Groetsca, which had a second entrance onto another street. As he approached it, a terse command in Russian made Josef switch direction to exit the way he had come.

Glancing over his shoulder, he stepped out into the street, only to trip over a Pomeranian. It barked and snapped at his ankles as he staggered to his feet and then broke into a run, for a short distance, before ducking left, deciding to head through the chemist, out of which he could enter into the Victory Arcade.

Coming out of the arcade, he headed straight across the busy street, slowing his pace to snake between shoppers, veering left as he crossed to the archway on the other side, where a group of men were cheering in Ukrainian outside the Happy

Milk Bar. He straightened up, composing himself as he prepared to pass by, looking in the other direction, avoiding the attention of those communist sympathisers who would give no thought to informing the Russians of his passing should they come that way. Anxious too that the traitors might have taken note of his hand pressed suspiciously under his coat, he upped his pace as soon as he had passed by.

The moment he entered the archway, he kicked straight into a sprint, heading past the tenements on the other side, and out onto the road that led to where his good friend Pietrosz lived. Then he forced himself to walk, albeit brusquely. Josef figured that Pietrosz, being lame in one leg from polio, might be overlooked by the Russians.

Abruptly turning left into a shortcut, he slipped along an alley, keeping to the shadow of the high wall, the stones so familiar to his feet, having gone that way many times before in his youth, not concentrating now immediately in front of himself, absorbed for a moment - mapping out a new route in his head - a half a glance back over his shoulder, and then *smack*, he walked right into someone!

With a stifled cry, he took one step back, shoving his gun deeper into his coat, but in that instant recognised his own wide-eyed look of fear in the eyes of someone he was sure he recognised from the lumber yard.

Cutting short the apology in the other slightly older man's eyes, he motioned with his hands not to go the way he had come and carried on, brushing past the man, patting the local's arm to come with him. A few steps and they were out of the alley, Josef instinctively heading left, but, from behind, his fellow hightailer grabbed hold of the collar of his coat with a terse shout of, "Uh, uh!" and directed them the other way.

A headspin of twists and turns and the two of them were up against a wall, taking a moment to recoup their senses, catch their breath, and figure which way they were going to go. One look was enough to say that they had decided to head in different directions. So, with a simple tip of the head that wished good luck and safe journey, Josef remained only long enough to watch out for his compatriot, as the man clambered up and over a wall, and was gone.

Josef kept his head as close to the wall as he could, peeking from the edge of the house, checking the street for signs of the enemy. All clear.

A minute later, he had got to Piotrosz's apartment without being spotted; with a cocksure smirk at outwitting the Reds again, he knocked on the door. He should have known not to knock a second time, should have looked carefully through the window first, but there through the pane, a glimpse of a black uniform in the corner of his eye was all he needed to turn and bolt. Pietrosz was not in mourning and there was only one set of people in Lwów right now who went around wearing black.

The NKVD.

The People's Commissariat for Internal Affairs. Always announcing themselves - handheld, Tommy-gun style PPS-41 at the ready - with a bang! bang! bang! on the door and shouts of, "En-Ka-Va-De! Open up!" The fear of that infamous knock carried its own stories of fathers, husbands, sons, and daughters even, taken away, most likely never to be seen again. Yes, it was routine that they had to be severely questioned first, but no one ever seemed to have the right answers. Everyone knew it could go only one way. If it was not your door being knocked, do not look out the window. If walking past, keep your head down. If you hear a gunshot, do the sign of the cross. But keep it quiet, keep it down, do not interfere. Each to their own when the NKVD comes knocking.

The black-clad thugs had filled the streets of Lwów, arresting as they went. The city was infested with them. The NKVD had spread through the streets and into people's houses, and now it was clear to Josef that there was nowhere to hide, nowhere to run.

Nevertheless, Josef was running. When he caught sight of a uniform he would switch to walking, calmly, all the while racing in his head for options: the narrow almost overgrown paths between buildings, the routes along the rooftops, the secret haunts of his youth; anywhere he could hide his gun and get back to it later.

He was going to head to the right, down the street to the flats where his friend Bogdan lived, but they were crawling with black uniforms, young men being pressed against the railings. One of them, Bogdan himself - waving his papers in his right hand and shaking his fist with the other. The barrel of a PPS-41 pressed to his chest.

With a skip of a heartbeat, Josef had gone left instead. Internally he hit himself on the head, what was he thinking, his friends were all young, of fighting age, of course the

NKVD would be targeting them. He needed to find someone older, someone who was not a threat to the Russians, someone who would not be noticed.

It seemed like fate then that he was now headed in the direction of the old station master, his mentor. It had been three years now since the old man had retired and handed over his keys to the new station master, who disliked Josef, who viewed his humour as arrogance. Threatened by Josef's initiative, the new master had made his life at work uncomfortable, to say the least. Josef would not be surprised if he was right in there with the Russians now, drinking vodka and working out what was in it for him - the fox had been killed and he would want his bit of the tail, his cut. Ambitious świnia.

There was no sign of the NKVD where his mentor lived, in the old quarter, but Josef hunkered low anyway. A slip down a shady street, pressed against a wall, invisible, stealthy, then through the gap in the hedgerow. All of it was second nature to him on the streets where he had been brought up, where the cobbles of the city began to give way to the decaying edges of the original town.

He cut across the embankment and out onto a dusty road, knocking over a hoop that some lad had rolled. Josef picked it up, jolted by the normality of it. He handed it back to the rusty-haired boy who grabbed it with a grin, and off he went with his stick and hoop. A smaller girl and boy laughed after him, as though it were any other day.

His eye caught a fleck of black cloth and he was suddenly aware that he had let his guard down, but it was just an old woman's shawl. Josef composed himself and looked around. No sign of the hunters here. Yet.

Chapter 4

The Team

1975 Pacific Ocean

Everyone knew about the HMS Edinburgh. Any salvor worth their salt knew that what she had inside her belly was worth nigh-on £50 million, a prize big enough to keep everyone in the field talking. At the same time what they were painfully aware of was that this treasure lay at the bottom of one of the most treacherous seas in the world. Furthermore, it was deeper down than anyone had gone before. As if the odds were not high enough, the ship had gone down behind the veil of Communist Russia, and at this point, in 1979, tension had reached a new high between the superpowers, who were building up their arms at an alarming rate, raising the threat of nuclear war to heights not seen since the Cuban Missile Crisis.

This was possibly the worst time in history that anyone could have considered going for that prize. Yet the race was on to see who could engineer a way to get to it and, beyond that, who had the tenacity to see such a project through. For a good few months now, Eddie had been testing the waters to find just such a group of extraordinary men.

For his own part, Eddie's job on oil rigs was to head down in diving bells to inspect the installation and integrity of the drill housing on the ocean floor; once completed the rig could commence drilling for that lucrative substance. Having done this job time and time again, Eddie had been taken to greater and greater depths.

He had been working for the likes of BP, Texaco, Shell. These were the big boys. It was a multibillion-dollar industry wherein the necessary investments were made to go further out to sea, and to drill ever deeper, always pushing the boundaries in search of that black gold. The time was taken to test and perfect new equipment and methods which Eddie and the diving teams would then put into use. It was time-consuming and expensive. People say that time is money. But not to these guys: oil was money.

Lives, on the other hand, were expendable.

Back then, Eddie's work as an inspector was mostly on jobs in the North Sea, and he would often quip that out there it was like the Wild West. This was the New Frontier of the oil industry, each company investing in equipment that would allow them to drill deeper into the seabed to reach new oil fields, always pushing the limits on how far and how deep they could go. The demand was just that high, and the opportunity for companies to make billions was too alluring. Nevertheless, as much money as the industry threw at innovation, there were still unknown variables at the depths they were trying to reach. Experts were in the process of developing the industry, to make it safer, but diving was still a high-risk career. Despite being at its peak, regardless of reaching new levels, week by week, month by month, the technology was still catching up. It was a dangerous game. An average of two divers were dying every year.

One of the most frightening causes of death was embolism.

Nitrogen and oxygen would only get a diver up to 90 metres underwater, at which point oxygen becomes poison. To avoid that poisoning, other gases were introduced to the mix. Heliox - a helium and oxygen blend - was applied. As the diving bell was lowered to the required depth, the body would then begin to absorb the gases being breathed in. Divers would therefore have a time limit before they would need to be brought back up to the surface and be transferred to a decompression chamber. A team would have to work in shifts, moving between time underwater and time in decompression, tag-teaming, so that half the crew were under while the others were in the chamber. Timing was imperative here: in the move between the diving bell and the decompression chamber you would only have seconds, minutes at most, or you could get the bends.

Decompression was all about equalising pressure. A chamber was pressurised to place the same pressure on the diver's body as that of the depth they had just come from, and then, slowly, over days, possibly even weeks - depending on the depth and length of the dive - the pressure in the chamber was released, incrementally, until it matched the air pressure at surface level. But it was the *combination* of gases and pressure they would be worried about.

A diver's body was still full of helium and nitrogen when they came up - the gases that they had just absorbed at the bottom of the sea. The human body is neither designed to take those gases in nor safely disperse them. Left to its own devices the body would expel the gases far too quickly, therefore they introduced a pressurised chamber, allowing for the gases to be released slowly, removing the risk of embolism.

"Take a balloon, for instance," Eddie would say, in his thick Yorkshire brogue, "Blow it up full and now take it under water. At 10 metres the size has halved, at 20 halved again, at 100 metres it's the size of a pea. It's the pressure. Take that balloon back up and, because it's elasticated, as the gases expand within it will accommodate them and go back to its original size, right? The body is not a balloon. It's not elasticated, is it? If those gases were simply allowed to expand within you. Well. Pop. If you know what I mean."

To put it differently, a diver's body would be a bit like a bottle of fizzy pop, absorbing the gases. One would have to let the gases settle and unscrew the top slowly to release them. This, essentially, was decompression. If a diver did not decompress properly, it would be like popping the top on a shaken bottle. This, in layman's terms, was an embolism. Everywhere the diver had a concentration of blood vessels - their muscles, their organs, their spine, their brain - the vessels themselves would expand and the bubbles would explode. If they were lucky, they would be paralysed.

Hence decompression was not simply left up to a machine. It was an engineer who ran the show; a gas engineer who regulated and monitored, precisely, the balance of the gases, turning the knobs, watching the dials, equalising the diver to surface level - making sure they did not pop. Their lives were in his hands.

The gases were known to soften the bones over time too. That was why divers had, at most, a ten-year shelf life. "Any longer," Eddie would jest, "And you'll start losing your teeth. Forget about eating pork scratchings. So, ideally, make your money as quickly as possible and get out. Move on."

That was why he was going after a decent salvage, and nothing shone out quite as brightly for him as the HMS Edinburgh. The money he stood to make as a finders' fee would not necessarily amount to a retirement plan, but it would certainly be a good financial platform from which he could start the next stage of his life. There was decent money to be made in the Barents Sea.

At that point, however, Eddie was not in the Barents Sea. He was not even in the North Sea, he was in the Pacific. The day before, he and the crew had taken the bell down. It had been a windy day. It was always a windy day in the Pacific. Despite the adverse weather conditions they had managed to reach an unfathomable depth of 761 feet - a record for the diving industry. To say it had been tense was an understatement. But this was a crackpot team.

Going to such depths meant more time in the decompression chamber, which had been just as well for Eddie, as it had given him all the time he needed to work the crew around to his way of thinking. After sitting with them for hours on end, Eddie had earmarked a particular member, a fellow Yorkshireman, as the leader, the one who could bring a team together and keep them going when things got tough.

"So, Geoff, you've been at this game for a while now, haven't you?"

"Yeah, but this is not the only thing I am into."

This was Eddie's in. "Of course, you have your own salvage company, don't you?"

Geoff Craddock had a company in his name that had been doing well enough for itself to be a viable enterprise after he retired from rigging, however, he too was after something more substantial than the smaller finds he was often contracted into retrieving.

"Beats working in an office though," he sniggered, after all but admitting that he was aiming for bigger fish.

"Or being home with your wife," jibed Eddie to a burst of laughter, before he went on, telling a tale about trying to negotiate with an octopus over a certain pot of gold.

"I'm at 35 metres with 15 minutes of oxygen left, and now I spend five minutes in this losing tug of war, when suddenly out from behind the pot this huge bloody conger eel sticks its head out! The octopus and I both clock it and then the octopus and I clock each other and, I swear, I don't speak octopus, but the look in its eye said, "I'm off. It's all yours mate," and he bolts, kindly leaving me in a cloud of ink so I can't see where the bleeding eel is, can I? The ink begins to clear and, now, it's the conga eel that clocks me, and that's when I decide *I'm* off too! I got back to the boat. We'd already done two dives earlier and this was our last - so whatever was down there, is still down there. And that's that. Most men would let it go..."

"Well, sure, but you can bet that if I saw gold in a pot," Goeff retorted, "I'd be back there as soon as I bloody well could."

"I've got you there," conceded Eddie, satisfied that he had his man. "In for a penny, in for a Pound."

In accordance, Rob, the Driver, piped up with his own tale. Geoff and Rob. Peas in a pod. They had been on so many dives together that they were practically brothers. One would start a story and the other would finish.

"I did this one job, off the coast of Penzance. There was this net of brass, stashed no doubt - the way it had debris stacked on top of it. This is what I think, couple'a divers went down, they bagged the brass, right, then hid it to come back for it another time. The harbour master there, I'm telling you, he's shrewd, he is. Tighter than any hole an octopus can squeeze through." Everybody laughed at that one. "You can't get anything past this harbour master - we've had, uh, a few…*run-ins*, shall we say. There're harbour masters out there who are lenient - they know everyone needs to earn some way or another - so's you can make a deal with them, they're pliable. Not this guy. He was beyond negotiation. He's a hard-liner."

The surveyor, Tom, looked puzzled. "What's the score with harbour masters then? Why can't you keep your finds?" he asked earnestly in his no-nonsense Essex accent. He was good with details and did not like it if anything was missing.

"Well," Eddie answered, "a harbour master works for the Queen, see? Anything left below British waters belongs to the Crown. So these masters are out to make sure no one sneaks any valuables past them. Their official title is actually H.M. Customs Officer but they're mostly known as R.O.W's - Receiver of Wreck. One of my old mates was an R.O.W for

Scapa Flow, where WWI German warships were scuttled in 1919 - a ripe target for amateur divers!"

Geoff butted in, "We're all privateers, you see, son." Everyone talked to Tom in those terms. He was "kid," or "son," or "lad," but it didn't bother him - he looked up to these seasoned divers and he was a nice-natured fellow, easy to get on with. Took direction well too, which already had Eddie thinking of bringing him into his scheme.

"It's like you and me, Tom, planning a weekend dive in Cornwall," Rob continued. "Just amateurs, going down to Prussian Cove, say, and doing a few dives to see what we can find. You start out just doing your local dives in and around Cornwall, and then move on to good dive areas around the UK and then further afield…"

"You only realise after several dives that there is actually money to be made," Goeff pitched in, "You could even make a living out of it," he said, to knowing nods from Rob and Eddie. "And *that's* the bug, the drive to go bigger. Sooner or later you start to get professional about it, you go in for a boat of your own, start investing in better kit. Next thing you know, you've got a full rig, with a winch and a team, and you all know what you're doing. Nobody is going to stash some brass without you finding it! But that bloody harbour master..."

"Yeah," continued Rob, "this one is beyond negotiation. And that's why they stashed the brass, see? They were obviously familiar with this tight bastard. So they were likely planning to return another time, to get the loot out a different way.

But, leave that kind of thing too long and someone will find it."

Geoff summed it up, "£160 worth, and that's just brass. There's silver out there, and gold, so when you get savvy to this stuff, you realise that you're going to need to do your research, if you want the big dosh. So you end up spending more time researching than you do diving. If you're just going in for a dive, you're going in blind. You could find nothing or you could find a pot of gold. Lucky dip. More often than not though you find nothing. But there *are* pots of gold out there," and at this, he raised a conspiratorial eyebrow at Eddie. A cue, if you like. Eddie shared one of the tiny double bunk pods with Geoff and had already talked at length with him about the possibility of going for some major finds - putting a deep-sea salvage team together.

So Eddie finished off in agreement, "It pays to be prepared. You've *got* to do your research. Be *over-prepared* is what I say."

The conversation was going in exactly the direction Eddie would have it.

Rob raised an eyebrow and glanced at Geoff and then back to Eddie. "Are you talking about the Edinburgh?"

There was silence then. Only for a moment, everybody adjusting to what had just been asked. It was a bit like the Holy Grail, the HMS Edinburgh.

Tom was the first to respond, "I heard about that. So you think it's true: there's really gold on it?"

The gas expert, Janick, finally chipped in, "You mean rumours."

Rob looked over at Geoff, "Same conversation, different d-chamber. I've heard this story before. Russian gold sunk to the bottom of the Barents Sea. It's a nice bedtime tale."

But Geoff came back with, "No. You know this is no tale, mate. I've done my research on this. The Edinburgh was carrying 1.2 million, the equivalent, in today's terms, of *fifty* million."

A longer silence this time, until Tom questioned, "You mean five million, right?"

To which Geoff simply said, "I mean what I say."

The young surveyor gave a low whistle.

Rob got up, as though, if he were not in a decompression chamber, he would go storming off, but he had nowhere to go, "Fine, fine, there's gold there, but you can't get to it. It's unreachable. Too deep."

Compression engineer, Mike, a quiet guy who seemed to be perpetually in his own world yet, when on the job, was razor sharp, asked, "What depth."

"About 800 feet," said Rob incredulously.

Geoff corrected, "800 feet *exactly*."

Eddie stepped in, saying, "Here's the deal," he leaned forward and paused to look everyone in the eye, his voice smooth - he knew he was nearing his mark. "Right now, we are confident at 750, we're making headway to 770 feet. We're getting deeper all the time. It is not *whether* we will be able to go that deep, the question is *when?* More to the point, the question is *who?*"

Bang. And that was the hook.

For Eddie, it was all an equation. The potential problems that would be faced on the job he had in mind all summed up to a total figure that needed to be balanced out by the crew. He had talked with each man, approaching the problem from every conceivable angle and, so far, what they had to contribute added up to the sum total he was after. At this point, when Eddie had brought them together, once he had all eyes on him - the whole group primed so that he was surrounded by the glint of greed in every eager grin - he began to present his plan, like payday. An idea so obvious, it was right in front of their eyes: it mattered not that they were in a chamber on the wrong end of the world, they were the right people, in the right place at the right time.

Ever since his research had come together, Eddie had been waiting for this moment, for his chance to tell the whole story.

Once he finished, everyone looked around the chamber, and suddenly, silently, with little nods of confirmation and smiles of approval, they all realised that they were in the room with just the people who might be able to pull off just such a job. Geoff winked at Eddie and it may as well have been a handshake. Deal done.

Now all they needed was a boat.

Chapter 5

The Station Master

1939 Lwów, Poland

Opening his old mentor's white wooden gate, Josef took one last look left and right and back the way he had come. No danger. All clear. Then he looked up to see that the sun was at its highest point and smiled at how perfectly he had timed his visit.

Most people lived in tenement flats in the city. You had to be quite established to own a house in the suburbs. Josef's mentor, Adash Politowski, did not think of himself as wealthy but certainly fortunate to be part of a line of men who had been in railways since the beginning, his forebear having overseen the work on the very first major Polish railways.

Right now he was tucked into his usual routine, gathering eggs and feeding the chickens, who were pecking about noisily at the odd heads of wheat left purposely by Mr Politowski, who had long since harvested what he could from the strip he had sewn in spring. He stood up and pressed his hands to his back, to relieve his ache, looking up to confirm that the cherries in his tree were ripe and ready to pick. If so, his good wife could make kompot preserve - to be stored in the cellar with the rest of the cold meats, barrels of sauerkraut, cheeses, chutneys and jams that she would be stocking up to help get them through the hard winter months.

She had already prepared the red currants, blackberries and gooseberries and you could hear her now in the cellar, the clink of the jam jars and bottles being shifted and organised to make room for the next batch. This was the way her mother had handed down to her, and her mother before that: a practical and conservative tradition of stretching out what you have. Needs be, if they were short on anything it could be bought from the store. As a rule, though, they would do this rarely, only keeping to their regular trips to the butcher and baker, otherwise opting to use what they had.

Mr Politowski still sported the wise white beard and twirled moustache of his working years, along with his old station master's dark woollen waistcoat. Without thought he pulled on the chain of his pocket watch, the simple time-piece swinging neatly into his palm - ever faithful, ever reliable, never let him down - as he clicked open the plain silver cap with a press of his thumb and glanced down at the bold roman numerals to be sure the midday Krakow express was due.

Back in the old days when he was station master, regular as clockwork, you would see him step up to Platform 1 daily, at 11:59, to see the all-important express train from Krakow enter Lwów Central. He would thread a coin through his fingers, little finger to thumb, and reverse the motion, all the while cocking his eye toward a distant point. The sooty young lads, who earned a few złotys as unofficial baggage handlers at the station, would bet exactly which landmark the old man used to gauge the timeliness of the express. Station Master Politowski would know, before you even saw the great bull bar pressing round the last bend a long way off from the station, before you even heard its proud whistle, with a small curl of his lip and a half a glance at the betting boys, he would know whether the train was on time.

If it arrived on time then the train schedule was on track, and, with a nonchalant look over to Josef, letting him know that he and the staff could get on with their allotted lunchtime tasks, the station master would toss half a zloty to the kid who won the bet, and make his way to the restaurant to dine with one or other important regular passenger from the train, all too happy to hear their opinion on the latest news which invariably passed through the station.

If the Krakow to Lwów was late, due to discrepancies that had arisen along the line, these would need to be remedied. The lads would know, seeing the old master slip the coin back into his pocket. As a concierge, Josef would be just as neatly on time, stationed at the centre of the platform with his crew, ready to give orders to the porters, restaurant runners and bellboys. He too would know, seeing the station master turn on his heel and head straight back into his office, that it would be his duty to cater for the delay, sending a message to the kitchen to hold the meals, telling the bellhops to replenish only the first class bar, giving orders to strip down the cleaning routine, calling on extra porters to speed up the change-over to shorten the delay on departure.

Even now, Mr Politowski regulated his life around that central point of the business day, so that today he had the same look on his face as he would have had so many times back then, when the structures of station life were all in place and everything was ticking over as it should. The cherries were ripe and now, and no later than now should they be picked. Any later and the sap would begin to move down to the roots, any earlier and not enough juices would have risen to the fruit. Anybody else would simply pick a cherry, but not Mr Politowksi. Everything had to be timed meticulously. He, as with everyone else, knew that the best time to pick a cherry was between new and full moon, in the morning, with the sap rising, however, Mr Politowski would wait until *all* the juices had risen so that he could pick the plumpest of cherries to make the best of compotes, such as his family were well known for. You were blessed indeed to receive a jar of Politowski kompot on your doorstep at Christmas.

Mr Politowski picked a small handful of cherries and cocked his eye toward the cellar door, trusting that his wife would emerge on schedule to come and test the stock with him. This was their autumn routine. Since they had been married, year by year, each mid-September without fail, the two would share this moment, their little ritual. Mrs Politowski would emerge from the cellar and join him as they delicately, silently, tasted the cherries he had brought over. Placing a cherry in each other's mouth, they would smilingly move the small fruit round from one cheek to the other, carefully pressing its flesh, sucking, smacking their lips, testing their palates like wine connoisseurs. Then they would spit out the pip and close their eyes, allowing the taste to settle. Without further ado, they would open their eyes and look at each other and know, instantly, whether the moment was right to prepare their beloved kompot.

Standing there, cherries in hand, Mr Politowski looked up and spotted Josef. He beamed instantly. Just before twelve, precise as always, on time to see in the express. And then just as quickly the old man slumped his shoulders and said, quite uncustomarily, "Shit."
You did not get to be the station master of a large city station without knowing how the world worked. The appearance of his protege, sweaty and flustered, flat cap pulled low over his eyes, clutching to his chest what could only be a gun, could only mean that the war that he had hoped would take a long time, or never, to come his way, had now entered into his front garden.
"You'd better come inside for vodka. I've a nice bottle of Krupnik I've been saving. Let's toast to our last days, huh?"

In the living room, Josef glanced at the framed photograph on the mahogany sideboard. It was Mr Politowski's retirement gift from the staff at the railway, a picture of everyone together, staggered in five rows, with the Krakow Express behind - the only day he had ever turned a blind eye to its delay. With the proud station master himself in the centre of the front row, Josef stood right there beside him, with his chest puffed out. It was an honour he had not forgotten to this day. Mr Politowski looked down at the photo too.
"Waistcoat fit me then," he said with a chuckle, flicking his eyes to his belly, now too big to do up all the buttons, and as he turned to Josef, he saw the lad was still gazing at the photo, lost in it before he came back to himself, suddenly

realising that he should have been at work and it hitting him once again, why he was not.

With an uncertain look on his face, he said, "What am I going to do?"

"Nobody needs to be at work today. All you need to do is have a drink with me. Make yourself comfortable, I'll get the Krupnik."

Josef was left gazing at the wall above the photo, the reality of it all hitting him in waves. For a moment the red and gold stripes of plush velvet wallpaper blurred. He put his hands to his sides and looked up, taking in all the familiar smells with a deep breath. All of those scents layered on top of one another: Mrs Politowski's homemade potpourri doing its best to remove the smell of tobacco, coal and smoke, with little success as always, and there too a wisp of last night's Krupnik. As he blew out a long breath to centre himself, he let his eyes roam around the room, picking up all the signs of a comfortable night spent in good company: there were the kieliszki, the shot glasses left on a table with an empty bottle of the honey vodka and a crystal bowl full of sunflower seeds, the husks piled in a smaller bowl next to it.

His head spun a little, he needed to sit down. Massaging the bridge of his nose and squeezing his eyes closed, he slowly opened them and waited for everything to come back into focus, first, the brass beading running along the side of the deep red carpet, revealing the zigzag of parquet wooden flooring around the edge of the room, bordered by the high ornate skirting board. Hands on his hips, Josef lifted his eyes to look at a gold-framed oil painting. It was a copy of part of the famous Racławice Panorama, depicting the Kościuszko Uprising - the Polish rebellion against Imperial Russia and the Kingdom of Prussia in 1794 where, even though they lost the war, the Poles that day had driven the enemy away. The painting itself had become a visual call for comradery, to keep up spirits when, as usual, enemies were coming in from all sides.

He could hear Mr Politowski in the kitchen, closing the squeaky szafka door, saying, "This will do. This will do nicely," as he came back through the hallway. The floorboards creaked in harmony with his footsteps, like so many times before when a meal had been being brought in, usually with his wife's calls echoing from the kitchen, insisting in high-pitched motherly tones of concern, "That boy must eat, he's too thin!" as though his mother had not been feeding him properly.

Josef turned to face the large room, the sofa beneath the chandelier looking a little too inviting, as drained as he was. Better to sit up straight, he thought. He looked longingly at Mrs Politowski's chair by the fireplace, thinking it was a better option. It was high-backed to keep the drafts off, and the tired lad could feel a hint of winter brushing against the hairs on the back of his neck. To preserve the precious maroon leather, the chair was draped in blankets, making it look all the more welcoming, despite how rude it would be to sit down in her chair without invitation. As though to answer his thoughts over whether he could sit in her chair, there was a movement outside the bay window catching his eye, where the thick velvet curtains were only half-closed to let in a slant of autumn sunlight. The grand woman was gleaning the peas she had allowed to go to seed for next year. She was not going to be sitting down any time soon.

A tad unsteadily, Josef went over to her chair by the fireplace, where the cat and dog were taking up the best spot, curled up by the fire that was already lit to keep off the end-of-season chills. The high-ceilinged room, like the rest of the dark old house, never felt warm at the best of times. The Politowskis were getting older too, and feeling the cold all the more.

Josef stooped down and stroked the fluffy, pale-brown Persian, and it stretched its paws out and purred in contentment. The cat regulated its heat by distance, shifting ever closer to the warmth of the coals as they reduced, and was lying almost against the grate now, in perfect rapture. Nice to be a cat, thought Josef, leaden with exhaustion, as he sat down heavily opposite Mr Politowksi's smoking chair - the pipe sat ready on the arm. Wincing, Josef pulled out Mrs Politowski's knitting that he had just lumped down on top of. Before he could nod off completely, Mr Politowski came into the room with a shimmering bottle. Walking over to his chair, he reached down to a triple table set and pulled out the smaller of the three, shifting it over between the two chairs, and placing the bottle down on the table. Then he went over to the komoda, opening the glass doors where there was an assortment of glasses, and, shifting some sherry glasses out of the way, took two kieliszki and brought them over to the table.

Mr Politowski sat down and leaned forward. For a few moments, he let his eyes rest on the bottle - the liquid inside magnifying the settling flakes of gold within. This was no Krupnik, Josef noted, it was Goldwasser from Gdańsk. An expensive vodka, a gift perhaps, that had surely been set aside for a very different occasion. Yet, with a slight nod, he let out a small "hmm" with eyebrows raised in resignation. He turned the bottle upside down so that, just like a snow globe, the glistening flakes of gold swirled and danced around the bottle. He turned it back upright, unscrewed the cap and poured some into the two shot glasses.

Passing one of the glasses over the table to Josef his old mentor toasted, "Na zdrowie."

In keeping with the old ways, they each flicked just enough drops to tickle the flames, waking the cat so that it lazily opened an eye a touch to reflect the blaze, before curling ever more tightly in a ball.

The two men looked across to each other, but just before they drank, Josef, hearing the almost imperceptible tell-tale sound of the clock about to sound the hour, glanced left to look at it, when he looked back to Mr Politowski, there was a knowing grin on his face as he said, "We're on the Express now, lad, it is a one-way ticket. No stops, no getting off from here. Let's drink. This could be our last."

Steeling themselves for the storm to come, the carriage clock on the mantelpiece chimed. Twelve 'o' clock. The eleventh hour was over. They both knocked back the first shot.

"You didn't come here to tell me you aren't going to make it to work today, and I don't think you came to wish us a happy anniversary either…"

Josef reached into his coat and pulled out the gun and placed it gingerly on the table, beside the vodka, "I don't know what to do?"

Leaning forward and putting his glass down, Mr Politowski placed his elbows on the arms of his chair, cupped his fist in his hand and put it to his lips, closing his eyes in thought. In the seconds that passed, Josef waited, not even knowing what advice he was hoping for.

Mr Politowski's father was a man made hard by hard living. He had taken no prisoners. Step out of line and Adash would get a swift clip around the ear. Say something wrong and Adash would get the same. Mr Politowski often remarked on how tough his father had been on him but admitted, too, that it was because of the austerity passed down to him that he had moved steadily through the ranks in the army, to become a high-ranking officer in the war. Even though he never said it outright, it was clear that Mr Politowski was grateful to his father for how he had brought him up. All of that familial discipline and directness, after all, had enabled him to climb to the top of the railway company too. Yet, underneath the unflinching exterior was, ultimately, a giving nature. When you got to know him, as Josef had, he was a warm man. Adding his well-earned discernment to the mixture, what you had was a brilliant mentor. If you had a problem he would listen, would not come back at you, would instead, sit back and put all the pieces together and formulate a rational answer, just as he was doing now.

Opening his eyes and shifting his clasped hands down to his lap, the old man looked Josef squarely in the eye and said, extending one index finger to point at the gun, "You leave that gun with me, and when they find it - and they will find it - they are not going to waste their own bullets on an old sobaka like me, they are going to shoot me with that very gun." When Josef started to protest, his old friend cut him off, saying without a hint of fear, "They *will* shoot me. Whether it is with your gun or theirs. Take it and they will shoot you too."

Josef's brow creased and seeing it, Mr Politowski continued, "What? You think I am too old for them to kill me? We are all in the shit together here. There's no escape for any of us. Cholera jasna! I've made it onto their list, of course I have: I know *many* people. I know too much. The gun is not going to help you in any way. If they catch you with the gun you might as well say goodbye to your wife too..."

Josef's eyes lit up with anger and determination as his mentor went on, "Get rid of the gun and get back to your wife, go to Maria," and now, stabbing back and forth with his finger, he pointed at Josef's chest and with all fatherly concern, saying the last statement in a short staccato rhythm, "And this is a must - you *must* listen to me: Bury. That. Defiance. The only thing you need to hide now is that fire - keep it, yes, but don't let them see it, you need to become small in their eyes, you have to *live*. If you don't. If they see it. Your train will come. It's already here. Chances are, you'll be on that train anyway, but at least you'll live." When the younger man made to interject again, Mr Politowski raised his voice a little, not allowing the truth to be curtailed, "And *that* is when you use what you've got. They will take many of us. Stay small, but *not* invisible. Do not get lost in the miserable masses. If they cannot see you, then they will leave you to die. Use what I have taught you: make yourself useful. Not just to anyone, make yourself useful to whoever is in charge. Then it will be harder for the others to kill you. And watch for a chance to escape."

Josef blew out hard, the reality of what Mr Politowski had said playing out graphically in his mind's-eye.

Seeing that his message had hit home, at least to some degree, the wise man sat back with a sigh, finishing with, "No point in being a dead hero, eh? A man knows when he needs to back down and when it is time to fight."

"Thank you," Josef mumbled. It seemed like the only thing he could say.

They both stood and hugged hard and then Mr Politowski pulled away and gripped both Josef's shoulders. "I know you will not leave the gun. But listen to everything else I have told you, mój drogi. It is probably for this that God put you under my wing," he said, finding his inner sage in the face of death.

Chapter 6

Hustler

1939 Lwów, Poland

Lusha was good with the cards, but it was more than that, she knew the game well. More than well. The young woman understood that what she had to play was not just the cards, it was the boys. She knew how to work them. Not showing too much too soon, she would reveal herself bit by bit. For now, her posture was withholding, it was all in the eyes and pouting lips. Bait is what she was. Waiting for the moment that the lads were hooked. The sign was always the same, Lusha knew she had them when they leant forward on their stools, almost on cue, and then she would give them a little more, slowly undoing the top buttons of her blouse with one hand, while fanning herself with the cards in the other, as though it was too hot. As the temptress then leant down to let them have a look at what they wanted to see, let their imaginations roam a little further, that was when she knew that their attention had left the cards, that all their focus was now directed on her. The temperature would rise in earnest, the boys wiping their brows. Without them realising it, from this point on they were not playing to win at cards, Lusha had them playing to see who could win her. Now they were vying against one another by placing higher and higher bets, trying to impress her.

But Lusha was kind, letting them line their mouths with Wiśniówska, the cherry vodka easing the way for them to part with their zlotys. They were well into the game now and the bottle was half empty, but the money pot was half full, which was still not enough for Lusha. This would be the point where she would sit back, removing that wonderful view of her chest, and fan her glowing cheeks with her cards once more as if flushed with desire, and that was it, game over. She had won. But she would drag the game out, doing whatever was necessary, until the pot was full. Which was why, now, she was feigning to stall, as though she had a bad hand and was trying to figure out whether to fold. She leant back further, craning her lovely neck through the kitchen doorway to speak with Maria.

This was all second nature to Lusha, all the lithe movements and gestures and hints at the body beneath her dress, the flowing vodka and the cards, the testosterone-flushed boys and the money in the pot, so it was nothing for her to keep up a conversation with Maria and at the same time use it to deadly effect, showing just a little more leg as she leant back.

"He's not that bad, you know; he's been a good husband, a good provider."

"I know," said Maria, blowing a little raspberry sigh, as she wiped salt from her hands that she had kneaded into the cabbage, for her second batch of kapusta, the sauerkraut that would be ready for winter. "He thinks he knows everything - he never listens."

"Look, Maria, he might not listen, but he will never let you down."

"Not so far," she replied, "but where is he? It's not like him to just not come home." She took up a dull knife, gently curved and almost completely worn down through two generations of use - in keeping with the thrifty sensibility handed down to her with most of the utensils in the kitchen. She used it to gouge out the eyes in the apple she was to add to the kapusta along with the fennel seeds in the earthen bowl beside the marble slab, where she had prepared dough earlier.

Just then Josef came in, looking hot and a little furtive as he took his hat off and his coat, but did not hang them up, and made straight for the kitchen.

"Oh, Josef, speak of the…"

But he had no time for Lusha, cutting her off as he said to Maria, "I've got to hide this gun."

He reached into his coat and pulled out the gun and started looking around the small, galley kitchen for somewhere to hide it. His eyes fell to the old black range, Maria half-thinking that he was going to put the weapon inside, when she saw his eyes go to the bowl of fresh dough that she had left on top of the range so that the warmth would aid its rising, and she interjected, "Don't even think about it."

"But no one would think of looking in there…"

"Don't even *think* about it," this second time she said it with a prodding of her knife at his chest.

"Okay, okay," he conceded as he backed away and looked at the sugar jar.

"Josef! Get that thing out of my kitchen, I'm making kapusta already!"

He did not have time to argue with her and went back into the front room where the game was still in full swing, the pot of money now near full and the men vainly trying to concentrate on their cards, all the while entwined in Lusha's glamour so that they barely even took note of Josef as he shuffled around the cabinets and shelves against the walls of the room, still looking for a hiding place.

One of the guys, Urban, two years younger than Josef and more of a neighbour than a friend, noncommittally offered for him to fasten it underneath the card table, starting to dip his head as if to show Josef where he meant, but Lusha was on to him. "I'll raise you, 50 zloty," she said in a sultry voice, averting his mind back to the game and away from whatever he wished to see under the table.

Urban's brother, only eleven months younger, and nigh on his twin in looks, let out, "That's a small gun."

"*Some* guns are bigger than others," said Lusha, with a smirk, not looking away from her hand, knowing very well that the boys would be looking that little bit more lustfully at her.

To deflect the comment on his manhood, Urban's brother suggested that Josef hide the gun in the ceiling. "My uncle did that back in the war. As far as I know, it's still there."

The lads all looked up as Josef dumped his coat and cap and climbed on a stool, reaching for the ceiling.

Just then, with a smack of her lips, Lusha kissed her cards and placed them down. The boys' eyes returned to the table to look in dismay at the winning hand, Lusha all but stroking the full pot of money as she took it up in both hands and cradled it like a baby. She turned to the guys and said, "Thank you, boys, that'll be all for today, better luck next time," as she demurely did up the top two buttons of her blouse, officially bringing the session to close. "See you next month, same day, same time - and bring more gotówka!" she said with a wink and the dazzling smile of a starlet.

Ushering the lads out the door, the brothers arguing with each other, as per usual, Lusha closed the door and looked straight over at Josef, who was moving the stool over to where there was a crack in the ceiling, and asked directly and full of concern, "What's going on?"

Distractedly, while looking around for something to ease open a hole between the lath and the plaster, he answered, "I ran into Stefan Robinova on the way home, his dad was arrested for having a weapon - NKVD came in the middle of the night and when they found the gun they took him. They just took him. He's gone."

"Gone? Gone where?"

Maria, hearing the tone more than the words, came in and also asked, "What's going on, Josef? What's wrong."

Josef stepped down and collapsed onto the stool, all his courage deflating the moment he looked at Maria. Close to tears and feeling like he had nothing left in him, he shivered as Lusha handed him a kieliszka of vodka, which he downed shakily.

"Josef," asked Maria more emphatically, "What's wrong?"

"Mr Robinova is gone. They put him on a train - Stefan said it's headed for Siberia…"

"You're not making any sense," Maria said as she knelt in front of him. She laid a reassuring hand on her husband's forearm. "Calm down, Josef," she soothed, and then said more slowly, "Explain to me: What. Is. Going. *On*?"

That got his attention. He looked from one to the other and asked Lusha for another glass full, and while she poured it he said, simply, "The Russians are here."

"W-where?" stammered Maria.

"Everywhere. They're in Lwów. Now. I can't believe they're not here yet," he said in genuine surprise as he took the kieliszka from Lusha and carried on, "When I finished my shift yesterday, I couldn't cross the high street, there were crowds, everyone finished work and just standing there, staring at the Russians. Just marching in. They just…walked in. Nobody stopped them. There were no shots fired. There was nothing. They just walked in." Still coming to terms with this, and all he had been through since then, he knocked back the vodka and then sat gazing at his feet.

Maria looked at him and to Lusha, hoping that someone would start making sense. "What are you talking about? I don't understand. They *couldn't* have got here yet?" she asked almost frantically, and Lusha quickly poured her a drink too.

"You're not listening, Maria: it's not the Germans, it's the *Russians*," and he watched her eyes go black with fear. "That's right, Maria. That's right. You know what they say: I'd rather be shot by a German than a Russian; Germans kill the body but the Russians kill the *soul*." He shivered at his own words, hoping to God that he would not get to find out whether that saying was true.

"Matka Boża," said Lusha, slumping down and, methodically, pouring herself a drink as well and throwing it back in one, "What are we going to do?"

Josef, feeling more composed, remembering Mr Politowski's words, said plainly, "There is nothing we can do. I've got to hide this gun - they're going to come - they're everywhere." Then he stood up and looked at the ceiling again.

"No! Just - just give them the gun! Maybe they will let you go?" implored Maria, visibly shaking.

"Maria. This is the Russians. It's not about having a gun, anything is an excuse to arrest us - I stopped at Tomasz's place last night. They…took him too - and he didn't even have a gun," he slowed right down and looked at Maria. "They will come here. And they will take me."

Maria, still kneeling, clasped her hands together over the kielieszka, dropped her head for a moment and then looked up at Josef.

"When I come back, and I will come back, Maria - at least I will have this gun if we need to use it."

Maria got to her feet and, half to herself, asked, "Where?"

Taking her cue, Josef stood, looked over to a shelf and stepped over to it, suggesting, "What about the hollow book?"

"What? The one I made? You showed everybody that book!" shouted Maria incredulously, then she sighed. "They'll find it there; listen to me: maybe it is better to hand it in?"

"Listen to Maria," piped up Lusha, who had stayed out of it, allowing the two to work it out, but she could not hold her tongue over this, voicing the thoughts she knew Maria was having, "She's right, it's not worth it: *everybody* knows about your gun."

"Maybe. But they *won't* find it."

"You know what the Russians are like," Lusha said with a little venom, "they've got *ferret* in their blood…"

"Walls have ears, Josef," Maria implored.

"I know, I know," he argued. "Do you think I'm stupid or something?"

Maria and Lusha looked at each other.

Josef went ahead and hid the gun in the hollowed-out pages of a large red book, his eyes defiant as he turned to Lusha. "It's done."

There were three short, sharp knocks at the door.

"An-Ka-Va-De!"

"Russians," gasped Josef, as the three exchanged glances, all dread and the whites of their eyes.

"Open up."

"Quickly, come here," Lusha hissed as she grabbed hold of Maria's arm and tugged her down into one of the seats the lads had occupied. She hastily whipped out three sets of cards, not forgetting to deal for Josef.

Once again the door knocked three times with its adjoining command of, "An-Ka-Va-De!" as Lusha, with that same presence of mind she always managed to maintain, poured out three glasses of vodka.

"Okay, won't be a minute, hold on!" called Josef as he searched for a place to hide the book, lamely choosing to simply put it back on the shelf before going to the door. He took a breath, looked over at Maria and Lusha, took another breath, and then opened the door.

Two black uniforms entered the room, one short, one tall.

No one dared breathe.

The short one smirked, knowing he had made the impact he desired. The room was his without even trying. He sized them up then his eyes roamed the room. Almost sauntering, he moved around looking at everything with half-hearted disgust, shifting an ornament here, pulling a book back there, lifting a glass then in two fingers, as though it was a dirty rat, and dropping it to the floor, taking a look over his shoulder to see how everyone reacted to its smashing. Then he looked at a photo of Josef standing in his uniform, looking proud as a button. The officer raised his head to look Josef in the eye as, with a flick of his finger, he let the frame fall on its face, enjoying Josef's involuntary flinch. Then he stopped and looked down at his hands, twisting a gold sovereign ring on his little finger, before parting his oil-slick coat and resting his hands on his protruding belly. Lifting his chin, he dipped his head to the side, feigning interest in the card table.

Walking over to Maria and Lusha, he took hold of Josef's hand of cards and, with a cocked eyebrow, dropped them again, tilting his head the other way to look at Maria's cards and letting out a little puff of disbelief. Now he edged toward Lusha and dipped her cards back with one finger, giving that smirk again, and said, "Do you always deal a fresh game when someone knocks on your door?" as he scratched at his stubble, his eyes falling momentarily on the pot full of money.

Not missing a trick, Lusha came back, sharp as a razor, with, "Yes, good timing. I can cut you in too, if you like." Her confidence hinted at sexiness. This was just another man after all. Same game. Higher stakes.

But the officer was not playing. His pupils turned black with menace. He swivelled on his heels, tucked his hands behind his back as he straightened up, tensed his paunch and said coldly to Josef, "We have reason to believe that you have a firearm. You have not handed it in."

"No. Not me," Josef said too quickly, flicking his eyes to Maria who in turn looked at Lusha, the two of them sharing a gaze of despairing unsurprise.

The officer looked a little disappointed: the sassy young woman had offered a taste of excitement to an otherwise interminable day of house searches and arrests, and now here was this chump coming out with the usual, predictable denial. He was bored. "Search the premises," he spat at the tall one.

Lean, clean cut and only memorable for his unusual height, the other officer went straight over to the shelf, pulled out the large red book, and handed it to the short one. All this time, they had been toying with them. They knew exactly where to look for the gun.

The short one let his eyes rest on Lusha, most uncomfortably and theatrically, opening the book slowly with that one finger, the gold ring twinkling like the glint in his eye as he looked over at Maria, letting the book fall open. Then he looked down at the gun and just as slowly pulled it out and pointed it at Josef, relishing everyone's intake of breath as he cocked it. All eyes were on the gun in his hand as he dropped the book with the other, the loud bang making the three start and close their eyes putting their hands up to their faces.

"Arrest him," he said, Maria only opening her eyes now to see that Josef had not been shot, "Take him to the cattle train heading for Siberia - he can finish his life there."

The tall one pulled his gun from its holster as he went over and opened the door, holding it in one hand as he stood to attention and raised his gun to point at Josef.

With Josef's gun still pointing at him too, the commanding officer gave an unmistakable gesture asking Josef what he was going to do, daring him, almost hoping it seemed that Josef would do something stupid.

Powerless, Josef found it difficult to contain his anger, as Mr Politowski had advised, hoping it did not show in his eyes, as he looked to the ground and walked to the door, pausing long enough to look apologetically at Maria before he was ushered out, the tall one following straight behind him.

The portly officer followed, but before he was out he stopped, took a step backwards and looked over at the pot of money. He casually stepped over to the table once more, picked up Josef's cards and, deftly fanning them out, laid them face up on the table to reveal the winning hand. Then he looked at Lusha with absolute childish triumph as he said, "You see, I win." Not even bothering to point the gun at either of the women, he simply grabbed the pot of money and walked out, ignoring Maria's sobs.

Lusha got up from her chair and took Maria to her chest. She let Maria cry, resting her cheek on her friend's head and crying a little herself, but it was not long before she lifted her head and gave it a quick shake. Sucking up her tears and centering herself, she pushed Maria away slightly and took her head gently in her hands, the poor woman still sobbing and mumbling about them taking her husband. Then Lusha dipped her head to one side, looking into Maria's eyes, trying to get her attention.

"Maria, look at me. Maria! Look. At. Me," she said emphatically, "Did you hear what he said? They're being put on a cattle train..."

Maria just looked confused. "Cattle train?"

"Maria! You've got to listen to me!" Then she lowered her tone a little. "Are you with me, can you hear me now?" Lusha said, moving her hands down to Maria's shoulders as they stopped jerking and she began to breathe more steadily. Sniffing, and then wiping her nose with a handkerchief she took from her sleeve, Maria looked up at her friend.

"The NKVD said they're taking Josef on a cattle train...Do you understand?" Maria was not completely with her yet, so Lusha added with urgency, "Maria! We haven't got much time?"

That brought Maria round, and seeing this, Lusha explained, letting each word come out slowly to make sure that they would register, "They're putting Josef on a cattle train. A cattle train, Maria - they're treating them like fodder!"

Maria's eyes widened as Lusha carried on, "They're going to pack as many of our boys...God, probably women too...as many people on there as they can. Think about it, Maria, this is the Russians. They're not going to give them any food or water, probably for days. Who knows how long it will take - it...it's a long way."

"What am I supposed to do?" asked Maria, looking as though she was going to break down again, but Lusha stopped her short.

She said with conviction, "You have to take him food, Maria. You have to go to the train and take it to him, or he'll starve."

That was all it took to get Maria on her feet and heading for the kitchen.

"Right," she said as she sniffed up her tears, took a large linen napkin from a hook on the wall, laid it flat on the kitchen table, and started moving quickly around the small kitchen grabbing a hunk of smoked cheese, kiełbasa, an apple and whatever else she could find to pack and take to her beloved husband.

Lusha gathered her lucky playing cards, put them back in their box and stepped over to the kitchen just as Maria was about to tie the bundle. Without a word, she prised the napkin open a little and placed her cards in with the food, winking at Maria, who tied it up and headed out the front door. Lusha looked on sadly, not believing for a second that she would see either her cards or Josef again.

Chapter 7

The Train

1939 Lwów, Poland

"Josef...Josef...*Josef*," called Maria in a nervous half-whisper, as she made her way to the next carriage, her voice high-pitched, fraught with nerves: if she was caught she would be on one of those trains herself. She was not even sure how many trains there were. On the first one, people had been packed in like animals for the slaughter, and she had also seen enough women on the carriages to know that what Lusha had said was true.

Having slipped through the bull yard to the middle of the first train, when she got to the cattle and cargo section of the railway, a little way from the main station, Maria had searched along as far as she dared. Not wanting to be seen by the guards at either end of the trains, she called out in a strained whisper for Josef, to find that there were only women on that first train. Some of them responded to her calls, peering through the gaps or reaching out their hands to grasp at her, as though she could save them. Reeling both from their clasping hands and from the clawing sense of fear and the mixing odours of sweat and cattle, it was all she could do not to break down at the shock of it all, but on she had gone.

To her horror, when she leaned her head out to look from between two carriages to see if she could make it across to the next train under the revealing glare of the full moon, she could now see that there were trains and trains beyond, and by the sound of the scuffles, cries and shouts coming from them, they all seemed to be full like the first.

Hearing a shriek of steam from one of the trains as it began to chuff, chuff out of the station, following on from another that had left only minutes ago, Maria felt all the more desperate. How was she going to find Josef before his train left and without being taken herself?

Moving up and down the carriages and between the trains haphazardly, holding the long rosary that hung around her neck like a prayer, she became more and more frantic, not even aware of the September chill that had set in.

"Josef...Josef...Josef," she called desperately through her tears, for what seemed like the millionth time. Exhausted and overcome with despair she finally slumped onto her haunches, her back against a carriage, and dropped her head.

Above her she heard Josef call her name, "Maria, I'm here."

She looked up to see his hand reaching through the iron grill. Jumping up and taking hold of his hand, she held it to her cheek, kissed it several times and called up to him, "I've brought you some food - I don't know how long this train will be here for - I have to give you some food, eat, eat - save some for later," and she handed the bundle of food to him. As soon as he had taken it into the carriage, he pulled with his other hand on the iron bar to press his face to the small hole in the grate.

"Oh, Maria, thank you. I heard one of the guards saying that we're going soon. That Ankavagista wasn't lying, they *are* taking us to Siberia…"

"Siberia!" She had not wanted to believe that it was true. "But that's days and days away! Boże, boże. I-I'll come back later - bring you more food."

"No, you shouldn't come back. I can look after myself, don't worry - I'm a Krupinsky. At least you are still safe - you must stay safe; I'll escape and I'll get back to you," Josef boasted, that ingrained cockiness coming through his fear. "Now you shouldn't be here, it's dangerous; if the guards see you they could arrest you - you *have* to go."

A rush of crunching stones underfoot coming closer and closer revealed that it was too late, Maria had been spotted: a young NKVD guard was walking quickly towards her with a rifle pointed, another one not far behind.

"What are you doing here?" he asked tersely.

The second one caught up and simply said, "Name and address?"

Josef called out from the carriage, "Leave her alone, she's done nothing wrong."

The second guard slammed the butt of his handgun against the carriage, making Josef shrink back.

"Grayznaya krysa!" shouted the guard. "Get back! I've had enough trouble from you."

"Wha…" Maria grasped for a response, but then that old Polish defiance kicked in, "I was just giving my husband some bread and water - it's not a crime to feed my husband."

"It is not permitted; this is not allowed," the second said without properly looking at her, his eyes still on the train, when out of the corner of his eye he glanced at Maria, and there was a pause. Now he turned and studied her more carefully, and that was when Maria recognised him and dropped her eyes. This was the tall officer who had come into her home and arrested Josef. "You live near here. By the station, by the bridge, yes," he stated more than asked.

"Yes." There was no point denying it, she knew that he had recognised her too.

The officer looked back over the way he had come, into the shadows where Maria could just make out the red-lit tip of a cigarette, and then a puff of smoke, before he said, "If I see you here again, I will arrest you. I could arrest you now. Understood?"

"Yes," Maria said, subserviently, and then made her way back the way she had come, between the carriages of the next train.

She heard the younger guard calling after her but he was cut off by the tall one, saying, "Let the *suka* go. Back to your post." And then there was only the receding sound of their crunching footsteps as they walked away.

Maria did not wait long before she turned around and snuck back towards Josef's train and whispered, "Josef, are you still there."

A small scuffle in the carriage and Josef's despondent voice came through, "Yes, I'm here, I'm here, I'm not going anywhere, am I? But you shouldn't have come back."

"I had to come back. I had to say goodbye," Maria said. It was easy to tell that she was crying.

"Shh - I heard something," Josef said, but in the pause, there was nothing, "Go, Maria, go, be careful."

"When will I see you?" Maria asked desperately. "How will I find you?"

"I don't know - you have to go, it's too dangerous," was all he said.

"I'm going, I'm going, I love you husband."

At that, Josef reached his hand out of the hole on the grate again and Maria took it once more and kissed it.

"I love you, wife," Josef said tenderly. "Now go, you *must* go."

Maria pulled herself away from Josef's hand and stepped over to the next train. Before she clambered between the carriages she turned to see Josef's face pressed into the hole in the grate, gazing at her with an unreadable expression.

Across from Josef, down from where Maria had slipped between the carriages, in the next break between carriages, the red tip of a cigarette burned bright as it was sucked on hard. It was then thrown down onto the moonlit ground and, stepping forward to twist his foot and crush the butt end under heel, was the NKVD commanding officer. He looked up at Josef with a smirk, running two of his fingers across his pencil moustache and down his stubble, then put his hand on his pot belly and, lifting the other hand to show off his gun, he turned on his heel and walked the same way that Maria had gone.

Lusha was still at Maria's flat above the railway station when she got back, clearly shaken, whispering nervously as she closed the door, "Lusha, I've seen Josef, he's okay," and then to answer Lusha's raised eyebrows of concern, "I haven't been seen."

"Good," said Lusha. "We need to be careful..." but she didn't get to finish what she was going to say because, in that instant, there was a forceful knock at the door.

"En-Ka-Va-De! Open up!"

One look and a shake of her head from Lusha showed Maria that her friend knew she had in fact been seen.

"En-Ka-Va-De! Open up!"

They didn't call a third time but simply came in, the same pair as before, the short one resting his hands on his stomach, with the look of a man who had laid his bait and was here to claim his catch. He lifted a hand and ran two fingers across his moustache, clearly savouring the moment. Finally he said, with cold satisfaction, "Maria Krupinski, you are under arrest for giving food to a prisoner; come with me."

"Oh my god!" shouted Lusha and started to cry, the short one relishing her tears - now she knew who was boss. "She only wanted to feed her husband - that's not a crime is it?"

"*Zatknis*, woman, or I will arrest you too," he said, gratification written all over his unshaven face. "Is that understood?"

Lusha nodded, sucking up her tears as she stood tall and stepped up to him and slapped him in the face.

"You know I could make you pay for that, but what I am going to do instead, is make your friends pay for it. Unless you decide to behave from now on. Is *that* understood?" His imperious tone made Lusha's eyes widen as she stepped back and then dropped her head in acquiescence.

With that, the men ushered Maria away.

Chapter 8
Bribery

1976 Birmingham, UK

In his office, Eddie sat with pen in hand, looking blankly at the wall, as he thought through his research on Russian special forces in World War II. Anja, his wife, had mentioned the NKVD often enough when telling the story of her parents, Joseph and Maria. What Eddie was trying to understand was how the involvement of that select unit of Stalin's militia related to what could be found on the wreck of the HMS Edinburgh.

The NKVD, as a Soviet governmental organisation, was still undergoing structural changes in 1939, ever-shifting under the paranoid gaze of Stalin, however, the work that it did was already routine by the time its black-clad officers marched into Poland. By then, untold numbers of Russian citizens had already been killed by them, mass executions of people deemed to be a threat to the dictator. Not only those seen to directly oppose the establishment but those associated with free-thinking: artists, writers, poets, teachers and gypsies. Plus those who could be seen as a hindrance: folks who were mentally ill or disabled. Anyone who might taint the new bloodline of subservient soldiers and workers was removed. NKVD officers carried the authority of the state, empowered to subdue, arrest or kill anyone fitting the Communist Party's broad description of a person who would weaken or come against Stalin's rule.

Just like Germany, it seemed to Eddie, in terms of gross domestic product, Russia looked very much as though it had been gearing up to extend its empire, if not to rule all of Europe. Alongside an invading army, such a grand venture required manpower, both as a workforce and as police to keep said workforce in step. It appeared too as though Stalin and Hitler, both brought up on a diet of old glory, had been versed in the same dogma of imperial rule: leading with an iron fist of discipline, wiping out any competition, silencing every voice of opposition, requiring absolute loyalty to them alone.

It takes an uncanny focus - and years of refining - to temper such a dedicated force: an unconscionable army of men who will obey every order, any order. Stalin himself had witnessed such unquestioning devotion in his training as a priest. His new religion was communism. Marx was its progenitor, Lenin had been its prophet, Stalin was God. Now what was being preached was this new political dogma, not just every Sunday, but every day, in every newspaper, through every door, on every street corner billboard, and broadcast on every available air wave. Even coming from the sky itself: cluster bombs filled with tens of thousands of leaflets each, dropped across the Soviet territories, extending the reach of information to the most remote corners of any state. This was a large-scale logistical effort and, once again, because businesses would have been involved in the venture, people had to get paid.

Eddie sat back in his chair and stared at the wall, pen in hand, tapping on the table, mumbling out loud, "Follow the money…"

For Eddie, everything his wife, Anja, had told him about her parents, Josef and Maria, left a trail of money too, starting with those cluster bombs. Before the Russians marched into Poland, leaflets had rained from the sky, announcing their imminent arrival and telling the Poles to hand over their arms. To make that happen would have required the reverse-engineering of the bombs, paper, printing, aeroplanes, fuel and pilots. Even those services run directly by the state would require financing. What Eddie was interested in, was whether this trail would lead to evidence of the infamous gold in Stalin's possession.

A thought coming to him, he leant forward and began to write figures on one of his notepads and then to tally them up, adding up the cost of the airborne leaflet operation alone and coming up with a sum that made him whistle out loud, knowing that this was only one small area within the propaganda rollout. There would still have been scores of people who had to get paid along the way, from business deals to backhanders - one would have to grease palms if one wanted to bypass bureaucracy and be top of the pile on someone's worklist - even in communist Russia. All of this added to vast amounts of cash, and a lot of people being paid. Even where some people were working on the basis that they would get their cut at some point, one would still require the hiring of people to do the coercing, make the deals, talk the talk. Eddie himself did not work for nothing.

So a question was forming in the back of his mind: where was Stalin getting all this dosh?

Take, for instance, Eddie thought, this twisted guy who was in charge of rounding up prisoners to be sent to the gulag, like Josef and Maria. Sure, there must have been a good stock of hatred for the Poles in him, according to what Anja had recounted, however for Eddie there always had to be more for people who sought positions of power, especially the ones who took the dirty jobs to get there. There had to be a substantial pay cheque each month, and extra on the side too. He had read and witnessed enough to know that communism was never so all-pervading as to secure loyalties without payouts, sums that went beyond the state portions. There were, after all, a good deal of wealthy people in Russia. Bribery was a force within business under any form of political rule.

Eddie also noted that to then run a gulag, as that arresting NKVD officer had gone on to do, meant not only that he had been ambitious but that he had the aptitude, and probably the experience, to take on a major directorial role. The gulags were not simply prisons, they were being run as large-scale labour camps. And the prisoners were not just breaking rocks: the gulags were the mines and the manufacturing and forestry centres which underpinned Russia's industrialization process.

It made sense to Eddie that Stalin would not have believed that Hitler would settle for taking Europe alone, so that even before the tides turned on their alliance, he had been forced to move up a gear in terms of arming. This had meant expanding his workforce to build his arsenal, which, in a sense, is precisely what was going on with the arrests of thousands upon thousands of Poles. It was, at the time, the Russian equivalent of recruitment.

As a businessman, Eddie could imagine Stalin and his boys doing the sums, just like him, and realising that, with what they had in their coffers, the calibre of the munitions that they could produce would be inferior to what came out of dedicated German engineering. So the Soviets had opted for bulk rather than quality, cutting the cost of labour and maximising productivity. To hold back the threat of being engulfed by the Third Reich had meant amassing a cheap labour force and then getting as much out of them as humanly possible. It was just accounting.

In the name of protecting their manufacturing tools and equipment, so the papers had read in Russia, several hundred trains transported machinery to Siberia, where the additional workforce also resided.

Taking into account the fact that a great deal had to have already been put in place before the Poles even got to the camps, by Eddie's estimations, the bill for setting up and running the gulags would have amounted to the cost of an entire industrial revolution. The venture had required the laying of train lines and running of trains, training and mobilising a whole army of secret police to arrest a Russian and then Polish workforce, and then maintaining prison staff, to name some of the most substantial expenses alone. The tally would have been unfathomable. So once again he sat back and stared at the wall, wondering just where these mountains of money came from.

Eddie picked up the phone. His question had triggered the fact that he had recently met a man who would now come in most useful.

Within the wide spectrum of people whom he called friends - people whom he had a use for, in other words - it was natural that Eddie's path had dovetailed with an economist. At the charity function where they first spoke, it had only been a surprise to the economist to find that he and Eddie held a mutual interest in the same kind of investment opportunity. Eddie had, as he often did at such affairs, already factored in how this man might be of some use to him before approaching him, so he had quickly got to the subject of what they had held in common. This was always Eddie's in-road.

First he worked on the fact that the eloquent man's first passion was investigating the history of the world wars from an economic standpoint, a subject he had written two books about. The real skill had been to then slip in the idea that an investment opportunity the economist was presenting could be boosted by funds coming out of a risky, yes, but *lucrative* salvage operation already in motion. After making the blatant suggestion that this salvage, involving a large find of property that essentially belonged to the Crown, would certainly attract the attention of high government officials and royalty, the economist was in. Status and money. Easy target.

Eddie had already managed to squeeze a tidy sum of money from the erudite fellow, what he needed now though, was the man's educated opinion. He needed to know for certain that what lay at the bottom of the Barents Sea was the real deal.

On the call, his economist acquaintance dished out the percentages that, at first, seemed to answer Eddie's question: just before the war, forced labour in Russia provided 46.5% of the nation's nickel, 76% of its tin, 40% of its cobalt, 40.5% of its chrome-iron ore. And 60% of its gold.

The base metals were for making the machines, the tanks, the guns and the bullets, and the gold may well have covered for the paid element of the workforce, but, as for feeding the army and paying both them and the police force, never mind the whole propaganda vehicle, all of Russia's gold stocks would still not have been sufficient. As far as the scholar's opinion went, Stalin did not have enough in his reserves to finance holding off the might of the Third Reich.

"For that, they would have needed even more gold than had been mined," the economist commented. "Stalin had gold galore to pay for his industrial climb, but only so long as he was allied to Hitler."

"Unless he had an unknown supply of gold," Eddie mused.

"Unless he had a substantial storehouse of the stuff," concluded the economist. "But then, it is fairly well known that the Soviet Union paid for their end of the Lend-Lease Bill in gold bullion. It just isn't represented that way in the ledger - only in a few mentions within the diaries of low-ranking navy crew. One of those accounts is from the

Edinburgh, actually. I can only imagine that your associate, Mr. Craddock, would be working on just such information."

History told Eddie, in a brutal tally of amassed bodies, that Stalin did not trust anyone. If there were discrepancies in anybody's behaviour, he would have them detained, questioned and in many cases shot. This was not tens of people, it was not even tens of thousands, it was hundreds of thousands. He was certainly not about to trust a self-professed megalomaniac like Hitler. However, up until the point when Germany invaded his country, Stalin must have thought that he was on the winning side. The question of how the spoils would have been divided when the war was over would have surely occupied his mind - whether that would have been decided over the table or at the end of a gun, or even guns on the table - but he could not have seriously considered the Führer turning on him, and certainly not so soon, otherwise he would have surely been preparing earlier. But, of course, Hitler lost his patience with the alliance: unlike Stalin, he already had his arsenal but he had limited fuel supplies. And this was, ultimately, to cause the turning point in the war.

Part of the coalition deal between the two countries was that Russia would provide oil to Germany. The Communists must have figured that they were offering enough to maintain the relations with Germany as a combined force and, as a backup, they would have believed that Hitler could not win the war if he added Russia to his list of enemies. So Eddie figured that Stalin must have banked on his alliance holding out, that he would have seen himself in a strong position. The fearsome autocrat would have been caught completely off guard and unaware.

Regardless of having a massive workforce, Russia was trailing behind Germany in terms of technology and munition stockpiles. Now they were twice vulnerable, considering the hasty retreat Communist forces were having to make, burning crops as they went to starve the encroaching Nazis. Russia could not make up for the produce it was losing or make munitions overnight.

Stalin was forced to look at his options, and quickly. Considering that he was an aggressor to the rest of the Allied forces whom he was now going to have to side with, simply to survive, he was going to have to make the kind of deals that were backed with some serious collateral.

But, as is the Russian way, the bargaining would involve *vodka*. It was not a drink, it was a way of life. Eddie considered that it was a common saying in those parts never to trust anyone who did not drink vodka.

Churchill was sent a formal invitation to a meeting in Moscow. There was no way Stalin would leave the safety of his own realm to make any deals and, as it was, the Allies needed Russia too. So the British prime minister was flown over to Moscow in an escorted Lancaster Bomber to look at a proposed treaty with Russia. This would have been a tense affair. Yet, afterwards, Churchill is famed not only for having partaken of a little vodka but for having a good ol' drink with the Soviet premier. This was, after all, how one consummated a deal with a full-blooded Russian. Not to mention an Englishman worth his salt.

Where Russia was concerned, the Allied treaty went hand-in-hand with what Eddie could only see as an American business deal: the U.S. would supply Stalin with everything necessary to repel the German forces, but they would be billed for the process. This was not charity. Over *four million tonnes* of supplies - including tanks, fighters, bombers, ammunition, raw materials and food - were transported to Russia over four years.

In response to the offer of this aid Stalin wrote to Roosevelt, "Your decision, Mr. President, to give the Soviet Union an interest-free credit of $1 billion in the form of materiel supplies and raw materials has been accepted by the Soviet government with heartfelt gratitude as urgent aid to the Soviet Union in its enormous and difficult fight against the common enemy – bloodthirsty Hitlerism."

The USSR received a total of 44,000 American jeeps, 375,883 cargo trucks, 8,071 tractors and 12,700 tanks. And it was not simply armaments that were delivered to the Soviet Union, they were also sent 1,541,590 blankets, 331,066 litres of alcohol, 15,417,000 pairs of army boots, 106,893 tons of cotton, 2,670,000 tons of petroleum products and 4,478,000 tons of food supplies.

The delivery of these goods had presented a daunting predicament for the allies, in that these supplies would have to be transported primarily by ocean. What was more, only *non*-military goods could be transported via the Pacific, because of the neutrality between Russia and Japan, which left only one route for armaments to be taken, and that was via the North Atlantic and Arctic Seas. This meant passing Norway, which was Nazi-held territory. Its coast was occupied by the strategically positioned and formidable German U-boats, which, now that Hitler had severed his loyalty to Stalin, were facing both in the direction of England and Russia, with a single mission: to break these lines of supply.

And so began the arduous Arctic convoys. A vast supply chain of cargo vessels escorted by fleets of heavily armed warships.

By this point, the German U-19, U-20 and U-23 submarines were a terrifying presence beneath the waves of the far northern oceans. Sea Wolves. They were a reckoning, a serious force to be dealt with. Had the Germans more of those awesome underwater terrors at their disposal the tide may have remained in their favour.

Along with the raw tonnage of food, materials, munitions and machines immersed in this deal, a huge number of the ships themselves were provided by the United States. This meant only one thing to Eddie: the American government was not going to jeopardise such an expensive flotilla for nothing. Britain needed Russia as an ally, whereas America, as a commercial entity within the partnership, was acting on behalf of the *companies* making the ships and providing the other goods, and *they* needed to get paid.

Whatever project it was that Eddie was working on, you would only ever see numbers and figures on the notepads in his office, however, now, as he put his pen behind his ear once again, Eddie leant back and looked at the words he had written amongst the scrawl of sums: Lend Lease Bill?

Eddie was well-read and versed in many topics. His frame of mind was to always be in the know, to have the edge, to have the knowledge to back up his words. He had a large library with a broad range of reference books. To save time he had developed the ability to speed read, scanning works for relevant information, and he had an aptitude for remembering what was most relevant and calling it to mind when needed. One did not get to win people over the way he did without doing a lot of homework. Eddie knew it paid to be armed, which was precisely why, after speaking with the economist, he set to read more about the deal done by the Americans. He was interested in who got paid and, more importantly, what they were paying with.

One historian had made a point of highlighting the log references to ships within the convoys. The logs recorded dropping supplies at Murmansk, in the farthest northwest of Russia but did *not* record the covert location up the channel, where they remained just off the coastline for the arranged pickup of payment. 'Select hands' were mentioned to have loaded such payments onto the cargo ships travelling back via England and on to America. The nature of payment had been a closely guarded secret. No one was to know.

Chapter 9

Secret Cargo

1942 White Sea, Soviet Union

"You have your orders, men," the first mate said, with a curt nod. The gesture was all the sailors required to bolster the understanding that the usual cargo loading procedure was to be coupled with both vigilance and confidentiality. It was just before midnight, a most unusual time to be taking on a shipment. Moreover, the load was to be taken aboard at an undisclosed location, not in the Kola Inlet, where the shipment of munitions and the supplies had already been dropped off, but out in the White Sea. And, alongside the officers, only a handful of up-and-coming petty officers had been employed for the task, each one feeling the weight of responsibility to have been chosen by the Captain personally. "Up on deck in five minutes."

"Yes, Sir," said Start and Walkey.

Supply Petty Officer Arthur Start and his mate, Petty Officer Bob Walkey, two years into the conflict, were already old hands in war terms. They had survived the seas together aboard the HMS Edinburgh. And not just any seas, but the severe waters that lay between the Finnmark countries of Norway and the Karelian shores of Russia.

The area they had to pass through on each run belonged to the Arctic Glacial Ocean, with a sub-arctic climate that made the waters closest to the pack-ice in the north up to a paralysing -25 degrees Celsius, and in the south, closer to the continent, up to -8. The North and the Barents Seas were not only violent in terms of weather, but they also, at that time, contained the largest concentration of warships, submarines and planes seen in any area of the war.

Departing time and again from Scotland and heading through the North Sea past the Orkney and Shetland Islands, favourite haunts for Nazi spies, then on to the Barents Sea. Widely manoeuvring around Norway, to avoid the elusive U-boats, the convoys then made their way through the freezing Arctic Sea, keeping as close to the ice as possible. When they finally headed down past Bear Island and around into Polyarny and Murmansk, the German bomber command would do their utmost to destroy the fleets, all of them aiming at the cargo. As soon as the convoys met the Folkawolf they knew that they would be honed in on by U-boats. The whole crew would be on standby, the attacks starting there and then.

That any ship should have made the journey came down, to a large degree, to the well-orchestrated Allied sea and air cover, which maximised the defence of the fleets and, to a far greater degree than one might have expected, came down to the weather - especially in the winter months. There were many times when those on duty could hear the Germans flying overhead yet remained unseen under the cover of fog, the sea frets often covering the superstructure and even the masts of the ships.

Nevertheless, it had not taken Start and Walkey long to learn the true meaning of the words "sitting duck." The bulk of the convoys were cargo ships, which were fitted with cannons and guns, but were not built for speed. Standing on any of those freight ships, the feeling of vulnerability was not only palpable but real: it was a great, big, floating target. That slow sea-train of ships, passing through U-boat-infested territories and icy waters, often dogged by German fighter planes and bombers, meant that one's survival relied heavily on intelligence received, and thereafter on sea and air support.

Sunderland flying boats were deployed to keep watch over the fleets, communicating U-boat sightings with the men posted to lookout on the ships. One of the advantages of the Sunderland was their flight time of up to 14 hours. They were in the air so long that the planes were decked out with their own kitchen, fitted with a kerosene oven, a toilet and bunks so that the crews could rotate between one another. The flight crew needed to be completely alert to see approaching U-boats, their slender hulls camouflaged against the murky seas. Sighting one would be more like spotting an irregularity in the water. In many ways, they were as good as ghosts: even at surface level they blended in with the grey-green, choppy waters. So one needed sharp eyes to discern whether what one was seeing was not simply a whale or the shadow of a wave.

Once a Sunderland had determined a sighting they would immediately relay the position of the U-boat to the convoy, and it would be all hands on deck, the whole fleet would be on high alert. In the meantime the plane could deploy its bombs, but with little success. Hitting the narrow hull of a

U-boat was the equivalent of winning the lottery. It was potluck.

However, the moment that U-boat rose to torpedo level, the ships were in its sights and fleeing was no longer an option. The wolves were upon them, the hunt was over. All the men could do was fight hard, sit tight, and pray to Mother Mary.

When the ships had moved past the point of no return, when they were beyond all other support, outside of what artillery they carried, steps had been put in place to reduce the vulnerability of the convoys. Desperate measures were taken to protect the cargo. Trawlers, whose main job was to pick up men who had fallen into the water during battle, were fitted with a giant catapult on the bow of the ship. Onto this catapult, a Hurricane was set. In the event of a battle, where no air support could be called in, the plane would be launched off the deck, and would then do as much damage as possible before its fuel ran out and it was forced to ditch in the sea! Fast and low in the water, and decked with as many guns as the nimble vessels could carry, the trawlers would then do their best to save the pilots, but in most cases, the men would be lost.

Not only did the crews have to survive all of these onslaughts, they had to contend with the elements themselves. The dangers of the notoriously treacherous waters and strong currents that the arctic convoys had to navigate, where rogue icebergs and simply the cold itself were as much one's enemies as U-boats, only increased in severity as the fleets moved closer to their perilous drop-off point in Murmansk.

The visibility of an iceberg could be tricky in its own right, where above the water one may have seen a little or a lot, but the threat was beneath the water. This meant that ships required a seamless routine of surveillance - men in the crow's nest watching out, not only for U-boats but also for drifting icebergs. They were irregular but, in that sense, were even more of a hazard, because all it took was to be looking in the other direction when one hefty underwater mountain of ice drifted speedily in. A momentary lapse in concentration and it was upon them. A sizable iceberg could render them scuppered.

Then add that fog. Fog so dense that visibility could be anywhere from poor to near zero. It rolled in swiftly and without invitation, so that, even though the fog cleared the skies of danger, the odds were still stacked up against the convoys, because their enemies were all *on* and *under* the water. To have reached this far only to go down because of a natural disaster would have been, militarily, unacceptable, and would have, in terms of morale, been soul-destroying.

The most prevalent and unremitting enemy though, was the cold. Along with the usual naval duties, combatting the effects of the freezing conditions meant that there were added responsibilities for any seaman who was part of an arctic run. There was very little downtime aboard the convoys. Of the crew members, all were required: if a sailor was not sleeping or eating, he was put to task.

A major issue was ice build-up on board the ships. If it was not cleared away regularly, the ice could get so heavy as to sink the ship. Because of the incessant ice build-up there had to be a constant rotation of ice-breakers on deck to hack away at it.

Every inch of steel became a foundation, a platform for ice stacks to build upon. For example, the speed of growth of ice on railings, which acted as scaffolding for ice to collect upon, was such that, while deckhands hacked away with pick axes at the clumps of ice covering the deck, yet another layer of ice would build up. No sooner was one area cleared of ice than the area cleared before was covered again. It was a never-ending story. Then there were doorways and hatches to keep clear, along with turrets, guns, winches, pulleys and more. Some of the guns, like the two-pounders on the Edinburgh, had electric blankets placed over the barrels, which had to be routinely checked and serviced. The ship required the guns and cannons to be operational just as much as the deck needed to be cleared. Yet a cannon failing was not as dangerous as an icy floor. If a sailor slipped and fell into those polar waters he had seconds, minutes tops - in truth, chances of survival were very slim. And the waves were so tremendous that they could very easily sweep sailors overboard, more so if the deck was icy.

Here one could see the paramount importance of those crucial tasks of surveillance and ice-breaking coming into play: if approaching U-boats were not sighted, a ship was as good as gone, and if one was located it would be of no use to have frozen cannons, so it was imperative that these tasks were undertaken with determination and due care. It was the difference between success and failure, between life and death.

It should come as no surprise then, that in terms of men, machines and tonnage, the fleets suffered heavy losses.

What is surprising and sad is that the survivors of any one run did not, by dint of having outlived the odds together, become a united brotherhood, bonded by hard graft and absolute trust. There was, all too often, a marked difference between the calibre of men who had joined the navy before the war and those who were called up after its onset. This meant that, for many, the Edinburgh was not a happy ship. Crewed by a certain number of hostilities-only personnel who were green to the sea, had very little training, and displayed the traits of coming from tougher backgrounds than the pre-war sailor, bullying and theft were rife and trust levels were low.

Despite this, there was a rare camaraderie amongst like-minded seamen that was exemplified in the likes of Start and Walkey, two men who had become nigh-on inseparable upon their previous runs. Having already sailed several of them, they were now weathered seamen too. Good men. Hard workers who followed orders and got the job done. As steadfast as they were as sailors, and efficient as they were in their roles, it had only made sense to increase their rank to petty officers, to hold them up as examples to the other crew members with whom they had gained due respect. It was because of men like this, because of their determination, impeccable teamwork and willingness to do over and above what would be expected of sailors in any other seas, that, on the whole, the fleets were successful: they defended their ships, repaired them when damaged, delivered their cargo and retrieved the payment with discretion.

◇

Start and Walkey readied themselves to go up on deck. They had gone to sleep in uniform and now unrolled the outdoor kit that they had prepared, as always, tugging on the extra layers without thought - second nature to them now. They could do it in their sleep. The kit included a second layer of knee-length knitted socks, knee-high black Wellington boots - with their distinctive white woollen band at the top - woven fleece jumper, a dense duffle coat with more wool on the inside and resilient black oilcloth on the outside, to mark their rank - where deckhands would usually be in khaki. They were trussed up like penguins. The uniform of the Arctic. All blubber and stiff movement.
"It's freezing up there," said Walkey, which was quite something for a Scotsman to say. He was from Thurso on the northernmost end of Scotland, just next door to John O'Groats, where the wind was born. "The snow's been settling for days," he added, pulling on his duffle coat, bumping shoulders with Start who was pulling on his wool-lined balaclava. It was a cramped space. There was barely any room to manoeuvre in the tiny quarters, only big enough for two thin beds, a wall of drying racks and shallow lockers. To keep the narrow floor space between bed and

lockers clear at all times, everything was economically stored and arranged purposely for easy access. One never knew when they were going to be rallied up on deck, and every second could count in an emergency. They could not afford to be falling over one another or scrabbling around in search of some item of clothing or kit.

"Yeah, must be three inches deep," replied Start. Neither of the men was complaining, they were acclimatised to the elements - even their skin had adapted to the ice and snow, giving them a hardy look - they were simply observing the facts, preparing themselves for what they would have to face outside. The harsh nature of the Arctic Sea had conditioned them quickly. They had learned fast that it took a strong mindset for the body to survive such severe elements. It was Hell frozen over. Place one's bare hand on a frosted railing and it adhered, instantly. The only way to remove it was to leave the top layer of skin behind, and it would not stop there. The other layers of skin would be burned by the ice, and that hand, even if the nerves healed and the wound did not get infected, was never going to be the same again. That sailor would feel the strain he had put on his crewmates, who would have to take over much of his tasks. The mind had to adjust swiftly. One learned how costly a single little mistake could be; from then on they were not only careful, they listened to orders and instructions to the tee. Attention to detail was paramount. Yet through it all, they were just men, just sailors doing their job.

"Three inches and the rest," rebutted Walkey, then he leaned in and lowered his tone, "I don't like it. That Admiral's on board."

"Whaddya mean?" asked Start, as they stepped over the threshold of the chamber into the narrow passageway.

Walkey geared up to tell one of his notorious seafarer's fables, "Well, you know the story, don't you?" As the more experienced deckhand, Walkey was more accustomed to the workings of navy life, having already served in the navy for a few years before the war, and he always seemed to have a greater handle on the comings and goings on board the ship, so that Start had stuck close to him from the beginning. At first, it had been a simple case of a veteran seaman taking a lad under his wing - big brother, little brother - but it had not taken long for the age gap to disappear - everybody's an old man at war - and for Start to mature, to take everything on board and step up alongside Walkey as a respected sailor in his own right.

"What story?" asked Start, a tinge of concern to his Essex accent as he looked at his friend with slanting eyes.

"Well, he's a Jonah, isn't he?" answered Walkey, with emphasis on the name of the ship-rocking prophet.

Start did not slow his pace through the corridor but tilted his head back over his shoulder and repeated, "Jonah!?"

"Every ship that's been under his command has gone down," Walkey responded with ill feeling, undercurrents of fear washing up against the sides of his words like oil-slick waters.

"Every ship?" questioned Start, Walkey's trepidation transferring into his mind. The men were under such tremendous pressure, with so many odds pitched against them, that it did not take much to tip the scales, to break the spirit. The convoys were being attacked from every direction imaginable, by cutting seas and the U-boats beneath them - waiting, using their prowess to find the right moment to strike. Then there were the constant air raids, and whatever else came from the skies - stinging rain, sleet, snow, all of them driven by relentless winds. It just never let up. The mind could only take so much, and in the Arctic, as the hazards piled up, all the men had was their training and their brothers beside them, yet often the only way to keep grounded, to centre oneself, to maintain balance, lest one go under, was to remain focused on the tasks at hand. This is where the crew having too much to do was a *good* thing. It was better not to stop, to be completely occupied with labour-intensive tasks until their heads hit the bunk and exhaustion quickly saved them from thinking too much.

They could not be active every minute of every day though. And there were only so many sea shanties one could sing and jokes the men could tell to buoy up the tone. It was inevitable that those dreaded moments of silence would come, or that the mind would be allowed to wander during some mundane task, and that was when it could get them: the fear. All of a sudden it would be upon them. Each man would have to come up with his own ways to keep the darkness at bay, to allay the despair: the feeling of living on borrowed time. Listing one's tasks for the next day.

Recalling a letter from a loved one. Singing. Whatever it took.

Nevertheless, there were times when one simply could not avoid something slipping through the net: an idea, a thought, a rumour.

"Well, ships. Plural. How many do you have to sink before you're a Jonah?" This thought had been festering in Walkey's mind, the voice of uncertainty building up inside him since he had discovered that the Admiral was onboard. He had tried over and again to keep the fatalistic thoughts from surfacing, from allowing the questions to mount. He had done well to keep a lid on saying anything so far, but this command to take in a mysterious shipment at a secret location was just too much. Walkey could not help himself from connecting the dots, storyteller that he was: Why had the ship, an Edinburgh-type cruiser, been named after Edinburgh itself? Why the seal of importance? Why had so few men been chosen to do a task in the dead of night? Most of them officers? And why had they been told to keep their mouths shut? Why would one not want the other men to know? What new dangers were they heading into? This was, no doubt about it, unorthodox procedure in every way. Not in the fact that he and Start had been told that they were taking in a shipment of munitions, only that they would be doing so at the stroke of midnight. There were reasons why munitions were loaded in daylight, given the obvious danger of fumbling explosives. What were they actually going to be loading?

And then there was the Admiral himself.

"Sunk the very first ship he set foot on as Captain - everybody knows about it."

"Well I don't know about it, mate, stop messing with me: out with it," demanded Start.

"The HMS Intrepid, back in the first war. He's a climber, he is: for every ship he sinks, he gets put up a rank, gone from Secretary to Admiral, to Rear Admiral, to Vice Admiral, and now he's only in command of our fleet."

"You're joking." The mind's first defence against dark thoughts: humour. It had to be a joke.

"No," replied Walkey, as he put his foot on the last rung and opened the hatch, the cold hitting the only exposed part of his face, that small window around the eyes, "I'm not joking."

Both the Vice-Admiral and the Captain stood on the rear deck of the HMS Edinburgh. Behind them were ten men; six selected officers, armed with rifles at the ready, and four petty officers, including Walkey and Start, to help load the shipment. Everyone else, Walkey mused to himself, had been given duties below deck until ordered otherwise. None of the crew had complained, all of them only too happy to be out of the Arctic freeze. In the meantime, the officers had needed to clear a path through the ice that had built up since the last ice-breaker crew had been sent below deck, only minutes before.

Coordinates and exact timing had been exchanged between the leading officers of the Edinburgh and the delivery vessel alone, shortly before the rendezvous. Only loosely briefed soon afterwards, the selected men had been given their orders and were now standing by. All of them looking out through drifts of snow at a wall of fog.

Waiting.

Just waiting.

Finally, slowly and imperceptibly at first, lingering with the wash of waves against the hull, there came the undertones of a low, pulsing chug, echoing the crew's heightened heartbeats.

The shape of a vessel pulled up through the mist and snow, no foghorn to sound its arrival, nothing more than a floating blur, a secret shifting across the surface of the water.

The Captain raised a torch and let out a few dashes and dots. The reply came straight away, long and short beams of light breaking through the fog, a random string of words to the crew who knew Morse code, like any trained seaman would, but were not privy to the encoded message.

The signal was confirmed and the Captain gave orders for the loading lights on deck to be turned on.

As the vessel drew nearer, shapes became more distinct in the broad beams of the floodlights. The lines and edges took form, the spectre revealing itself to be nothing more than a barge. Nevertheless, it equalled its presence next to the Edinburgh; the warship sleek and ready, the barge thick and bulky, just as tall in the water yet wider at the front, its jutting nose approaching like a blade. Silhouettes of men slowly emerged too. About a dozen Russian soldiers, armed with Tommy guns, surrounded hessian-covered crates. The NKVD officers, as they came fully into view, were still little more than shadows in their oil-slick uniforms and black hats, juxtaposed against the swirling white flakes that battled to find purchase on the hard leather of their red lapelled trench coats.

The Captain had already given directions for the petty officers to assist the Russians in bringing the cargo onto the Edinburgh. He had primed his armed contingent, his chosen few - men who had proven their worth on previous missions - to have their rifles cocked and ready, but faced down, to show no aggression. All said and done this needed to be a low-key, swift and unassuming transaction. Load the cargo and go.

Yet an intense pressure built up very quickly, as the barge steadied itself beside the Edinburgh. Men went inwards on themselves. The still-point of no return. They were in it now, in a space that was not readable. Previous relations with Russian soldiers had not exactly garnered favourable relations.

No one moved.

There was a stillness. Part discipline, part perfect-pitch adrenaline, creating that heightened awareness every soldier experienced in the face of danger.

The barge got to within distance for heavy ropes to be cast aboard from the Russian vessel. Two men went forward to tether the barge and, rather than running out the main loading platform, a simple sturdy gangplank was lowered into place between the two vessels, wide enough for two men of either force to stand and shift crates; this was the neutral zone: Russian and British sailors could step upon the plank, but not beyond it onto each other's ships. Things could get messy if one had other militia on board one's ship. And the idea here was to keep it simple and swift.

There was absolute silence and the tense stillness held out, broken only by the motion that quickly set in amongst the NKVD officers aboard the barge. Under the shifting eddies of fog they pulled back the canvas to reveal a stack of ammunition boxes, from which one was taken down by two men and carried over to the plank where they swung the box by the rope handles to the next two Russians on the plank, then, keeping the momentum, they swung the boxes over to the Brits.

Both petty officers instantly registered the sheer weight of the box - so much heavier than it should be - their eyebrows raising for a moment, but they simultaneously pulled themselves back into the job at hand with a neutral regimented look. Swing the box on, take the next one, keep moving. Show nothing.

The undercurrents of tension still gripped the men even when the last box was being stacked, the final card placed on top of the pyramid, and no one dared breathe. The adrenaline peaked and all went into slow motion: the gangplank being retrieved, the ropes untethered and pulled back, the deckhands stepping into formation, and then, as quickly as it had come, the barge was retreating, being swallowed once more by ghostly swirls.

Yet, as the shapes began to lose their distinction, and as the men began to breathe once more, Walkey tensed suddenly as a figure he had not spotted before emerged from the shadows on the barge. A short, portly officer with hand on belly, puffing hard on the last of his cigarette, looking straight at the English Captain, expressionless as he dropped the butt, crushing it underfoot and letting out the smoke to mingle with the fog into which he disappeared. And the barge was gone. The men eased up in time to the fading thrum of its engines, which receded steadily, until there was nothing but the image of that officer in the fog, a sinister silhouette forever etched into Walkey's mind, taking on ever more malevolent forms in his imagination throughout his days at sea and even beyond.

Chapter 10

Blood Payment

1942 White Sea, Soviet Union

The attending officers and the first mate had headed below deck and were making sure the path through the ship was clear all the way to the bomb room, where the ammunition boxes would be stored. With the familiar hum of engines, the Edinburgh headed out, through the straits of the White Sea and into the waters of the Barents.

The Devil's Run.

There was no joy in the fact that the ship was now back in formation, making its way, along with the rest of the convoy, back to Old Blighty. In the men's minds, they might just as well be on their way to the bottom of the sea, to Davy Jones Locker.

It was always a slimmer convoy that made its way back to Britannia, with the amount of ships lost on the journey in. That meant less support on the return leg. Arrival at Murmansk could be kept secret from the Germans to some degree, however once there, re-entering the Arctic was impossible to mask entirely. The Nazis knew the ships had arrived and were waiting for them to leave again. For this obvious reason, ships were more likely to go down on the home run, and the numbness set in as Start and Walkey retreated into themselves, with nothing in mind except doing their job.

"I want these ammunition boxes loaded in the bomb room now," ordered the Captain.

"Yes, Sir," chimed Start.

"Yes, Sir," echoed Walkey.

The four petty officers settled into a workable routine, Start and Walkey getting the boxes through the door and stacking them there, while the other two took the boxes down to the ammunition room. The momentum kicked in, a steady shift of boxes from the pile near the ship's edge over to the door, with the other two men back near enough to grab the next box. Satisfaction welled up in the small team as they set into their cargo-loading routine, all muscle memory and monotony. Just get the job done. Smooth and efficient. That was why they were chosen.

Two-thirds had already been loaded and the men were enjoying the second wind that comes from seeing the end of a task in sight. Paying no mind to the sleet that cut in diagonally across the deck, they slogged on, when all of a sudden, as they hauled a box off the pile, one side of Start's rope handle slipped from its socket. Even though he still held the rope firm in one hand and quickly tried to steady the box with his other, it tipped to the side and the contents, clearly too heavy to be held in by the stapled lid, broke through, and to the floor they dropped with metallic clanks and thuds.

Bars of gold.

"Jesus - it's *gold?*" Start blurted out, the whites of his eyes showing as he shot a querying look at the Captain.

Walkey looked over to the rest of the boxes, remembering his count when they had been loaded, and he instantly began to do the maths but was cut short by the Captain.

Stating, with no hint of surprise, he simply said, "You saw nothing, seamen, right?"

"Yes, Sir," chimed Start.

"Yes, Sir," echoed Walkey, mollified for now by the steadfast tone of the Captain. Nothing unusual here. All according to plan. Hush-hush and all that. Get on with it.

"Good. Pick it up and take it to the bomb room, with the rest," he finished, setting the men back on track, as they quickly placed the bars back in the box and pressed the lid in place, Walkey pushing the tacks in as best he could with the heel of his boot, his mind digesting the sight of all those crates, each one painted with hammer and sickle.

After putting the box down in the entrance to the portal, and letting the other two men know the handle was broken, Start said to Walkey as they headed to get the next box, "Look at my gloves, there's blood on them?"

"It's just paint from the boxes, look at the rain, it's transferred," the other said, almost convincingly, though Start could see that his sly friend was analysing the situation - he would ask him when they returned to their bunks. "Let's just get it done," Walkey said and the two set into motion again, as one by one they shifted the heavy boxes to and fro until the job was complete and they stood up to attention.

"Finished, Sir," chimed Start.

"Finished, Sir," echoed Walkey.

"Right then; back to your bunks," ordered the Captain.

But as they peeled the layers off and readied themselves for bed, having managed not to say anything to each other so far, Start could hold out no longer. "What was that all about?" he whispered.

"Don't ask," said Walkey curtly, not wanting to go there, trying to press the terrible tales of the Russian revolution from his mind.

"But there were 93 boxes there," Start pressed on. "How much would that come to?"

"I don't know. *Don't* ask...but...I told you it was going to be a bad trip," Walkey replied, clearly unnerved, as he slammed his head down onto his pillow, his back to Start.

There was a pause, as Start changed tack. "So…" he started, the mirth obvious in his tone, "you think this has something to do with our Admiral Jonah the Boner?"

"I'm not messing, lad," said Walkey as he turned over to look the younger man steadily in the eye. Counting reasons on his fingers, he said angrily, "First, this Jonah, yes, but then, second, all this hush-hush around the load. Third, midnight, and, fourth," his tone dropped to a whisper, as he added conspiratorially, "you've got NKVD officers...with fuckin' tommy guns...work it out, man."

Start began to visibly assimilate all that his friend was saying.

"And let me tell you something," Walkey added with finality, "that wasn't paint on your hands...that *was* blood."

Chapter 11

Clinching the Deal

1980 Birmingham, UK

In order to support Stalin with his hefty order of supplies and munitions and also, no doubt, to account for the cargo that would inevitably be lost along the way, the price that the United States demanded from their Russian counterpart was, apparently, no less than gold.

It came as no surprise then, to Eddie, that the contract agreed for there to be "no interest" applied. The increase in the value of gold, as a long-term investment, would far outstrip anything that could be gained through a percentage of interest over the same amount of years.

In Eddie's mind, it was *unlikely* that the word gold would have been mentioned in the deal. Gone were the days of piracy and treasure chests overflowing with doubloons. This was commerce. Basic accountancy. It would have been expressed as figures in a ledger - the pluses, the minuses, the add-ons, etcetera, etcetera - which all amounted to a hefty final payout after the war. However, he could imagine that before those vodkas were knocked back and everyone smiled for the camera, the word "gold" would certainly have been spoken, because it turned out that, in one case for sure, five tonnes of Russian gold were said to have been placed on a ship called HMS Edinburgh, at an unrevealed location on the map.

But what gold? By Eddie's accounting, in an economy still based solely upon the gold standard, all of Russia's gold supply coming out of the gulag mines was locked up in paying for industry and the war machine. Russia was already in debt for this mechanisation process. Stalin simply did not have reserves of gold enough to account for the amounts said to have been shipped in payment for his end of the Lend-Lease Bill.

Eddie was not going to put in his full financial commitment behind a treasure hunt that did not end in treasure. He had to know where this extra gold could have come from because his sums told him there was none left in Stalin's pot. But what if the gold was not Stalin's in the first place, what if it had belonged to the Tzar?

Rumours had spread that, back in the days of the Russian Revolution, when the fledgling communists took over Tzar Nikolai's palace, they had rounded up his family and then lined them up, family portrait style, in a room full of the Tzar's prized collection of gold bars, against which they shot them. It was more likely, both to scholars and to Eddie, that Stalin's stockpile had been garnered by stripping the opulent palace of its gold and processing the precious metal coming from the various ornaments, statues, crosses, chandeliers, candelabras, furniture, picture frames, crockery, cutlery, jewellery and more. But was this the gold that made its way to Murmansk and then aboard an English ship?

Things were not adding up and nothing troubled Eddie more than unbalanced books. He stood up and began to pace back and forth, stopping now and again to peer absently through the Georgian window that overlooked the courtyard, where his nephews were playing - as oblivious to his world as he was to theirs.

Anja brought in a cup of tea but placed it on the table without saying anything, sensing a storm brewing and knowing well that it was very likely that both the cup and its contents would end up being thrown against the wall, like so many times before. You did not stick around when Eddie was in one of those moods, but just as she made her way out of the office she caught him blurting out, "The journal!"

Turning on his heel, Eddie went straight for the phone.

He did not greet Geoff when he picked up on the other side but went straight into questioning him over the journal he had spoken of, as to whether it mentioned the actual word 'gold.' The reply was even better than he had hoped for - there were two words: *blood gold.*

The conversation grew heated however as Edie argued the validity of the journal, saying that if the writer knew that it was the Tzar's gold, then there was a strong possibility that the coordinates in the journal were correct. In contrast, Geoff was not so sure that was enough to go on. With each point he tried to put across, Eddie banged his fist even harder on the desk.

Eventually, Eddie gave up and told Geoff to fax him a copy of the journal, only to find that Geoff did not have it on him, that it was in his office in England while he was in a hotel in Helsinki, en route to the Barents Sea to do scouting trips to check out possible locations for the Edinburgh. Eddie took a deep breath and composed himself, requesting Geoff to have his secretary get the journal out - he was going to pick it up right away.

He put the phone down and looked at his watch, calculating how long it was going to take to pick up the journal, considering whether to book his flight to Rotterdam before he left, but realising instantly that if his hunch about the journal was right, that having the journal in his hands might just give him the leverage he needed to clinch the deal on a salvage vessel, which was what he would be doing in Holland.

It was getting late; he might miss the chance to get a plane to Rotterdam that night and, that being the case, he could not call ahead to make an appointment with the shipmaster. A meeting which he should have already had days ago.

Time was money.

And the way Eddie now saw it, money was gold.

It was at this point that the cup, and its contents, met the wall.

Chapter 12

Running the Gauntlet

1942 Arctic Ocean

The Arctic Convoys were a colossal undertaking.
This was not dropping off cornflakes.
In total, between August 1942 and May 1945, around 1400 merchant ships transported vital supplies to the Soviet Union. They delivered, on the whole, nearly 4,5 million metric tons of cargo, making up for a quarter of the entire Western Allies' total aid. This included over 7,000 aeroplanes, plus 5,000 tanks and cars, as well as ammunition, metals and raw materials, fuel and medicines.
Taking into account the logistical effort required to fulfil the quota of supplies contracted to be delivered to Russia, the magnitude of this enterprise was monumental. The amount of manpower required and tasks involved in getting even a single shipment out would have been no mean feat. With all the training, mining, manufacturing, transportation, preparation and loading that each run would require, convoys could only go out once a month.
On a single run, arguably the largest, codenamed PQ-17, up to 150,000 tons were shipped, where that tonnage broke down to 300 aircraft, 600 tanks and more than 4,000 trucks and trailers - enough to supply an army of 50,000 - and had an unbelievable net worth of $700 million. For one run.
And there were 78 runs in total.

The losses suffered by these convoys were harrowing. As a shocking example, when PQ-17 left Iceland with 35 merchantmen, it arrived at the port of the USSR with only 11. To put it another way, only one-third of the convoy reached its destination. Sinking to the bottom of the sea, with the vessels that were destroyed, went 210 combat planes, 430 Sherman tanks, 3,350 other vehicles and nearly 100,000 tons of additional cargo. That was in terms of supplies. Then add the 120 seamen who lost their lives, not forgetting that, of those who survived, many were crippled and maimed.

By the end of the arctic convoys, 85 merchant vessels and 16 Royal Navy warships were lost.

101 ships.

Over 3000 men.

Depending on the route taken and the considerable effect weather might have on a run, it could take from ten to fourteen days to get from Allied waters to the Russian ports of Archangel and Murmansk. The longest two weeks of a sailor's life.

Even though weather conditions sometimes prevented German reconnaissance aircraft from operating at all, there was simply no time when the fleet was not exposed to attack on the arctic convoys. The threat was constant. The Nazis occupied Norway, with troops 400,000 strong holding it fast, and no fewer than eight air bases covering almost the entire stretch of coastline from Stavanger, opposite Orkney, to Petsamo, just short of the Kola Inlet itself, offering German U-boats ready access to support from the Luftwaffe.

The allies were squeezed between pack ice too thick to the north - their ships not built to plough through solid layers of ice or to withstand collisions with icebergs - and a wall of Nazi aggression to the south, forcing them to run the gauntlet.

Once they had left the docks, a convoy was committed. From the moment the Allied ships left either Hvalfjord in Iceland or Clyde in Scotland they had entered enemy territory. After an air reconnaissance flight had been deployed to scan for enemy planes, ships or U-boats, the convoy could commence their departure, escorted by a second deployment of planes for as far as their fuel range could allow. Then the ships were on their own.

With no other support thereafter, other than the naval escort itself, analysts had formulated the best convoy configurations to maximise protection and minimise losses, however, this was almost futile, since the speed of any convoy could only be as fast as its slowest ship. Unlike a streamlined and agile assignment of military craft, the bulk of the convoys were made up of the large, lumbering merchant vessels, with achingly wide turning arcs, preyed upon by swift and, for the most part, invisible U-boats. The merchant ships were nothing less than slow, hulking whales, setting off into waters inhabited by killer whales. The odds were against them. There was simply no way of avoiding confrontations with German forces.

As a tactical procedure, a staggered line of ships maintained station in a long zig-zagging column. The practice of frequently altering direction to port or starboard was designed to disguise a convoy's true course and confuse the enemy. All ships followed the same pattern: one of several top-secret zig-zag diagrams created by admiralty anti-submarine experts.

When bound for the Soviet Union the convoys could take alternate routes, but only to a painfully limited degree. Very little leeway could be found in that narrow approach to Murmansk or Archangel. Staggering the times each convoy would enter the final leg of the journey also lessened the odds of the enemy being aware of its approach, however at some point they simply had to enter the arena. There was no way of hiding their arrival at the Kola Inlet. As far out as possible from the inlet, Allied Russian forces would provide air cover, however, rest assured, the convoy would be entering battle. The Nazis would have rallied their Luftwaffe upon the convoy's approach and the hammering would commence. Losses would be inevitable.

Having certainly sustained losses on the inward journey and then even more at the Inlet, what ships remained of the convoy would then dock at the Allied ports, where the battered crew would begin the laborious task of offloading the consignments. The pressure would be on and there was little time to centre oneself. Two days rest, refuelling and loading of supplies later and the convoy would begin its return run. There was no point in delaying: whatever happened, the Gerries were already alerted to the convoy's presence and they would be waiting.

On Tuesday 28th April 1941, having taken in the special consignment of gold at midnight, the HMS Edinburgh, along with convoy QP11, entered the Barents Sea at first light.

The unavoidable peril awaiting a convoy as it entered the straits presented major challenges to convoy commodores, escort commanders and watchkeepers on the ships' bridges.

One of those challenges, considering the drastic losses of trained staff that the convoys sustained, was to continue training other men who could take over their roles. A single, well-aimed or unlucky hit from a German bomb and one or more officers could be injured or dead, yet the determined continuation of the convoys gave no option but to keep the training in motion.

As a standard procedure, Captain Faulkner was on the bridge for this foreboding part of the return run, the light cruiser positioned to protect the merchant ships, the main target of the Germans. They had made it out of the worst part, with excellent air support from the Russians, and were moving into wider waters.

He was using the opportunity to take Supply Petty Officer Bob Walkey through the command routines with the Crystal Radio Operator Edward Anderson when onto the bridge stepped Vice-Admiral Bonham Carter. The men stood immediately to attention but the Vice-Admiral simply told them to carry on while he turned his back to them, looking out over the deck, portside.

"Bloody cold morning, Captain," he said. There was a moment of quiet, where no one replied.

The Vice-Admiral continued, "It's an opportunity is what it is...My wife wants pictures of some penguins and, seeing as we're not far from the pack ice, I say we head up under cover of snow and take a few snaps for the old lady, eh?" This was said while the man in question looked out to sea, hands behind his back and privileged belly pressing against the counter on the bridge, and not a hint of irony in his voice. Behind him, the Captain, who was busy instructing Walkey on night-shift bridge commands, paused. Both of them looked over at the figure and then at each other, questioning whether they had heard right.

"Penguins?" queried Faulkner. "Sorry, Admiral?" The Captain stood upright, straightened his tie and gave his shoulders a roll to loosen up, then walked over to the console to stand next to Bohnam-Carter. Without the option of invisibility, Walkey suddenly felt the need to pay extra careful attention to the command book, as the Captain said clearly, "Please excuse me, Vice-Admiral, Sir, I need to ask you to clarify."

Stuart Sumner Bonham Carter was fairly new to his post as Commander of the Fleet. Essentially he was only a passenger on the HMS Edinburgh, however, even in that capacity, he outranked the Captain.

"You heard right, Captain, *penguins*," said Bohnam-Carter as he turned his face to look Faulkner in the eye, "I want to get some pictures of penguins. It's said at the Zoological Society that there aren't any left, but I'd be darned if we can't find some. I want to seize this opportunity. I might not get another chance like this. "

In a firm tone, Faulkner responded so that Walkey and Walsh could clearly hear what he had to say, both of them sensing immediate tension between the two leading officers, "Vice-Admiral, I'm under strict orders to maintain course with the convoy."

"Ah pish!" said Bohnam-Carter with a dismissing wave of his hand. "It's the crack of dawn in the bloody Arctic - who's going to miss us?"

The Captain took a step back and stood to attention. "Permission to rebut your request, Admiral."

The Vice-Admiral let out a shallow breath. "Granted," he replied as he dipped his head and turned his eyes to the sea again.

Faulkner looked over his right shoulder at Walkey, the sailor immediately registering the intensity in his Captain's eyes, telling him to take note of what was going to be said next, and then the Captain did likewise to the Crystal Radio Operator, then squared up to Bonham-Carter once more, spelling out each word emphatically as he spoke, "Admiral, by leaving the convoy we will render the fleet susceptible to attack, and alone we will be vulnerable."

Whether it was simply the Captain's tone or whether anything of what he had just said had registered with Bonham-Carter, the portly man straightened his own back and turned to glare at his subordinate.

Now that he had the Vice-Admiral's attention, Faulkner made another show of looking at the other two seamen again before looking back at his superior and saying, "With all due respect, Sir," his left fist, with pressed forefinger and thumb, emphasising his words, "we'll have to notify the convoy and log the change of course." Seemingly disregarding the fact his superior's face was reddening as he spoke, the Captain then slowed down and deepened his tone to finish, "I *strongly* object."

"God, man! No need to make a fuss!" bellowed Bonham-Carter, waving his hands in the air with annoyance, spittle flying from his mouth, saying animatedly, "I'm talking about a quick jaunt across the water! My wife wants pictures of penguins and she'll bloody well have them!" Then he sighed and seemed to soften, his shoulders relaxing as he said with almost fatherly tones, "I'm not asking the whole convoy to go, just this ship."

With little option left, very calmly, in the same lowered tones, Faulkner stated his position again, "Admiral, I'm obliged to reiterate, my orders are to stay with the convoy; to get my men and my cargo safely home at all costs."

"Noted, Captain," said the Vice-Admiral, swivelling on his heel to face the sea once more, and for a moment Walkey thought that the Captain had managed to get the message across, and he stifled a sigh of relief.

There was a long pause in which it seemed that everyone would return to their tasks, when the Vice-Admiral turned fully to add, declaring with finality, "Captain, this ship is under *my* command," and then from a great height, "Find me some penguins."

"Admiral, there are no…"

"Enough! I will not tolerate insubordination! I'm in command of this vessel!" Red-faced and fist-clenched he spat out, "Set a new course!" At that, Edward Anderson stood to attention and Walkey, dropping the command book as he jolted upright too, took a look at it then decided to leave it be and stay at attention, not daring to move while the Vice-Admiral went on, "We will head to the pack ice and then rejoin the convoy. Those are my *orders*." He thrust his hands behind his back and glowered at everyone in the room with disdain. Then, with a smug roll of his shoulders, he lifted his chin and headed for the Captain's cabin.

Before he got through the doorway, the Captain called after him, "Sir?" which stopped the Vice-Admiral in his tracks, "Permission to speak freely?"

The Vice-Admiral did not turn and face him this time but simply stood where he was on the threshold and nodded.

Obvious that he was speaking more to Walkey and Walsh, the Captain stated, standing steadfastly, hands at his sides and chin up, "For the record, sir, I strongly disagree with these orders: by leaving this convoy we will render this ship vulnerable. My objection will be noted in the captain's log."

"Acknowledged," replied the Vice-Admiral, weary now, it seemed, before he told the Captain, "Follow me," and disappeared into the cabin.

"Right, Walkey," said the Captain, with a small, deflated smile of respect on his face, "Go through the commands for coordinate reset. Walsh, hold current settings until I return."

No sooner had the heavy metal door to the cabin shut than muffled sounds of raised voices began to reverberate through the steel walls, the sheer volume of the heated argument between those two stalwarts of the sea coming through.

Walkey and Smith each had an ear to the door, staring wide-eyed at one another, their mouths slightly parted, holding their breath to try and catch any of what was being said.

There was no mention in Bob Walkey's diary of whether or not the two men did pick up on the Vice-Admiral and Captain's words, however, what was certain to both of the crewmen was that the outcome of that argument could mean life or death for them and their friends.

Chapter 13

Rumours on Rigs

1980 Manchester, UK

The split-flap display of the flight board renewed, a rushing staccato cascade of clapping thick plastic slats being rolled into place to show the current outgoing flight times. With it, the background echoes of a final call for flight 436 to Rotterdam came through, but this and all the other goings on in the departure lounge of Manchester Airport were lost on Eddie.

He sat at a white coffee table, stabbing his pen at the numbers he had just circled on a page in front of him. His free hand went to his forehead as his eyes closed and he began to rub his temples, then pinch the bridge of his nose. Taking his hand away and opening his eyes, he waited until they focused and then looked down again at the copy of Walkey's journal, where he had drawn a circle around the final coordinates that the crewman had put down for the HMS Edinburgh. He tapped his forefinger on his top lip as his eyes flicked left once more to Captain Faulkner's log where he had also circled, three times now in emphatic blue ink, the final coordinates that the commander had put down.

The two positionings did not match.

Dropping his pen and taking his credit card from his wallet, Eddie began to tap and roll, tap and roll it on the table in rhythm to his thoughts. The card itself was nigh on maxed out, as well as time, but so far Geoff's dive team had come up with nothing on their scouting trips. Tap and roll, tap and roll. But what if that was because they had the incorrect coordinates? Eddie glanced back over at the two sets of coordinates he had come across, tapping and rolling. Two disparate numbers in a sea of words. But which one was right? There was only one way to find out. The card stopped rolling. "Right, that's it," Eddie said out loud, with one final, conclusive tap of the credit card.

He stood up, scanned the flight desks across the hall until he found the one he was looking for, put the strap of his leather satchel over his shoulder, scooped up his paperwork into his briefcase, snapped the clips shut, taking the case and his tennis hold-all in one hand and with the other, still holding the credit card, took hold of his ticket and walked directly to the counter he required.

Before he even reached said counter, he had made the impact he always did on people. With his confident step and easy demeanour, he paced over to the two ladies standing there, already capturing their full attention.

To both ladies at their respective counters, separated by a thin divider, one with a dark blue hat pinned perfectly straight to her impeccably combed hair and red British Airways scarf neatly tied, the other with a Lufthansa badge pinned squarely above her pocket and tidy blue eyes looking alert, he said, with his unique brand of charm mixed with respect, "I wonder if you can help me, Ladies? I have a bit of a dilemma," as he held up his British Airways ticket for both of them to see from their respective cubicles.

"How can I help you, sir," came the efficient reply from both women at once. There was a pause and then all three of them laughed.

"Thank you. Here it is, the dilemma: I have booked a flight to Amsterdam but I've had an unforeseen change to my schedule, so now I need to get on the first available flight to *Frankfurt* instead," he said, as he looked from one to the other, his eyes saying that he was aware that he was asking a lot of them and that he would understand if they turned him down. It was one of his favourite looks. So earnest was his open face and his God-Honest working-class manner of speaking, that it worked just about every time. "I'll take whatever is available, I don't care if you stuff me in a suitcase and put me in the cargo hold, but what I really need," he grimaced apologetically, "is to know whether you can help me exchange this here ticket?"

In one voice the flight attendants said, "I'll do what I can, sir." Another pause, another chuckle, and Eddie was all set.

Eyes sparkling, and his smile genuinely grateful, Eddie took his Lufthansa ticket in hand but before walking over to the barrier to board his flight, he made one more request, "I wonder, I haven't been able to make any arrangements for when I get to Germany, could I be cheeky and use your phone?"

Looking down at his watch, Eddie saw that, light as it was this stifling summer's evening, it was already one minute to seven as he waited at the pick-up point outside Frankfurt arrivals. As he lifted his eyes he saw a car slowing as it approached and wondered whether it could be for him. Rather than giving him a description of the car he would be picked up in, on the phone his friend had told Eddie that he would know it immediately when he saw it. Eddie's eyebrow raised and he muttered to himself, "Well, *that's* got my number on it," as he smiled and made a point of scanning the mustard Lada Vaz pulling up, recognising his beret-clad friend in the driver's seat, also wearing a big, cheesy grin.

Eyebrow still quizzically raised, Eddie threw his sports hold-all and satchel in the back and then climbed into the passenger seat with his briefcase and, without greeting, asked, "So, is this the S.E. then?"

"Ja," his mate agreed, "This is Special Equipment indeed; what were you expecting?"

To which Eddie replied, "I thought you had a desk job now, Jens, where's your Opel Senator?"

"On what they're paying me?" Jens guffawed, "Besides you don't get to where we are going in a German executive car, my friend. No such luxury for us, this elegant piece of Soviet workmanship is standard equipment for getting anywhere near the wall. So, how have you been, my friend - want a drink?"

They headed to Jens' local, where, over a couple of Steins, they caught up on each other's travels. Even though engineering was a world industry, one wouldn't necessarily get to see all kinds of places, whereas in the oil industry workers were far more likely to have seen some of the far reaches of the world, from Aberdeen to Argentina, from Alaska to India, so they had plenty of stories to tell at the bar. Yet, when all was said and done, Eddie and Jens were interested in one story more than most: The Edinburgh.

Jens had been a project manager in a Scottish rigging company when Eddie had first worked with him, a good few years back. They had butted heads, in that usual wrangling that ensues between engineer and project manager, but when Jens had held his own, time after time, in the face of Eddie's obvious disrespect for his position, Eddie had started to like the guy. More so because Jens was a *doer*. Unlike the other managers who sat behind their desks and asked for updates from the engineers, Jens was hands-on. He had been a diver himself and would not hesitate, if solutions did not seem to present themselves, to head out to a rig and speak in person to the men on the job, and then deal personally with the issues. Jens had even been known to go down to the dive sites himself so that he could get eyes on a problem. And he was resourceful too, getting whatever was short on-site from wherever he could, always before the pressure mounted. Other project managers were firefighters, dealing with issues as they arose, while Jens was always one step ahead. This work ethic and attitude, and the simple fact that, on occasion, he had sat in his fair share of D-chambers, had placed Jens within the inner circle of the hard-core set of people employed on oil rigs who lived and breathed diving.

They never left the water, these divers, even when they were on land. These guys were real-life treasure hunters. It was all maps and the Queen's gold for them. Days off studying charts, reading up on maritime history, scouring shipping archives and pouring over old ship blueprints, gathering information and formulating plans, touching base with partners and crew from previous salvages. All of them well-versed. Everybody after the big one.

Coming back from their days off, having heard tidbits on the radio, having picked up on something or other in the newspaper, or having read it in the latest issue of Diver Magazine, having made a phone call or two, they would, in between giving each other the rundown on the task change-over, bring each other up to speed on industry banter: improvements in equipment; the latest salvage find; how some salvage job or other was unsuccessful and the goods were still up for grabs; whether it was true that a wreck in Orkney had any valuables worth retrieving or whether it was turning out to be a myth; was a job in Peru cost-effective considering the length of the journey, hiring and transporting kit, local facilities; and what of those wrecks further off the Cornish coast - had the latest advancements in equipment on the market made them attainable?

All of these divers remained in the circuit, keeping up with the inside news, and with knowledge of locations and equipment, to have the upper hand in reaching the wrecks everybody knew were there, but no one had been able to get to because they were just too far, too deep. In this industry, being ahead of the competition was the difference between breaking the surface with a couple of brass trinkets, or working away to haul up several chests of jewels and doubloons from a Spanish galleon. What made the real difference in this game was *reach*. How far out, how deep salvors could go. And one had to stay within the flow of information in case something came up because the waters of the deep were getting shallower.

In the oil business, there was always an undercurrent of stories and urban myths shifting around, just like they did in any other large industry. The most valuable information to the likes of Jens and Eddie was, however, kept within that small circle of professional divers with whom they had worked many times before - just the sorts who would find themselves living on top of one another for days on end in decompression chambers. These men excelled in their fields and, for that reason, they were hired over and again for projects all over the globe. This being the case, even if they occasionally worked on separate jobs, it was only a matter of time before they would be working with one another again. Hence, a familiar rapport had built up between them so that when they saw each other they would simply slip into conversation once more, and in so doing, each of them was kept up to speed on goings on in the salvaging game.

Naturally, this was where Eddie, and Jens in turn, had come across word on the escalation towards going for the Edinburgh. There had been whispers and rumblings for some time before it had reached the point where the guys in the inner circle had been making confirmed reports on movement towards a salvage operation. They were on the cusp. It was about to roll their way.

So the idea of obtaining the gold was not exactly anything new to Jens, however Eddie now explained how the possibility had suddenly shifted from being an impossible stretch to a workable reality. He told of how the tipping point had come when he had dived just short of the depth required to get to the Russian gold, and how everything had lined up rapidly after that.

"Now there is a ship with the equipment and gases to work the bell at those depths. Everything in one package," said Eddie, sounding like he was wrapping up the tale.

"And how exactly does coming to my beloved landlocked country help you to secure this boat of yours? Didn't you say there was another team after the same vessel?" Jens asked, having waited this long for Eddie to get around to why exactly he was there, and why on earth he would want to go anywhere near East Berlin.

Ever withholding, Eddie's only reply was, "I'm after one last thing - something I don't think our competitors have. I might just be able to win the use of the ship using what I've already got, but the fact is, Jens, without the piece of information I'm hoping to find, even with the right ship, we might not get the *gold*."

His friend was right to allude to the risk Eddie had taken in heading out to Germany, knowing that the Norwegian team would be after the same salvaging vessel that his team needed to complete the job. But, as he had mentioned, there was more at stake here. So, the next day, after staying over at Jens' house, the two of them would go through the false border into Berlin, heading for the old *Wehrmacht Information Office for War Losses and P.o.W.s*, and Eddie would find out whether his gamble had paid off.

Chapter 14

Swimming with Sharks

1980 Frankfurt, Germany

Eddie sat at Jen's kitchen table, working through Admiral Karl Doenitz's treatise 'The Conduct Of The War At Sea,' from which they were picking out relevant information. As Jens translated, Eddie was captured by the scope and eloquence of the essay. He noted that it had taken a good deal of time and testing before the U-boats emerged as the legendary threat they were now known to have been.

With the availability of U-boats being slim, it became clear to U-boat command that they could have very little effect on the UK's trade and military movement out at sea. Operational U-boats during the winter of 1939-40 only numbered as many as ten at any one time, sometimes reduced to as few as two. The only way to make a strategic impact on the Allied movements was to use surprise tactics, to engage in daring attacks, as often as possible, where they were most vulnerable: at "the concentration point of traffic in or near harbours."

Without the numbers to be able to make any serious dent in British naval manoeuvres, the limited German arsenal was directed to cause maximum destruction at weak nodes within the English fleet. A convoy could become stretched at points on the journey creating openings in the fleet, exposing them to attack. Aiming for these chinks in the armour, the U-boats would take the opportunity to cause as much mayhem for the English navy as possible, attacking and immobilizing the fleet, thus meeting their main objective of breaking the momentum and occupying the Brits' attention on keeping the convoys intact. This was designed to render the Allies incapable of concentrating their energies on modifying their defences, to formulate more vigorous approaches to the threat the U-boats posed. When all was said and done, all the Germans could do at this stage, it seemed, was to cause as much distraction as possible.

In time, however, the U-boat division would emerge as an intimidating force, tormenting the British fleet at every turn.

Of the 56 submarines Germany had at the onset of WWII, less than half of them were suitable for the first operations in the Atlantic. The accelerated production of U-boats during the war, however, led to over *eleven hundred* U-boats being built in total, of which 785 were destroyed and the remainder surrendered or were scuttled.

By comparison, their toll on the Allies was the sinking of 175 naval vessels of all types and *2,603* merchant ships, their combined weight coming in at over 13 million tons. This, of course, was the role of U-boat commanders, to stop supplies reaching the Allies at all costs.

Of the 40,000-odd men recruited to U-boats the human cost was 28,000 which nearly equaled the 30,000 men lost on the Allied merchant vessels. The carnage wreaked by the U-boats on Allied *navy* personnel, however, came in at a staggering total of 50,000 men.

To make clear the destructive abilities of a single U-boat, of the 1,418 men on the HMS Hood, that was sunk near the start of the war, only 3 survived. It was a huge morale hit for the British. Just as when the converted troop ship Lancastria was sunk in 1941 and over 3,000 people lost their lives in a single attack - the worst disaster in Britain's naval history.

Over the three years since the opening of the conflict, the Germans had steadily recalibrated their wolfpack tactics so that, by 1942, it was a successful operation.

Early approaches had the submarines gathered in packs ready to intercept convoys from several angles, however, all they succeeded in doing was alerting the Allies to a group of targets, resulting in the loss of all or most of the U-boats. The layered and focused protection of convoys was more than prepared to take on the attacking team of submarines.

Escorting the merchant ships were various armed cruisers, with one leading warship and two on either side of each merchant ship to provide maximum cover. These warships were practically floating weapons, with little room on deck besides the stacked and packed artillery: tens of surface-to-air cannons and machine guns, plus torpedoes below deck.

Despite this, the loss of U-boats was considerably less than that of Allied ships until the British and Americans joined forces with the Russians to turn the tide of the war, bringing all of that military might to those frozen waters of the North. Yet the number of Allied ships that were lost or damaged more than doubled when the Arctic Convoys began. From 1939 through 1941 around 500 Allied ships had been attacked by German U-boats. That number more than doubled when the convoys started.

Instead of taking on an entire fleet, with its warships and air cover forming a wall of protection around the cargo, a single U-boat could be better deployed against any stray ship. Better, in other words, a lone, lean and hungry wolf than a wolfpack. A rapacious brute in the ice, ready to pick off any stragglers. The weak, the slow, the damaged.

German high command had discovered that if they staggered the U-boats over a greater distance, they had more chance of engaging with an unattended Allied ship, cut off or trailing behind a fleet. The U-boat could fire off its torpedoes and sufficient rounds from its deck guns and quickly submerge before air cover could locate them. This new manoeuvre, the wolfpack convoy tactic *Strauchritter*, proved to be far more effective than previous strategies.

To be in the same seas as one of these prowling Leviathans from then on, was to be in danger from the moment you lost view of the land. Provided the U-boat was able to surface and attack with its deck guns, the advantage of using both surface cannons and torpedoes was a lethal combination. A single U-boat could be so deadly as to be able to take out anything from a partially armed merchant ship to a heavily armed destroyer.

"So, who is this Admiral Doenitz fellow, that we should listen to what he has to write?" Eddie queried.

Jen's face screwed up in disbelief, "What? You don't know he was? He only took over as president after Hitler did us all a favour and topped himself."

Eddie came back with, "Don't act so surprised, mate, no one in England, or the rest of the world for that matter, apart from Germany, cares what happened to your country after the war - save that bloody great big wall being built through the middle of your capital."

"Ja, well, I don't care what happened to England either," Jens agreed, albeit slightly defensively.

"What happened to this Doenitz anyhow?" asked Eddie earnestly.

"He was the one who signed the peace treaty," Jens explained, "Lasted in office for less than a month. Poor bastard got put in jail for ten years after the Nuremberg trials. He was only doing his job. Sure, he was known to be a hard nut, but he didn't do any of the crazy shit Hitler and his cronies got up to. I mean, take a look at his essay - this was a level-headed guy. Died last year, actually."

Admiral Doenitz had been the Supreme Commander of the Kriegsmarine from 1943 onwards, and his treatise offered an accessible overview of how U-boats and their tactics evolved through the course of the war.

At the onset of the war, U-boat commanders acted within the strict confines of orders issued by the naval staff of the German operations division, under whose direction unarmed merchant ships were not to be attacked. This was per the Geneva Convention. However, when Churchill declared that all merchant ships were to be armed for both defence and attack against U-boats, as well as have military escorts, this placed them beyond the protection of prize law. Hence, the German high command had granted their U-boats freedom of attack on all merchant vessels escorted by enemy warships.

Where Hitler was strategically placing his forces for the next leg of expansion after the first few months of war, and, quite possibly at this stage, manoeuvring towards Russian oil fields, German merchant ships were using neutral Norwegian waters to transport necessary supplies to Axis forces, via Polish and Russian ports. Keeping the Baltic open to Germany was therefore of great importance to the bulking up of their armies in the east, and Hitler had been taking advantage of Norway's neutrality and English adherence to international law within Norwegian territorial waters.

Yet with British naval bases positioned at propitious points near the coast of Norway and therefore easily able to provide interference to German shipping in those waters, the Nazis simply could not effectively protect its supply line. Therefore Hitler was using all the diplomatic means necessary to keep Norway from siding with England, as this would put an end to Germany's free flow of traffic in the Norwegian Sea and also jeopardise the entrance to the Baltic.

From the Allied point of view then, Norway's neutrality was a hindrance to their ability to put an end to German shipping. The English simply had to force Germany's hand, because the Nazi occupation of Norway would allow the Allied navy to openly attack German supply ships in the Norwegian Sea. Throwing the gauntlet down, the British destroyer Cossack cornered and attacked the German supply ship Altmark, rescuing 300 Allied prisoners. This altercation threw Norwegian neutrality into question, forcing Hitler to speed up his plans to invade Norway.

Whereas the focus of the German military machine was successfully aimed at achieving superiority on land and in the air, the development of their navy trailed far behind British sea power, hence the taking and holding of Norwegian waters, given the inadequacy of the German fleet, made their effort 'one of the boldest in naval history.'

Backed against the wall, the strategic value of taking and holding Norway at this point was not underestimated by Hitler's advisers. Under Allied control, it would have formed a blockade against Germany that would have proved far too detrimental to the Axis war effort. Conversely, as a launchpad for German naval forces, the Nazis could still have the upper hand. It was crucial that the German High Command pursue an ambitious invasion. So, throwing in all of their available units to secure the land and the sea, drawing in every U-boat from the Pacific and the Atlantic, they focused all their arsenal in and around those Norwegian waters.

Despite German naval staff and U-boat command promising great results in this operation, the actuality was embarrassingly lame. Insomuch as, at the onset of the war, Germany was concerned about the *shortages* of torpedoes, in the Norwegian expedition it became clear that torpedo *deficiency* was the core issue to be overcome.

Counting on the strength of their position at sea, Britain's calculated move of instigating German aggression against

Norway included pulling in their fleets for the foreseeable hostilities. With Germany doing the same, this made for the greatest concentration of Axis and Allied naval vessels in the war to date.

In the vast expanse of oceans like the Atlantic, the relatively sparse naval engagements allowed for U-boats to remain on the surface for extended periods, right up until enemy ships were spotted - after which they would submerge for a short distance and come back up to fire both cannons and torpedoes. However, there was no such luxury afforded to them in the close quarters of enemy-infested Norwegian waters. The concentration of Allied ships was so dense that U-boats were forced to remain submerged far longer than they had been designed for. The U-boats had never encountered such overwhelming proximity with enemy forces, and therefore never realised the effect that such long stretches underwater would have on their torpedoes. This protracted submersion caused pressure in the boat to penetrate the depth chamber of the torpedo. This markedly increased the torpedoes' depth setting, meaning that the calibration was affected and the torpedoes fired too low, missing their targets significantly, even at close range.

With German torpedo technology still far from being perfected, U-boats suffered heavy losses. Torpedos had only been meagerly tested during peacetime and, up until then, only been used in sparse confrontations, and even *then* they had been unreliable. Now other issues were coming to the fore alongside the pressure issue, one of which was an unrefined magnetic firing system which meant that, when the torpedo did reach its target, it would either explode too soon or might not even detonate at all.

◊

It was only when submarine crews were at significant depths that the enormity of the ocean's presence hit home. At those crushing depths, the unforgiving sea was unceasingly pressing against the sides of the tin can they were submerged in, reminding them every minute, with tics and groans, that its steel sides and rivets were taking strain. Often the only thing allowing crews to keep themselves together mentally was a steadfast faith in both the boat and their comrades and, holding it all together, trust-absolute in their captain.

U-boat crews were conditioned to be a tight unit - the men well primed for the job. Morale was crucial nevertheless. A crew needed to be alert for long hours and be prepared to take commands without hesitation. There was simply no time for debate in the meticulous running and, especially, the technical attack manoeuvres of a submarine. Everything had to be done in sequence and in a streamlined fashion for the vehicle to function. Underwater, the stress of turning too quickly or not releasing pressure at the right time, for instance, could easily compromise the integrity of the vessel's hull. Once a submarine surfaced and laid itself open to attack, the window of opportunity to fire off torpedoes accurately was a taught sequence of commands which required perfect focus and complete confidence in both the captain and the machine.

In the confines of Norwegian waters, with enemies constantly nearby, it is fair to say that the high degree of losses the Germans were taking was unforeseen. Add torpedo discrepancies, rendering the U-boats all but useless in combat situations, the effect on crews was obvious. It was all one could do as a U-boat commander-in-chief to keep their spirits up.

The German fleet, as well as ground forces in Norway, were at breaking point when, quite suddenly, only ten days after their victory at Narvick in April 1940, the Allies retreated both on land and at sea, withdrawing their forces to strengthen their failing positions in Holland, Belgium, France, and particularly at Dunkirk. This retreat was precisely what the Germans needed to defend, hold and fortify their position on the Norwegian front. Immediately work began on intensifying their coastal defence system, concentrating their focus on bolstering their arsenal.

At key points, economically placed at the closest possible intervals, bases were built within the extensive coastline as refuge points for the German navy and merchant vessels. The chief stations were kitted out as fortresses which provided the necessary base equipment for U-boats and warships, the construction of which was vastly accelerated. At the same time, German engineers had pulled out all the stops on ironing out issues with torpedoes, all of them now fitted with impact fuzes, which were found to be far more reliable.

With Russia then switching sides and the onset of the Arctic Convoys, fierce pressure was placed on U-boat command to hold its position and, at all possible costs, to neutralise and delay any aid being shipped to the Soviet forces. After it became evident that, despite the upturn in torpedo technology, German tactics were still wanting, the all-new and daring *Strauchritter* formation was put forward. Against the backdrop of demoralising U-boat losses, the High Command was nervous as to whether it could achieve any results, placing all of the burden on the strained U-boat personnel to make it work. The success of this bold new tactic, as well as keeping up the spirits of the seamen, fell on the shoulders of the U-boat commanders, who were often new to the field themselves - German naval forces only just managing to replace the sheer volume of officers who were going down with their boats. Yet some turned out to be just the right combination of cool thinking, character and experience to effectively take on the precarious role put upon them.

Chapter 15

Teichart on Target

1942 Arctic Ocean

Knowing full well that a convoy had entered Murmansk and had been reloading and refuelling, U-436 and U-456 had run the full course of their night patrol in readiness for the return run. The night had come and gone with no contact, so that now they sat on the 73rd parallel of latitude 33 degrees east, awaiting the arrival of the ships.

The stakes were high, where any daytime attack on the convoy would render the U-boats equally vulnerable, being more easily spotted from a crow's nest aboard the ship and then by the air support that the vessel would surely call in. Yet the Germans were willing to meet those odds head-on, accepting the risk in an all-out attempt to maim the convoys and delay the devastating support they were offering to the eastern front. Orders were given by U-boat command to seek out and optimise on any given advantage. In essence, the U-boats were there to create havoc, and they were succeeding.

Using the cover of night to move in close to Allied ships and then to recede to safety directly after firing, had proved to work in favour of the U-boats, whereas during the day they were completely exposed on their attack run, having to surface to fire off torpedoes. What was more, the new Type VIIC submarine had excelled in night-time attacks. So much so that the great U-boat aces of the German fleet were turning down offers to take up lead positions on larger U-boats, swearing by the reduced size of these new boats which offered better manoeuvrability. Never before had Germans on the naval front line been so convinced of the quality of their war machines as they were now.

With a few nighttime successes under their belt, the confidence of the crew of U-456 was increasing, the young captain having buoyed their morale through the desperate failures of the Norwegian campaign up until this point. It was, however, broad daylight, on a clear afternoon in calm Arctic waters, when U-456 and U-436 came upon a solitary warship, cut off from its fleet.

A golden opportunity.

Directly north of Murmansk, skirting the edge of the northern ice barrier, the two U-boats were making their way towards the Kola Inlet, in the hopes of intercepting the British convoy, having received word from German air reconnaissance that it had left docking.

On a map, the neck of the sea between the mainland of Norway and the polar ice barrier can look like a narrow causeway. In comparison to the open waters of the Atlantic, it certainly was, however, with the hard front of ice being 3° from the land and another 3° east towards Russian waters, that six square degrees on the map worked out to approximately 21,000 miles of ocean. Even the most tactical placing of U-boats could allow for an entire convoy to slip through.

The logical routes for convoys to take would be as far north as they could manage, to avoid being spotted by German air reconnaissance closer to the mainland, but neither of the U-boats had made contact with the enemy that far north. Therefore they were on their return run, with U-456 passing the midpoint between Murmansk and the ice sheet, and U-436 not far away, when the Edinburgh was spotted.

Coasting at surface level and still hunting despite heading back to base, the sonar operator called, though certainly showing his nerves at announcing a daytime find, "Got a ping, sir."

The captain was at the drafting table, head in one hand, eyes on the map, tapping his finger back and forth between nodes on the last known exit routes of the Allied convoys. At the radar operator's announcement, the captain's left hand dropped to take the sliding rule and shift it over to their position on the map. His right hand took hold of the protractor as his close-set, hawk eyes looked over to the sonar operator.

Three years into WWII, Kapitänleutnant Max Martin Teichert was already an experienced commander with an excellent record of achievements, having received the Iron Cross 2nd Class at the start of the war and then the Iron Cross 1st Class two years on. He had risen through the ranks steadily from his appointment as an officer in 1934, so that by September 1941 he was given the honour of commissioning the renowned U-456.

"Mark?" Teichart requested.

"72 degrees north by 32 east."

The captain marked the general location of the first contact on his map, then, with an educated guess he gauged the cruise speed of a mid-range naval vessel heading northwest en route to Iceland, he set his pencil point gently down a few nautical inches in that direction, giving the command, "2 degrees, half right rudder."

"Rudder at half right, 2 degrees," repeated the commander to the engine room.

"Ahead," the captain motioned for the U-boat to make its approach run in the direction of the vessel, to cross the U-boat's trajectory to the south at an almost right angle, "Pump. 200 litres forward."

"200 litres forward bearing 2 degrees," the commander confirmed.

Teichart traced the forward movement of the sub on the map, with a pencil in his right hand and his left hand held aloft, fingers splayed. Slowly, three fingers of his upraised hand closed into his palm and his wrist twisted so that his index finger pointed at the sonar operator, who took the cue to ready his equipment. The captain's finger then raised and held for a few instants, his eyes lifting from the map as he connected with his gut feeling, then the finger dropped to point directly as he called with conviction, "Radar, make a hand sweep on A-scope. Use mean scale."

"All clear to...thousand metres."

"Send ping."

"Send ping."

"Radar, track target bearing six zero, range one thousand metres..."

With heightened attention, each man at his station kept their focus on their task and equipment, in tense readiness for the next command. If a ping returned they had a solid contact and the whole team would need to work in sync, with decided precision, to prepare for an attack run.

Silence.

With clarity, the radar operator reported, "No contact bearing six zero, range one thousand metres."

The captain only paused momentarily, shooting a look at the radar operator, his eyes distant as he worked through the picture in his mind of where his boat and the enemy ship could be in relation to one another. His imagination was his only window, his men an extension of his reach, each of them working as one to drive this blind vessel through the blackness of the sea. Suddenly he gave a glance at the compass above the pilot and then back down to the map, where he recalibrated for a different speed and trajectory of the enemy vessel, and after tracing another imaginary line on the map his free hand came up again, this time forming into a point at the pilot, "Pilot, check speed fifty percent, hard turn to starboard, bow planes left forty-five degrees."

"Check speed fifty percent, hard turn to starboard, bow planes forty-five degrees."

"Ahead. 100 litres forward bearing four zero degrees."

"100 litres forward bearing four zero degrees."

The captain marked in his log the new approach angle, making a point of the fact that having missed the vessel on radar could mean that it was a smaller and faster craft - in that case, it would certainly be a military light cruiser, with similar speed and agility to the VIIC - a whole lot harder to catch and a great deal more difficult to hit.

A shorter wait this time, while the captain traced the forward movement of the sub on the map with pencil in one hand and his other hand held aloft once more until he pointed again at the radar operator and called, "Radar, make a hand sweep on A-scope. Mean scale."

"All clear to...thousand metres."

"Send ping."

"Send ping."

"Radar, track target bearing four zero, range one thousand metres…"

Everyone waited once more for the return ping, but to no avail, "No contact bearing four zero, range one thousand metres."

The captain marked the failed contact once again then set his equipment down and brought his hands up to rub his forehead and then temples, stretching his skin so that his eyes widened and watered slightly with exhaustion. He closed them and then opened them again until the blurr receded. A questioning, "Hmm?" left his lips as one hand scratched at his morning stubble, the other tapping on the location of the first ping. Then a look of dawning awareness spread across his angular face as his hand came down to stretch fingers across his chin, his eyes suddenly glinting with the inspiration his men had seen enough times to recognize that, in that short space, he had figured it out not only where they were going wrong but also how to get the upper hand.

Teichart's eager eyes scanned the faces of his trusty crew, standing ready with full confidence in the man and the machine, and he took in a lungful of air. The breath before the plunge. Then, with a voice full of startled realisation, he said, "It's going the other direction."

The commander queried openly, "It's going back to the Kola Inlet?"

"Ja. It could be in trouble. This might be our opportunity," was the captain's straightforward reply.

A swift nod from the commander to his captain, and then another from him to the crew, and everyone acknowledged by standing at the ready for the commands that were sure to come in quickfire now.

The captain's eyes fell to his map as he took up his instruments instantly and, working backwards from the initial zone where the first ping came from, he reformulated the possible position of the target going in the other direction, east towards Russia, then called out with urgency, "We must make up for lost time: Left full rudder! About turn!"

"Left full rudder."

"Rudder at left full."

"Steer due east, bearing one two zero degrees."

"Steering due east, bearing one two zero degrees."

"Full speed ahead!"

"Full speed ahead. 200 litres."

"More speed," the captain said firmly to the commander, who immediately took up the talker on the XJA handset to give the command to the engine room for more power.

A short relay of messages bounced back and forth between the commander and the engine room, while the captain continued to mark their progress on his chart and make notes in his log book.

"Answer bells on three main engines. Put one main engine on charge," ordered the commander, glancing over at the captain and justifying his decision with, "Retreat protocol."

The captain looked up with a raised eyebrow and said, with a hint of a smirk, "Since when have I retreated? *Full* power."

Without question, the commander smiled broadly as he gave these new orders to the engine room, "Answer bells on four main engines, that's *four* main engines."

"Standard speed will be seventeen knots."

"Answer bells on battery...secure the engines."

The captain kept the heading due east, making up the distance from where the boat had first left off to come in north of the vessel they were following. When they had reached that point, he had the boat turn due south and moved at full speed towards where he had calculated the vessel to be.

"Radar, you're up again," the captain called and put out for another sweep of the sonar as the crew waited anew, at the same time hoping and trusting that their brilliant captain had made his measurements correctly.

"We have a ping, sir," said the radar operator, unable to hide his surprise.

Teichart hit his clenched fist on the table as he whipped his head up, saying with eyes lit, "Game on."

He stood up, flattened down his uniform, looked left and then right, taking in all of the crew on the bridge, then stood straight and said, "All hands at the ready. Prepare for attack run."

At full speed, the U-boat made for its mark, a series of orders being given by the commander to the engine room, and orders for readiness being given to the torpedo room. The captain sent a signal via the enigma operator to headquarters to confirm the radar contact and notify them that U-456 was on the attack run.

Not losing any time waiting for their response, having got the boat near enough to its target, Teichart gave orders to drop just below periscope level.

Beside him, the commander now called to drop one engine and put it on charge as the speed was reduced. As the submarine got deeper and the pressure built, it took more power to maintain speed, with a maximum of 7 knots at the deepest level, engaging all four engines; rising nearer to the surface the lessening pressure allowed for more speed to be applied with less engine power. Not yet at the top speed that surfacing would allow, the U-boat was nevertheless making headway on approaching its target, which was coasting unawares.

The staccato tapping sound of Morse code was heard and a message was quickly given to Captain Teichart by the radio operator, read out in the terse, stop-start, language of Morse code: Target confirmed. Light-cruiser A-class. Four attempts from U-436. Failed. U-456 clear for attack.

Defying the tension rising in his crew, the captain was in his element, saying to the commander, "Excellent. Let's take a look at that prize then, shall we? Come to periscope depth."

Stepping over to the periscope bar, the captain gripped the handles and moved them into the upside-down T position, ready to pull the periscope down to eye level.

"All planes up 10," the commander ordered.

Instinctively, each of the crew leaned in to compensate for the inclining angle on the bow, the captain shifting to a forward stance, looping an arm around the periscope to stabilise himself.

"Steady at 2 metres."

"Both planes zero."

"Stern down 5."

Bringing the boat just beneath the surface of the sea, still stealthy below the waves, the crew straightened themselves to almost upright as the angle of the boat lessened. The Captain, now no longer having to hold himself up, had both hands on the grips, pulling the t-bar down so that the periscope would rise above the waterline. His eye pressed right up against the viewfinder, his hat tilting up against the periscope tube, he mumbled, "Okay. Where are you, my sweet." Not seeing anything yet, he nevertheless continued his commands to rise to attack level, "Come up."

As the boat levelled out to a depth within two metres, relieving a great deal of pressure from the hull, the strains of metal eased off, and at the same time, Teichart got his first clear visual of the surface.

"Clear skies. Calm waters...dead calm." It was all he needed to say for the crew to understand the position they were in. Visibility in the midafternoon on a cloudless day would mean that all it would take to be spotted by the enemy, once the U-boat made its attack run, was one keen eye on the ship lookout, spotting the periscope and then tilting the binoculars down to see the hulk of the attacking submarine. From then on, it would be an easy target for the ship's torpedoes and multiple surface cannons.

In a fluid motion, the captain turned the periscope, swivelling his body with the movement, until suddenly he stopped and said, clearly, "Eyes on target. Light-cruiser. Coming up on their stern, heading east."

The commander relayed this information to the torpedo room so that they could prepare the torpedoes with the correct calibration for the type of ship they were to engage.

A heartbeat.

"Stand by battle stations," commanded Teichart.

With a unified and resolute response, the crew replied, "Stand by battle stations!"

The commander then repeated the order over the tannoy, "Stand by battle stations."

The radar operator called out at the same time, "Target heading acquired, sir. Speed 15 knots. Range 700 metres."

In the meantime, the captain continued to scan the full 180-degree arc of the periscope, then quickly swung it back to the first target acquired, at which point he pushed away from the periscope and locked his arms over the t-bar.

Looking down, he tilted his head, speculating, "What are you doing out here, all alone? Where are you going?"

Just as he moved forwards again to the viewfinder the radar operator piped up, "Sir, what if their radar picked up on U-436' torpedoes and they are on the run?"

To this, the commander simply retorted, "You don't run at half-speed."

Teicharthad took another confirmatory look through the viewfinder to check the gyro-angle and then spun round to his desk to make calculations. U-456 was heading east-south-east at 120 degrees, below-surface speed of 7 knots, whereas the enemy light-cruiser was heading more towards due east at approximately 100 degrees but only at half-speed. The U-boat was approaching more or less from behind making the ship a narrow target to be fired upon. To come up to surface level and attack with torpedoes now would bring them into full view of the ship within its close firing range. Plus, not only was there a strong possibility of missing the ship's bow but also the fact that the ship could increase its speed to twice that of the U-boat and be lost altogether. The only option was for U-456 to continue forward at the same rate, purposely overshooting the enemy vessel when it made a turn in keeping with the Allied zigzag formation, then to alter course to the east and after doing so once again, come up on the enemy's port side.

"Maintain heading one two zero degrees."

"Heading one two zero degrees."

"Continue course for 2000 metres."

"Continuing 2000 metres."

"Sir!" the radar operator shouted, "Enemy checking speed. Turning starboard."

The captain launched himself to the periscope, and seeing the ship turn rapidly, could barely contain his emotion as he said, "Gott. They are turning right into our firing line."

Standing bolt upright, with arms locked and head turning sharply to his commander, the captain raised his voice just a decibel more, and in his customary fighting tones, ordered, "Flood tubes one and two." They only had two torpedoes left. Teichart would have to make them count.

The commander passed on the order to the torpedo room, "Flood tubes one and two."

"Level off, chief. Keep your bearing."

While the commander gave orders to balance out the boat in readiness to fire, the captain pushed the periscope up and slapped the grips back in place then stood where he was, hand on chin and mouth, mumbling calculations to himself.

"Both planes at zero," the commander reported.

Snapping his head up the captain ordered, "Open bow caps now."

"Open bow caps."

Over the speaker, in muffled tones from the torpedo room came the response, "Caps open, commander."

Then silence again.

The eye of the storm...

The captain clenched his fist.

Then, with the professional calm that made him the formidable foe that he was, he said with conviction, "Fire torpedo one."

Chapter 16

In the Shadow of the Wall

1980 Frankfurt, Germany

"What? *Patrol*. Bullshit," Eddie mumbled to himself, as he sat at the kitchen table in Jen's home, surrounded by various photocopies of wartime accounts and diaries.

Jens stood at the door unnoticed, coming in on Eddie's thoughts with, "Ja, and as you like to say: you can't bullshit a bullshitter, right?"

"You said it in one, me old mucker. And yet here it is. An established historical journal saying that the Edinburgh was 20 *miles* away from the convoy when she was torpedoed," Eddie explained, and then added with incredulity, "On a routine patrol? What a load of bullshit."

"So, hang on," Jens queried, catching on to Eddie's train of thought, "The flagship is on patrol? 20 miles from its assignment."

"Exactly. But where?"

"Show me those coordinates again?"

Rifling through a few sheets, Eddie pulled out the page from Walkey's diary and then Captain Faulkner's log and slid them across the table to his savvy friend. He went right to work locating the positions on Eddie's map, as the Englishman leant back, placing his pen behind his ear and crossing his arms.

After a minute or so, Eddie looked over at Jens and, with a small shrug of his shoulders and a little nod of his chin, asked, "So who are you going to believe? We have a ship carrying a pile of gold worth...what's the Pound to Deutschmark exchange rate at the moment?"

"Had a feeling you'd be asking that," said Jens without irony, "Call it 4 to 1."

"Hm, the good old British Pound, eh," quipped Eddie. Jens's eyebrow raised in mock objection. "So, looking at its worth against today's exchange rate, we're talking 180 *million* Deutschmark," which then had his German friend letting out a low whistle. "Which," Eddie continued, "nobody needs to know about. We have that same ship miles away from its fleet, off on some hair-brained adventure, which nobody needs to know about either. Somewhere along the way, most embarrassingly for everyone, it comes a cropper. And now all we have are these lame accounts of why it was out there, all by its lonesome, and two disparaging entries for where it went down: one from a seasoned and respected Commander of the Fleet and the other from a shiphand."

"Mm, see what you mean," agreed Jens. "Who did it serve to lie? I can tell you are leaning towards your top brass hiding the location."

"You know me, always going with the underdog."

"Ja, that's why we're still friends, right? Remember me when you are at the top, will you."

"Sure, I'll throw you a bone or two."

The tone eased off as they both smiled but then shifted back again, the weight of what they were trying to accomplish settling in once more.

"So, what we are looking for in Berlin is what? A third account?" Jens guessed.

"Spot on. This, uh, what's his name again?" he rifled through his notes, "Ah, Teichart, that's it. This Teichart, where's *his* log? Was he anywhere near the Edinburgh when it went under, and did he mark the position?"

Eddie put his pen down and, resting his elbows on the table, put his hands to his face, rubbing his forehead to keep his focus, then brought his hands down into a clasp in front of him as he explained, "Thing is, if the war records were all properly filed, then someone would have got hold of them by now. There have been a couple of attempts to retrieve the gold with no success - one of which was Russian, in the fifties. We're not the first ones here...but it's not like they're going to hand over their information to us and say, "Here, you have a go," so we've had to do our homework on this. Now I have these two sets of coordinates and, as you say, what I could do with is a *third* account to confirm which of them is legitimate. Only, when the war came to a close, what was left of the German war records - whatever wasn't blown to smithereens - was moved to a little town smack on the border of east and west Berlin."

"Where?" asked Jens, standing up and going over to his work bag and rummaging through for his map book.

"Wittenau," answered Eddie and gave the street address.

"Ah, in the French sector," said Jens with a gleeful glint in his eye.

"Dealing with Germans would be bad enough," said Eddie with no apology. "Why does it have to be the bloody French?"

"You're telling me, right? And when you get that close to the wall, everyone is a little…?"

"Tense? I can imagine."

"Ja. *Scheisse*. I can't believe you want us to go so near to the wall. It's a mess there. You don't know who the fucking enemies are. You have these patriot soldiers, the bloody *People's Army*, shooting escapees from East Berlin - they are shooting their own people! Just last week they shot some poor guy and his wife. They were *Germans* for God's sake, just trying to get back home. Madness," he finished, swinging his head from side to side. "Just crazy."

The two men stood looking at each other and, for a moment, that is what they were. Not a German and an Englishman. Just two men. Jens' outburst brought it home for Eddie: what it was like to live with the constant uncertainty of having enemies living in your backyard, what it was like living without any promise that the enmity would ever come to a real end.

The powerlessness of it.

It was just a moment and then the engineer mindset kicked back in and the two of them were looking at the map. "We just have to get onto the autobahn, heading west," said Jens as he traced his finger along the map to show his friend, "and it's pretty much a straight run until we get there. Though, saying that, we are likely to be stopped a few times, especially as we approach the border."

"Right," said Eddie, standing and packing away his papers. "Time is money. Let's go."

Jens and Eddie, a little beleaguered after having come through the checkpoints, were standing in the broad marbled foyer inside the imposing building that housed the German war records for officers and prisoners of war. A bookish Frenchman was explaining how difficult it still was to locate information in the archive - a substantial amount of records still not collated after being moved several times during and after the war.

"So, be my guest and do some filing while you are down there, huh," he said as he walked them over to an old elevator and pulled the gate aside.

After the Frenchman's comment, Eddie presumed to walk into a room with papers strewn all over it, only to find neat, high shelves, evenly spaced across the low-ceilinged room, with boxes and files orderly placed upon them.

"It will probably be in this row, what you are looking for," said the Frenchman in an apathetic drawl. "This is where most of the U-boat records we have found are placed. Try that group of green boxes over there. Good luck." And then he sauntered off, leaving them to it. No shifty-eyed guards watching over them, nothing of the espionage that they had prepared themselves for, the two friends giving themselves a look of pleasant surprise and walking down either side of the aisle.

It was only when Eddie and Jens each pulled a box away from the shelf and looked inside, that it dawned on them just how impossible it might be to find what they were looking for: instead of the contents of the boxes being neatly set in folders and labelled alphabetically, papers, folders and books had simply been dumped inside. Rifling through them, it was difficult to know exactly what was what.

Jens looked up from his box and asked, "Uh, so what is it exactly we are looking for?"

"Well, so, it's U-456, Captain Teichart...uh, we'll be looking for a diary or a log book. Suppose they shouldn't be too hard to distinguish, right?"

"Naturlich," agreed Jens, and, after a little rummaging through his box, pulled out a dirty, dark brown book with aged pages which he leafed through, "Right, here we are, this is a logbook - not the one we are looking for unfortunately - but you get the picture: here, one page, you have entries like yours, Mr Accountant, it's all numbers, times and brief descriptions with coordinates," then flipping the page back and forth, "and on the opposite page are his notes, handwritten notes…"

Eddie and Jens set to work then, looking for a phantom. The impossible find. A log book that may or may not have existed.

After some time Jens pulled out a single sheet and said, "Oh, so here we have a typed version…? Hmm, perhaps they wrote by hand and then when it was quiet they would type it out - from what I have read they spent hours upon hours on the water with silent nothing going on. Plenty of time to type things up."

"Okay, so we know what we are looking for then, but which bloody box is it in?" quizzed Eddie.

"Pick one," said Jens with a shrug.

Frustration lengthened time, as the two men went from enthusiastically piling into the boxes, shuffling through endless sheets of paper upon paper, leafing through file upon file and scanning through countless books, the concentration of the task taking its toll so that it was not too long before they moved on to stretching their backs and necks, to yawning, to sighing, to sitting on the floor. It all began to look like it was for nothing, doubt having long set in that they would find what they were after, the odds of finding it becoming slimmer as the hours went by.

Eddie looked at his watch, Jens seeing him do so; both of them were aware that time was running out for Eddie to get to the airport: he had given himself a day to search out information that would strengthen his position when bidding for the salvage ship. The only ship that could do the job, he reminded himself for the hundredth time. For all he knew, the Norwegian competitors had already made their pitch and won the boat. Time really was money. Or, Eddie mused unhappily to himself, time really was gold.

Time had run out though. The Frenchman had already come in to let them know that the building was due to be shut in twenty minutes, and they were also under pressure to get to the airport.

Eddie dropped his head into his hands and rubbed his face, and when he looked up, Jens was handing over his leather satchel, saying, "Time's up."

When they got back to the car, Eddie lumped himself into the passenger seat, totally deflated, leaning round and flinging his satchel onto the back seat in disappointment.

"So. I'll have to do the deal with what we've got."

Jens then reached over to retrieve the satchel, handing it back to Eddie, the Englishman looking back at Jens with a quizzical look.

Fighting back a smirk, Jens said, "Open it."

Eddie undid the buckles of the satchel and looked inside, a wry smile coming over his face as he shook his head from left to right. His smile broadened and he looked over at Jens and said, "You sly dog."

◇

Aboard KLM flight 563, heading up through the clouds on the small passenger plane to The Hague Airport in Rotterdam, Eddie did not even register the turbulence, so absorbed was he in the accounts he was reading about the HMS Edinburgh. He was en route to meet with the one man who had the only ship which had the capabilities to accomplish the salvage job in the unpredictable conditions of the Barents Sea. The ship in question, owned by one Rollie Visser, had all the facilities and equipment onboard that was required for this difficult salvage to be a success, where others in the past had tried and failed.

He was all too aware that he was on a flight against time, that the Norwegian contenders would be making their approach to Rollie, or already had, and that he may well have taken that one day too many on his hunt for additional ammunition to bolster his proposal. Eddie felt confident, nonetheless, that what he had managed to gather would help him to seal the deal.

For Eddie, there was no such thing as a no-win situation.

From the information he had gathered over the years and, more specifically, over the last few weeks, Eddie had turned his eye now to the salvage itself, looking to draw out any clues about the sunken vessel that might help the salvage team to know where it was that they could enter the wreck and locate the gold. It was not lost on him that such information might equally strengthen his bid for the salvage vessel.

As the plane broke through the clouds to reveal a stunning sunset, turning Eddie's notes and papers pink, he looked out of the window to the sky above, just like a clear blue sky on a fateful day in April 1942.

Chapter 17

The Black Death

1942 Arctic Ocean

At 4 pm on 29th April 1942, flying the flag of Vice Admiral SS Bonham-Carter, the HMS Edinburgh, in direct contravention to orders received on the 8th of that month, which required her to provide strong support for Convoy QP-11, was a distance of twenty miles away from any other ship in the convoy.

Reading the captain's log, Eddie looked up, tutted and shook his head, "Uh," he said out loud, "There it is again: twenty miles," as his eyes turned inward to the map in his head, where he circled the location of the Edinburgh in the blue ink of his imagination.

She was on her return run from what was put down in the log as a 'routine patrol', which flew directly in the face of the orders which required a 'close escort.' Despite these orders, the Edinburgh was leagues away from the other 16 ships in the convoy.

The protocol was to have a tight-knit layout of zig-zagging vessels. Among them were 4 destroyers, 4 corvettes and a trawler, the strongest escort yet allocated to a Russian convoy. In addition the Harrier, with 3 of her sweepers - Hussar, Gossamer and Niger - backed up the convoy screen set up to protect the 4 merchant vessels for the first part of the voyage. This flank guard would protect them, for that first and most exposed part of the leg, from enemy attacks coming from the shore of the mainland. An armada with more than enough firepower to protect the cargo, as well as one another, but they were no use to the Edinburgh, as far as she had wandered from the fleet.

Yet aboard the ship, there had been a general air of confidence.

The pipe had just sounded 'Fall out from action stations' and 'Non-duty hands to tea'. Most of the crew had been at 'Stand by action stations' for the last 48 hours. This was the earliest opportunity for some of the men to relax in the comparative comfort of their mess decks. For the first time since the ship had left Murmansk, the pipe seemed to dispense an atmosphere of relaxation. There was a natural buoyant air of optimism, a sense of security. The ship, after all, had not got a scratch on it - coming through every run clean so far - despite being in its fair share of battles. Yet it was in this unguarded moment that no one, not even the bridge lookouts, saw the tell-tale silver wakes of the deadly steelfish streaking through the Arctic waters towards the ship.

Leading Stoker Leonard Bradley was mock-sparring with the young amateur boxer, Taff Harrington, to the jeers and cheers of the other forty-eight men in the stokers' mess deck. They were making the most of their first chance to relax, when everything shook, and the floor, from one side of the mess hall to the other, split open right down the middle, and fifty men fell into blackness.

The first torpedo from U-456 had hit amidships, destroying the oil tank directly below the mess hall so that the crewmen were left to flail in pitch darkness as they tried to keep afloat in a wash of oil and water. The emergency lighting had failed to activate leaving zero visibility, allowing only the hollers and screams of other drowning men to go by. The temperature outside was easily a murderous 20 degrees below, if not colder, so that the water gushing in through the hole in the hull was menacingly cold, flooding in to take the men in its freezing grasp. All the elements were against the crew and the carnage wreaked by the torpedo left their surroundings just as precarious. Whoever was fortunate enough to have survived the shockwave of the blast was in danger of being cut by jagged metal and hammered by falling tables and benches and bludgeoning pipework - blood mixing readily with the oil slick and ice.

Bracing himself against the shock of crippling cold and sheer terror, Leonard Bradley eventually found footing and grabbed for anything to keep himself stable. Clinging onto a pipe that met with his grasp, he used the pipeline to navigate where he thought the hatch might be. His mate, Taff Harrington, called out from somewhere nearby and Bradley shouted in return, reaching his free hand out into the darkness and just managing to get a hold of his friend. It seemed the boxer was able to find his footing except that the oil, spurting out of the damaged tanks, was filling the room rapidly and had now reached the men's shoulders so that Harrington slipped and lost hold of Bradley and was gone.

After waving his hand about under the oil and water and calling out to Taff for some time, with no response, all

Bradley could do was continue to make his way towards the hatch.

When he reached a stanchion near the entrance, he knew that he was headed in the right direction and he continued to pull himself towards it, only to bump into someone else clinging to the stanchion. It was a lad named Harrison who managed to say, in a voice full of agony, "Help me, I th-think I've br-bro-broken something - can't hold on m-much longer." Bradley tried to pull Harrison above the rising tide of oil but the boy screamed blue murder, the stoker not realising that both of the lad's collar bones were broken.

"C-can...you...s-s-stand?" he asked Harrison.

"I c...ca...can't, can't, the pain - d-don't make me s-stand!" the boy cried.

So, changing his grip a few times, only for his crewmate to cry out, Bradley figured that both of Harrison's arms might be broken and he had to make a choice, "Jus-st h-hold on, I'm going to...to try..."

"N-no, I c-uh-can't," said Harrison, weaker now, "I can't h...hold on any m-more, m-meh...my arms..."

The only way Bradley was going to be able to keep the boy afloat was to let go of his only support and use both hands to lift Harrison's body above the oil line - by his estimation it was not far from the hatch now, and Bradley would just have to try and walk that slippery couple of metres through the thick blackness. It was a far-reaching few metres.

It was only then that it struck Bradley how quiet it had gone. Chances were, it was only he and Harrison left.

He would give it a go.

Pressing his feet to the slick floor, slipping once then getting his footing, he pushed his hands under Harrsion's broken body, the oil line reaching his chin, and said, "H-hold on, I'll g…I'll g-get you out," with all the assurance he could muster, trying his best to coax his faith at the same time.

◇

"Direct hit, Herr Kapitän!"
"Up periscope," Teichart said calmly.
"Up periscope."
The captain stepped to the periscope tube, pulling on the handles and shifting the viewfinder down to eye level. Eye on the viewfinder, Teichart swivelled the tube until he could see the target, the smoke rising into the unnaturally blue skies. He pushed himself away from the periscope and, for a moment, looking down to nowhere, his eyes closed to a slit, pupils moving left to right, as he absorbed what it was he had seen, then he quickly put his eye to the viewfinder once more.

The clear conditions allowed for good visibility, the stain of oil bleeding out from the ship so that Teichart figured where they had hit the vessel, "Mmm," he mumbled, "Got the fuel tanks, starboard…" then a small groan, "But she is still moving…"

Taking a step back, the captain drew a sharp breath in, then said aloud, "Report to High Command. Send coordinates. Direct hit. Light cruiser, second class. One torpedo remaining."

"Target turning to Starboard, bearing east-south-east, Kapitän," said the radar operator, "Still turning, hard towards due south."

"He's narrowing the target," the captain mused.

The commander asked, "Open bow caps?"

"No. Wait," commanded the captain, "We need to make this one count." He knew he had only that one torpedo left and that he could, by all rights, use it to blow another hole into the side of the enemy vessel, a kill shot that would surely sink it. Coming away from the viewfinder, he looked around the bridge, seeing not soldiers, but men, boys even, and decided to aim for the enemy's engine instead, as was his custom - it would cripple the ship, but give the men on board the enemy vessel time to be rescued.

Ignoring the questioning glances of his crew, the captain leant into the viewfinder once more and waited for the ship to turn, until he was looking directly at the stern. It was the narrowest angle, the chances of missing - considering unknown ocean currents - being far higher than they would be if he came alongside the ship again, but it was the engines he wanted.

"Keep bearing. Open bow caps."

"Keep bearing."

"Bow caps open."

Not waiting to be asked whether he was keeping the boat level, the commander reported, "Both planes at zero."

Now was the moment.

Clenching his fist, the captain commanded cooly, "Fire torpedo two."

Chapter 18

Going Under

1942 Arctic Ocean

Upon the bridge of the HMS Edinburgh, with steadfast presence and absolute focus, Captain Hugh Webb Faulkner was firing out commands. After a burst of relays back and forth from the engine room, confirming that the ship still had full capacity, he had given the orders to take evasive action: turning hard to starboard to avoid the next torpedo that was almost certainly already on its way. There would be no way of telling what angle that torpedo would approach at, or even whether they were turning into the optimal position for a second submarine to fire a kill shot. In a situation like this, one was blind. All the captain had to go on was a combination of experience and instinct and a bit of luck to boot.

Bursting onto the bridge, able seaman Joseph Bleakley took a second to catch his breath and then stood to attention, not waiting for any invitation to give the report he had been sent to pass on, "Captain. They've torn a hole in the hull. Starboard oil tanks. We're taking on water."

"Seal the bulkheads," the Captain ordered, "Let's make her watertight." Those inner walls, placed at intervals along the shaft of the ship, not only strengthened the hull but also created separate sections that could be isolated to stop inflowing water and restrict fire from torpedo damage getting into the rest of the vessel.

"Yes, Captain. Already on it. Any other orders."

Knowing the layout of his battleship back to front, the Captain had already calculated the obvious damage that the mess deck above the tanks could have taken, and he asked curtly, "Have you cleared the mess deck?"

"All dead, sir," said Bleakley, eyes dropping, but then taking a breath and returning to protocol, the training that had been drummed into him, had kept him and his shipmates alive time after time, he made eye contact with his Captain again and reported, "Walkey and Start are sealing the hatches to the stokers' mess deck now, sir."

"Right, seaman, back to your station," said the Captain, not waiting for the crewman to leave before swivelling on his heel to command the telegraphist, "Send message to…"

But his command was drowned by the almighty blast of the second torpedo ploughing into the ship, the men grabbing for whatever holding they could, jolted by the force of the impact that caused those sturdy steel walls within the vessel to shudder and wobble impossibly.

The brutal cold had taken hold of Bradley, reducing his ability to move, to even think where he was and what it was he was supposed to be doing. In moments of lucidity, as he came back to himself, it would feel as though he were two separate entities - the mind and the body, no longer a single unit, not responding to one another, disconnected - his mind reaching out to his frozen limbs, urging, "Move!" in vain, until, somehow, he was able to force his unresponsive body to wade through the freezing oil, managing to take just one more shuffling step towards where he figured the hatch should be.

Losing consciousness, his chin dropping down to his chest, as the ice lulled him into a frozen sleep, his mouth filled with oil and his head jerked up as he choked and spluttered. He returned to himself once more and realised with alarm that he had lost his hold on Harrison, letting the boy's body slump into the oil. With burning cold hands barely registering what they touched, he lifted Harrison above the slick again.

There was no response from the boy. Not knowing whether the lad was still alive or not, Bradley took one more impossible step, but could not take another, could not get himself to move any more, an invisible barrier blocking his way.

In his mind, his responses lagging, Bradley had lost all sense of time, thinking that he had only taken one step, maybe two, not registering that he had reached the hatch. It was only when he willed himself to lunge backwards, in a desperate stride, that his heel hit against a vertical surface...a wall. His eyes, which he had closed against the cold, fluttered open to see nothing.

Where was he?

Reaching his left arm under Harrison, to cradle his shoulders and keep him afloat above the oil, which seemed to have levelled off, Bradley tried to twist and move his right hand from under Harrison's back to no avail. His arm just was not responding, locked in place after carrying the boy forever, across the void.

Reaching deep within, Bradley kick-started himself with a dramatic call, "Come on!" The adrenalin worked its way through his body but the actual words escaped his stiff lips as a diddering, feeble breath. But it was enough. His arm came away from his injured friend and in stunted, jerking movements, slowly reached out beyond his cargo to feel for what was in front of him.

His palm pressed against a hard surface but it did not immediately register as such, as his mind sluggishly connected with the disjointed senses of his body. When it came to him that it was real, that he had got to the other side, he then had to rally against disbelief that in his staggered, stumbling, half-awake reach he had also managed to continue in the right direction. But hoping against lost hope, he painfully slid his hand left across the metal wall until his wrist hit something, and he suddenly jolted completely awake.

Pressing his wrist and the back of his hand against the object, to be sure it was real, he then shakingly shifted his hand back to feel what it was, the terrible stinging cold making his fingers fight against the action, but he forced himself once more, gripping onto an unmistakably cylindrical pipe...*no...not a pipe*, he thought, as his hands worked round, *a wheel*. The 'dog' - the handwheel of a watertight hatch!

Survival instinct negating the pain, he gripped firmly onto the dog to turn it. But it would not budge. He tried again and again, with every ounce of strength left in him, wishing inside that he could have use of both hands until he had no more to give, and sunk into the realisation that it would make no difference. The hatch was sealed. Possibly welded shut from the other side.

It was then that it dawned on Bradley once more just how quiet everything had gone. There was not a single movement to be heard. Utter silence. And Bradley began to wonder if he had died. As the cold and dark began to engulf him, suddenly the floor and walls shook and warped, the shockwave from the second torpedo strike surging through the ship.

Bradley lost his grip, his feet slipping as the floor seemed to come away from under him, and he and Harrison went under the oil, lost in its black depths.

The second torpedo tore into the stern, shredding the layers of tempered steel like paper, the fortified armour plating being twisted as though some great fist had scrunched it up, so that, from behind, the ship looked like no more than a crushed tin can. The entire quarter-deck was blasted up, peeling the shreds of ripped metal back to enfold themselves around the guns of 'Y' turret, leaving the barrels to jut out between the obliterated steel decking. All that was left of the rudder and two of four propeller shafts was a mess of mangled metal.

The unfathomable force of pressure wreaked upon the underside of the ship nigh-on destroyed its integrity, breaking the backbone of the vessel, bending the base plates of the ship backwards and reforming the sheets into a twisted fin.

The violent shockwaves and sound of buckling metal were drowned out by the deafening noise of tons upon tons of seawater surging into the ship under enormous pressure. An impossible volume of water forced its way through passageways, at relentless speeds, the deathly torrents pummelling anything in their path and carrying them off to form a fist of bodies and broken metal that slammed into everyone in their wake.

The cruiser ground to a tremoring halt and the ship listed to starboard, an injured man-of-war leaning over like a soldier in his last gasp. Yet, somehow, miraculously, she was still afloat.

Chapter 19

Courage Under Fire

1942 Arctic Ocean

Before the first torpedo hit, Petty Officer John Napier had been musing over how lucky the Edinburgh had been so far. He had been on duty on the starboard pom-pom, on the afternoon watch, and had gone down the Petty Officers' mess for his tea, poured himself a cuppa and sat down at the table when suddenly there had been a great thump! thump! thump! and all the lights had gone out.

Thankfully the emergency lighting in his mess hall had kicked in, and he had immediately bolted from the mess and gone straight to his action station, only for the ground to move below his feet, as the ship was hammered by the second torpedo. When he came to his senses, he half ran, half stumbled to the surface, to find that the ship had started taking a list to starboard. Looking down aft, towards x- and y-turrets where the quarter deck had been hit, he saw that the heavy gauge metal of the platform had been turned into no more than tin foil. It was curled back on itself and plastered round y-turret, so the guns of the six-inch were wrapped up - as if someone had come along with a sardine tin opener, opened the tin and pulled the cover back and crumpled it around the barrel of the gun.

Stepping up to his gun, Napier trained it away and scanned the horizon only to sight the periscope of a U-boat! He opened fire, taking note at the same time that none of the other gunners were doing the same from the bow. He tried to contact the bridge, to let them know what he had spotted, but communications were out altogether, so he used his initiative and continued to open fire in the direction of the periscope to attract the attention of the personnel on the bridge. He was fairly certain that he managed to hit his target, damaging the periscope. With its action periscope unserviceable the U-boat would not be able to fire its torpedoes accurately from then on. Odds were though, it was still close enough to land a direct hit, even with its sights damaged.

Able Seaman Joseph Bleakley had not made it far from the bridge, having flown down the two short flights of stairs and started to run along the top deck, when the second torpedo hit. Thrown onto the decking and stunned by the quaking of the blast, it took him a few moments to regain his bearings as his mind tried to register the sight of men being cast overboard, tumbling like ragdolls from the railings. Shellshocked, he stood and stumbled forward towards the entrance to the quarter-deck stairwell, not even registering where he was supposed to be going, automatically taking the route mapped into his muscle memory, having run this course so many times that his body knew exactly where it was headed.

It was only when he had run along the open passageway and turned to head past the laundry, that he came to, remembering that he was headed back to his petty officers to help seal the hatches. He raced down the stairwell at the back of the laundry only to stop dead in his tracks, it was pitch black down there and he could hear the sounds of men stumbling blindly through the passageway. It sounded like they were careening into one another, some cursing that they could not find the stairs. Reaching for the blackout lamp positioned near the foot of the stairs he switched it on, shining the torch down the passage and calling the men to himself. To the first sailor who reached him, Bleakley handed the torch and told him to light the way for the rest.

"Where ya goin'?" asked the new torch-bearer.

"I have to get back to my station!" Bleakley shouted back as he made his way down the passage, running his fingers across the wall to guide himself along the whole run of the passageway that led to the last bulkhead, where he would have to head down one more flight of stairs before he could get to where Start and Walkey were sealing the hatch to the mess hall.

It was tricky to navigate in the darkness and more so because the floor was sloping to one side where the ship was listing, and he was ankle-deep in water, sloshing through debris. He began to register, as he pressed on, the sub-zero temperature of the water seeping in through his galoshes and into his boots.

At the same time, a chaotic cacophony of sounds echoed towards him - groaning, creaks and ear-piercing squeaks of straining metalwork. The tail end of the ship's frame was twisted out of proportion in the aftermath of the explosions and the disconcerting sounds of snapping wires and tearing metal grew louder as he headed in that direction, the

Edinburgh seeming to succumb to the stress of the breaches in her hull. There too was a horrible, steady reverberation of what Bleakley could only imagine must have been seawater cascading into the ship, finding its way into every rip in the shell of the vessel.

As he spoke aloud a prayer, behind him he made out the splashing footfall and voices of two men headed in the same direction. He turned around only to be blinded by torchlight. Recognising one of the voices though, Bleakley called out, "That you, Dawson?"

"Yeah, which way you going, Joe?" asked the young stoker.

"Stoker's mess deck," answered Bleakley curtly, as the others caught up with him.

"Same goes," puffed Dawson as they all carried on.

The three men worked their way along the passage and down the next flight of stairs, holding the railing so as not to slip in the cascading water on the leaning stairway. Having picked their way as quickly as they could down the stairs it was not long before they could see Walkey and another stoker in the light of Start's torch. Dawson handed the other stoker the crowbar he had been sent to fetch so that they could try and prise open the hatch which would not budge because of how buckled the flooring was around it.

"Sir," Bleakley said to Start, "Did as ordered, the Captain sent me back down here. Are you sealing the hatch?"

"No, we're trying to open it," replied Start.

At which point the stoker with the crowbar blurted out, "There's no point," as he dropped his head with a heavy sigh, the hatch not seeming to move despite his effort, "they're dead. And we'll be dead too if another torpedo hits."

"Listen, stoker," said Walkey, "if they had any more torpedoes to fire, they would've done so already. Here," finished Walkey, holding out his hand to the lad who had spoken out of turn, "give it here - I'll have a go."

Arthur Start had been with the rest of the Chief Petty Officers and Petty Officers in their mess hall when the first torpedo had hit. All the lights had gone out but luckily Start had kept a torch in his pocket. Men had come running from everywhere, congregating around the light, and he had led them up to the flight deck where, in such an event, they had been told to gather. Realising that the mess decks below might still contain trapped men, and knowing that there was a vertical shaft leading to that room - through which the gold had been lowered - he had asked his friend, Walkey, to head down there with him to see if they could save anyone.

With a mighty heave and a shout from Walkey, the hatch opened a crack. Start and Dawson instantly dropped to their knees to help open the hatch all the way.

Shining the torch down the shaft they could see, low and behold, the whites of eyes looking right back up at them. As his own eyes adjusted to the light, Start could make out the blackened faces of the oil-covered men.

There was nothing in the trunking of the shaft to grab onto, so Walkey commanded, "Rope."

"Couldn't find any, sir," replied the stoker. "Just grabbed the crowbar and got back here."

Walkey sent Bleakley off to find rope this time when Start patted him on the shoulder and said in astonishment, "No need, mate: *look*," as he pointed to where one of the men below had got his way into the shaft, which was only two feet square, and was working his way up the shaft by pressing his knees and back against the sides.

As the sailor made his way up the shaft, a call from below sounded out, "It's w-working! R-r-right, m-mate, you're n-nuh…next."

By the time Bleakley returned with rope, several men had already climbed out the hatch and Walkey was calling to Bradley to make his way up, but the brave fellow refused to leave young Harrison behind.

"I'll wuh-wait for r-rr-rope," called up Bradley.

To which Walkey shouted, "There might not be time, you need to get up here!"

But Dawson handed him the rope, which they lowered and Bradley, frozen and numb though his fingers were, managed to tie it around Harrison's chest, under his arms, so that the lad could be pulled up the shaft. Then, finally, Bradley too was hoisted up and the hatch was closed.

Somehow, despite everything, he was alive.

Sending the rescued men and the stokers to the flight deck to congregate with the officers there, Bob Walkey turned to his friend, Arthur Start, and said, "The engine room isn't far. We're the officers on hand. The ship's stopped: we have to find out what's going on with the engines and make a report. The Cap'n will need to know."

With a heavy sigh and a smile of resignation, Start simply replied, "Ah, shit. Yeah, you're not often wrong, but you're right again. Come on then, let's go."
Start got the undyingly enthusiastic Bleakley and also the signalman, Dawson, to join them and off they went together, into the darkness, not knowing what would meet them.

Captain Faulkner had built up trust within his men and they held a deep respect for him, beyond his rank, knowing that on all occasions and especially in the situation they were now in, his main concern was for their safety and for that of the ship that carried them.
Immediately after the first blast, when the ship had ground to a halt, he had tried to hail the lower steering position and damage control, post right aft, to get a report on the state of the vessel on the starboard side of the ship, only the torpedo blast had taken the hailing system down so that the Captain could not raise an answer. With no electronic means of communication, the bridge reverted to a hub, runners being sent back and forth to get reports and relay commands. The Captain, like any worthy seaman, knew that if the ship had not gone down within the first few minutes then there was hope that she could survive several hours, long enough perhaps to be rescued. In the meantime, it was paramount for him to understand every detail of the vessel's current condition for him to plan any sort of escape strategy. Considering the still-present danger of the attacker and the condition of his ship, the main enemy now, was time.

Able Seaman, John Bamford, had just given his report regarding the plugging of holes in preparation for pumping out loose water in the cabins. He was about to report on the progress on the hailing systems when, entering the bridge came Gunner Jack Spence, who walked straight past the Admiral and stood to attention in front of the Captain, saying, "Damage report, Sir." The Captain had Bamford wait with the rest of his report, knowing the state of the ship's integrity came first.

The first torpedo had hit nigh on the dead centre of the ship, the bulkheads keeping most of the damage to the rear, the 50-foot breach leaving compartments all along the starboard side exposed almost through to the port side, opening the floodgates to the entire stern, the weight of water trying to gouge away at the remaining bulkheads that were buckled by the blast.

While taking in the report, Faulkner raised his binoculars and followed the firing line of the starboard gunner and spotted a periscope. "U-boat sighted. One hundred metres off the starboard bough, midships. Periscope level." He dropped the binoculars slightly, letting out, "Has he hit that periscope?" Gazing out in that direction and adjusting the focus on the lens, he took a closer look, and said, more clearly this time, his voice full of praise, "He *has*!"

The commander, looking through his own binoculars, lowered his and said, "Sir, we are still directly in its firing line."

"And there's not a thing we can do about it," the Captain responded. "With the action periscope damaged, they will want to get eyes on - it's only our gunner down there who's keeping them from surfacing. But that won't last. As soon as they come up, they will make the kill shot."

He looked down and gave a slight shake of his head before his eyes looked accusingly over Spence's shoulder to where Vice-Admiral Bonham-Carter stood, causing Jack to follow his gaze.

"What are you looking at?" shot the Admiral at the gunner, his belly protruding and his chin raised.

To which the Captain responded, dropping all pretence of courtesy, "He's looking at you, you pompous idiot. You've sunk the bloody ship. This is how it will be read in my report. You are just a passenger on this vessel. The best you can do is return to your cabin where you will be safe - I'm the Captain, leave me to do my job."

Ignoring the blustering of the Admiral and seeing the whites of the gunner's eyes after this outburst, he reassured him with a glint in his eye, "Let's keep her afloat, Spence: head down to the second and help to seal off bulkheads."

Turning his back on the Admiral, the Captain asked aloud, "Where's Bleakley with my report on the engines?"

Then, swivelling to face ordinary seaman John Bamford, the captain asked if the hailing system was operational yet.

"No, sir, all the electrics are still out for communications, they're working on it, sir," responded Bamford.

"Guns?" asked the Captain.

"All electrical power to gun turrets are out too, sir, except for "B" turret," said Bamford as he motioned with his head towards the front of the ship, "But it's not fully operational yet."

The Captain was looking down from the bridge at the two gun turrets, hunched one on top of the other, each with three cannons, taking up almost the entire bow - the unmistakable presence of firepower that made these light cruisers such a formidable vessel - the sea dog's muzzle, reigned in, with no one to bite.

Onto the bridge burst Joseph Bleakley and Stoker Second Class Patrick Beattie, who stood to attention and said, "Engine room report, sir."

The Captain wasted no time, "Engines and propulsion, crewman, what have we got?"

"Engine one and two destroyed, sir," reported Bleakley "Three and four damaged and we only have torchlight down there - as well as fixing engines three and four, they are salvaging, hauling in what machinery we have left to rig an alternate source of power - looks like we can get engine four operational. We have limited power for forward motion; partial propulsion, Captain."

"Good work, man," Faulkner said with genuine praise, then turned to the Commander and ordered, "Make headway, Commander, as much as you can with the limited thrust - let's at least make ourselves a moving target."

The Captain returned his attention to Stoker Beattie, who gave his side of the report, "Oil losses in compartments three and four - down to thirty percent - Petty Officer Start and Walkey are leading on extracting and redirecting what's left of the oil."

"Right, Bleakley, Beattie, the first port of call," Faulkner began his order, the import carrying in his eyes, "I need power and steering for an about turn - we only have one cannon operational and it's facing the wrong bloody direction. Our starboard pom-pom is doing his best down there to fire at the Gerries, not one hundred metres from the deck. If we can't go anywhere we may as well have firing capacity to buy time to get that engine properly up and running. We need to get rid of that submarine. Go." The two men did not need to be told twice, they were off.

Faulkner's left arm went to his bicep and right hand up to his chin, and his eyes shifted side to side. His men doing what they could for the engines, there was no need for him to give any further commands in that direction, therefore he was weighing up the other needs: they were likely to get the ship moving but it was listing dangerously to one side and, as she was likely to take on more water, that would only get worse, eventually taking the cruiser under. There was no protocol for this situation, however, his mind was rallying through options of how to counterbalance the ship's perilous tilt…His eyes suddenly scrunched, his memory hitting on a long shot. Left hand dropping to his side and right hand now pointing all fingers at able seaman Bamford, he ordered, "Fire the starboard tubes - we need to relieve pressure - then conduct controlled flooding of the tubes: let's try to get her steady. Double time, Bamford."

All the reports in, the Captain reviewed the notes that Edward Anderson, the Crystal Radio operator, had been taking, and, asking for his pencil, the Captain underlined relevant points and handed the notes to Hank Davis, the Petty Officer Telegraphist, to send the report to HQ.

The Captain then turned to his commander, Arthur Bailey, and said, "Nothing more I can do here, Commander, I'm going to rally the men. I leave you in command of the bridge."

Chapter 20

Counting the Cost

1980 Rotterdam, Netherlands

Eddie stepped into the muggy Amsterdam air, heavy with the cries of seagulls and the smell of the sea, and walked to the front of the line of taxis outside arrivals, climbing into the foremost car with his meagre luggage. "Rotterdam Savoy, please," he said to the taxi driver.

Fingers drumming on his satchel, Eddie hoped to hell that his credit card would not give out when he got to the hotel. Just like in Germany, he had friends and contacts in Amsterdam who could easily have put him up for the night, but choosing to stay at the Savoy sent out a statement.

It was seldom that Eddie worked this way, but even he knew that sometimes one had to look like money to win the deal. If he had stayed at a colleague's house or at a bed and breakfast, then he would not have had any way to show that he had the collateral to afford the hire of a salvaging vessel. When he arrived at the hotel he would call the owner of the salvage boat, Rollie Visser, and let the old seaman know that he had arrived in Rotterdam and was all set for the meeting they had arranged for the following morning. The expense of staying at the most desirable hotel in the area was all worth it for that one line he would say when he called: "You can reach me at the Savoy."

The fact was, Eddie could no more afford to stay at the Savoy than he could afford to buy the suit he had hired for the meeting, but what he required from this semblance of status was the *ease* to do the deal. He needed the only man, who had the only ship capable of completing the job, to feel *comfortable* with the notion that he would be hiring it out to a well-dressed fellow who could afford to stay at a top-notch hotel.

There would be no question that their competitors would also have approached Rollie for the use of his ship, even if they had not yet signed a contract to do so. It was the one ship that had the equipment to accomplish the salvage in a single stage, after locating the wreck, and it would not only have been Geoff's team who would have worked out that this was the best way to get down to the wreck and get the gold. Anyone who had any serious interest in a successful salvaging operation, and had done their research, would inevitably end up in Rollie Visser's office.

Everything Eddie had done up to this point, everything he and others had invested thus far, hinged on making a deal with Rollie. Everything rode on acquiring his boat. Yes, Eddie could not afford to stay at the Savoy, neither could he afford the suit he was wearing, and what was more, nor could he afford to look as though he did not have a pot to piss in. He simply needed Rollie to take one look at him and trust that this guy had the financial backing to hire his sought-after ship.

The first thing Eddie had done on walking into his hotel room, was to make that all-important phone call to confirm the meeting with Rollie. Then, almost on auto-pilot, he turned on the TV to catch up on the evening news and collapsed into the chair next to the bed. Elbows on the arms of the chair and hands prayer-like in front of his chin, he tapped his fingertips together, thinking about how much rode on getting this deal right. Oblivious to the sporting highlights that would usually captivate him - McEnroe to face Borg in the men's final at Wimbledon - Eddie was lost in contemplation; thinking through all that he had been through to get to this point.

Confined in the room, with nothing to do but think, it was not unlike being in a decompression chamber, where one's underlying thought, no matter how much one tried to distract oneself, was always about the pressure. Without a doubt, right now the pressure was on, taking Eddie back to that D-chamber where he had sat with the very men who would become the key players in this venture.

Back then, Eddie had long since cemented what he knew about the Edinburgh into something he could sell as a concrete opportunity; all he had needed was to find the men who could go that one step further than anyone else had. After putting the idea subtly out there with each individual, he had got them all together in the common room of the chamber and set the scene for the salvage of the century.

Everything had been there, laid out in front of them so clearly that they could almost touch the gold, the divers leaning in, bodily inviting him to say, "So. We all know that the time is fast approaching when someone will go after the Edinburgh. Let me ask you this then: if you were a company or an individual, and you needed a team to get the gold, who would *you* hire?" There had been a stunned silence as each of them had looked around at each other and realised, almost simultaneously, with small knowing nods of agreement between them, that *they* were the ones: this was the team who would get the gold. At that point, all eyes had fallen on Eddie, which was exactly how he had engineered it to begin with. With a curt nod, he had said, "Leave it with me."

Not only was the information that each of those men had shared relevant to what Eddie had held in mind for the job, but their skill sets and also their temperaments had been applicable too. Most engineers, in the weeks off between projects, would go home, kiss the wife and put their feet up, whereas these guys would take what little time they had off to go on salvage trips. In so doing they had built up into that tight network of people who knew the ins and outs of how to recover goods from the ocean floor, and, more importantly, how to make it a profitable endeavour. If there was treasure to be found, these guys could get it.

As the saying goes, where there is gold there are gold diggers. Yet going after the enviable cargo of the Edinburgh was to be no small feat. The scope of the project called for a fully developed plan and a serious amount of backers. Not only were hefty investments unavoidable, but there also had to be political and administrative backing to undertake an operation inside Soviet territory. Not to mention the inevitable wrangle for the gold that would ensue should it be retrieved.

Everyone in the game could be in the pipeline for the kind of valuable information that could bring them one step closer to bigger and better ventures, yet, as far as the gossip on the rigs had gone, Eddie had never caught wind of a workable plan to retrieve the gold. Aside from back in the fifties, none of the larger salvaging companies had shown any interest in going for the Edinburgh - probably due to the political aspects as much as the technological side of things. And, Eddie mused, quite possibly because no one had ever had the correct information for the location of the wreck. That said, it was always going to be an uncertain exploit even if bureaucratic and technical issues could be surmounted. The only hope of going for the gold, in that case, had fallen then to anyone who could put together a consortium of vested interests who were willing to fund such a risky enterprise.

All such ventures were a gamble, Eddie was well aware, however this was not funding a fishing trip. This was a pioneering salvage dive, a large-scale operation that would take tens of boats and vessels rigged with state-of-the-art equipment just to *find* and confirm the exact location of the Edinburgh. On top of the fact that Eddie's team would be reaching unknown depths, going far deeper than any other diving expedition had ever done before, they would be doing so in waters littered with the wrecks of umpteen sea battles.

Salvage dives were reaching near enough the depths required but certainly not in the extremes of the Barents Sea, where temperate waters from the Gulf Stream and cold waters from the Arctic meet, creating conflicting currents, making for unpredictable conditions. It was the surface of those waters that were so treacherous, frozen over at worst, choppy at best, but once you were past a certain depth, the sea was the sea. What was necessary, in other words, was a salvaging vessel with the equipment to handle the rough surface conditions and, after that, to reach the depths required *and* then remain in place for the weeks it would take to bring all the gold up to the ship, without being knocked off course.

The main leg of the operation could take a full three months, which, for Eddie and Geoff, meant building up, storing and loading supplies - from food to drinking water, from medicine to diving gear. As well as hiring equipment - from diving apparatus to helium tanks, from a backup compressor to high-density underwater lighting - they would also need to pay for specialised staff - such as gas regulators, medical staff and licensed diving bell operators. The hire of Rollie's ship alone, for all of that time, and beyond, when the team would have to remain in the decompression chamber after docking, would come to a substantial figure. With the securing of the ship, sourcing and hiring equipment and supplies, travel expenses for the team, medical staff and coverage, the bills would rack up and continue to do so as the project went on. The final estimated figure would make most men shrink, but not Eddie.

Someone could walk into a bank and ask for fifty thousand Pounds. They would be led by a member of staff to a table and have a bunch of questions asked while a credit check was conducted. Eddie would walk into a bank and say he needed fifty *million*. Backs would straighten, eyebrows would raise, whispers would hiss across the room, and all of a sudden the walls would have ears, and Eddie would be ushered to a plush waiting room outside the director's office, where he would be offered a coffee, fresh orange juice, a glass of prosecco perhaps. Eddie would ask for tea instead. He would lean back, rest his foot on his knee and drink his cuppa, unfazed by the movement his request had caused, the flurry of managers and directorial staff being roused to lend their expertise to the conversation. Soon he would sit across from the director, bank manager and their financial advisers and have their undivided attention. You can guarantee, he would walk away with what he wanted, even though he had jack shit to begin with. That was his knack.

The man simply approached things from a different angle to most people. The unconventional way in which he did things took people by surprise and yet, they would be drawn to him and absorbed by his showman's persona. He would not make an appointment at the bank, for instance, he would just saunter in, flash a smile, and ask for that fifty million. Literally. There would be no sharp suit or lawyer by his side, he would be casually but accordingly dressed, with a relaxed approach and no impressive language.

By rights, this approach should not have worked and would have made bankers nervous, but Eddie was a bit of a wizard. He would draw people into his comfort zone, where he was all easy talk and natural charm, effortlessly commanding the conversation with the absolute ease of someone familiar with talking about massive amounts of money. He would not go to them with plans for opening a chain of barbers. The endeavours he would put forward to the bankers were huge undertakings and he would boggle their minds with the magnitude of the projects, spouting out facts and figures so fast that, in the end, they just had to take his word for it. Should they have run checks at that point, they would find that he was right on the money.

He was precise about what he wanted, in ways that made one think he was the kind of man inclined to get his way. He had the air of someone who belonged on the rich list - the bank managers and directors would be puzzling over whether they should know this guy. Eddie was surely a fellow director of something or other, a millionaire. He was lord of a manor somewhere so grand that nobody knew about it. Affluent and connected enough to be off the radar. He just struck others as a person of influence. There was just something about his presence that was unquestionable. One would not, for a second, doubt that he had the collateral to back up a sizable loan.

When all was said and done, Eddie had balls.

Especially when the stakes were high. When all the chips were down and the only thing going for him was his dogged determination and, of course, his irresistible charm, Eddie would bring out his a-game.

Look up the word 'persuasive' in the dictionary, and next to it, you will find Eddie's name. Quite simply put, he would say whatever someone needed to hear to get them on board - often exaggerating the payout that the business opportunity would bring in return. To anyone under his spell, a prospect that Eddie was putting forward would be nothing less than the Pearl of Great Worth.

Eddie justified the way he tweaked the truth, knowing that what he was offering always had legitimate value. Knowing a good opportunity when he smelled one, all he ever needed after that, was the cash to go out and get it.

Bank loans aside, having the kind of people who you can work for money does not happen overnight. He had an entirely different mindset when it came to friends, family and business partners: all of them, aside from a rare few, were assets from whom he would most certainly, at some point or other, require money. For those who knew him best, it was never about who Eddie owed, it was about who he did *not* owe money to. Nevertheless, he had the gift for getting the dosh he needed.

It was the idea that would draw folks in. The way that Eddie presented a concept made it tangible - put it within their reach. It was not an idea, it was already a fact. All he needed was that last bit of money to conclude the deal and then the proceeds would be theirs. He was driven and passionate about what he was doing - it was contagious - once he was rolling he was unstoppable. A magnet. His talent was to get others on board: he would use his flair to entice them, bring them in, and he would be so convincing that this was a win-win situation that they would start lending money. He could work people around to the point where they were willing to put their *homes* on the line.

Eddie would approach someone he knew with an investment opportunity, and tell the person that the ten thousand Pounds they would give over would become *one hundred* and ten thousand by Wednesday, but, come a month Wednesday, he would have told twenty others the same thing. He would have them stacked and packed behind him, waiting for him to finalise the deal. Some folks would be patient, others not so, turning up at his office angry, threatening even, but it did not matter whether they were only shouting or whether they had Eddie up against the wall by the scruff of his neck, they would always leave laughing.

Every time.

It was like some sort of magic.

And this time was no different, except for the fact that this was the largest undertaking he had ever been involved in, by far. That being the case, there were a good deal more people waiting for the return on their investment. He had called in favours that he would never have a cat's chance in Hell of paying back if he did not get the gold. And the job was far from being done.

He did not even have a ship yet.

In fact, all the funds he had sourced so far were almost depleted, having been spent on the scouting trips - Geoff's consortium and his team trying to ascertain the location of the wreck.

Say what you like about Eddie, whatever he got others involved in he was right in there with them. He did not do things by halves either. Once a decision had been made to enter into a deal he would go all out to finalise it, so now he was in the same boat as everybody else: he had remortgaged his own home to add to the funds which retained his dive team, and he had maxed out on all his credit cards, both personal and business, to keep the project afloat. There were some areas which required payment upfront - flights, hotels, insurance, permits - and it had come as no surprise to Eddie to have to pay gratuities to relevant individuals who would ease the way for the salvage to take place in Soviet waters.

So far, despite being Her Majesty's gold that they were intending to retrieve, the British Government had been less than forthcoming in helping to fund the operation.

And then there was time. The Norwegians. Who knew how far they had got? Geoff had mentioned that the Norwegian team had stopped scouting and there was no way of knowing whether that was because a major funder had pulled out or whether they had found their mark. Either way, Eddie was up against the clock. Once a team had located a wreck, no other salvors could go for it.

His gamble had been based on finding coordinates from the German side to back up either Faulkner's or Walkey's coordinates. Then he would have a true location, which would give his team a far stronger position to obtain Rollie's ship than any other competitors held, and, of course, would clear the path to finding the Edinburgh.

Even though Eddie knew fine and well that locating the wreck would be a tricky task even *with* the correct coordinates, he could not stop a simple version of events from playing out in his imagination, over and again. The fantasy was just enough to keep him going whenever the odds seemed stacked against them: the team would head out to the correlated coordinates, run the radar, confirm the find and, bingo, they would be away.

Finders. Keepers.

Chapter 21

The Competition

1980 Rotterdam, Netherlands

The next morning, just before heading to the all-important meeting to acquire the salvage vessel, Eddie gave one last call to Geoff to get the latest information from his end. Geoff had been pinging back and forth from the UK to Russia for the last several months, working to get royal backing for the project and going out on scouting trips.

Geoff's distant voice came through the headpiece, "There's only one man who would call collect from the Savoy. How's it going, Eddie?"

"Aye-up Geoff, sorry about that - staying here damn near broke the bank. But I've got to look the part, right?"

"I'd know better than to argue with you, mate. You on your way to see Rollie?" asked Geoff, to get the conversation rolling. Calls from Russia were expensive.

"Yeah, I'm all set to do the deal," Eddie said, then paused, almost not wanting to ask the next question, "Any new developments before I go ahead?"

There was the usual delay, as Eddie heard his question repeat, and waited for Geoff to respond. Calling from the Soviet Union, at the height of the communist regime, meant that nothing could be said outright. All operational terms had been strictly coded so as not to give the game away to anyone who would undoubtedly intercept their conversations. This was real. This very phone conversation was being listened to. No question.

You could feel the tension over the static.

"Operation 60 Charlie - Whiskey - Hotel - Approx," was Geoff's response.

Sitting with Roget's Thesaurus in hand, Eddie began to rifle through, finding the words to correspond with the code.

Then, holding back all emotional content from his language and voice, Eddie simply said, "Understood. I'll let you know how the deal goes," and replaced the receiver.

Geoff had done everything he could at his end, whether his team got to go all the way, rode entirely on Eddie's performance with the shipmaster.

Heading down to the counter to hand in his key, the receptionist put down the paperwork and stapler in his hand and greeted Eddie politely. Taking the key from him, the receptionist then asked if Eddie would like a taxi ordered, but Eddie was lost in thought, his gaze going right through the receptionist so that he had to ask again, "Sir?"

There was no turning back now, this was the moment of truth: Eddie would not have another shot at getting the deal done, and without Rollie Visser's specialised ship, there was simply no going ahead with the project. After speaking with the Dutchman, they would be all in.

Eddie came back to himself and, with that devil-may-care smile of his, said, "Yes, thanks, go ahead and order that taxi. The docks, if you please."

The receptionist requested, "Do you have a port code, sir?"

Eddie handed over a slip of paper with the address and gently rapped his fingers on the counter as the receptionist arranged his ride. Then he slipped the young man a ten Guilder note and asked if there was any chance his luggage could be stored in the reception's cloakroom while he went to his meeting - his whole look would be broken if he had to lug a tennis hold-all with him. That done, the smart young man said to Eddie, "I trust you enjoyed your stay at the Savoy, sir. Have a good day."

Eddie glanced down at the satchel clasped tightly in his right hand, and then looked back at the receptionist with a glint in his eye, "Thank you, I'm banking on it."

Though he would never say so himself, before being a diver and even before being an accountant, Eddie was a salesman. He knew that, when offering a sales pitch, the first few seconds were paramount. First impressions and all that. Those precious seconds could buy him thirty more, which was all he needed to lay down his customary charm and read the body language of his investor. That, in turn, bought him the only three minutes he required to have them, hook, line and sinker. The ten minutes that followed would all be for the investor to catch up with the fact that he had been sold.

"You have to hook them in, yes, but you can't let go of the line until you have reeled them in all the way, and only then can you be sure that they will sign on the dotted line," he was fond of saying.

Eddie already knew that the first three seconds were in his grasp before he had even walked in the door, being one step ahead by making a call from the most expensive hotel in the area, and knowing too that he would walk into Rollie's office looking like a million dollars. All judgements that could be arrived at about a person were made within seconds of seeing them walk in the door. It was all about presentation. A position could be settled based on being attired appropriately. It was shallow, it was sad even, but that, Eddie would always say, was the way of the world.

There was always the chance that Rollie, seasoned seaman that he was, would take one look at Eddie and think, "Here we go then, another suit with an attache case. Same old, same old," and that was where the charm would have to kick in. Thereafter it was the facts that he would present about the job and the strength of his team that would keep the conversation going. Eddie had all angles covered. The only thing that he did not have, of course, was money.

Eddie's taxi pulled up beside a hulking warehouse on the docks, scattering a bawdy gang of seagulls - screeching their annoyance at him like a bunch of old hags as he got out and paid the fare. He walked through gusts of drizzle, doing his best to shield his suit by holding the satchel above his head as he peered through the rain to try and locate the door to the building, when out of the mist stepped a man who could only be the lanky figure of Rollie Visser, looking everything like a whaler, gum boots, yellow oiled-waterproofs and all.

"You Eddie?" Rollie half-shouted over the din in the docks.

"That's me," replied Eddie, "Though I didn't quite recognise myself when I looked in the mirror this morning." The suit was too much after all.

"Ha-ha! Follow me then, let's get that nice suit out of the rain," he said with a wry smile.

Rollie took Eddie round the other side of the warehouse and up a steep, weathered-metal stairwell to a cabin attached precariously to the side of the building. Once inside Eddie could immediately see why this would be Rollie's office: it was the crow's nest. With a vantage point over his ship in the dry docks and the port beyond, he would be able to keep a keen eye on everything underway, both on land and at sea.

Scanning the room to get his bearings, Eddie instinctively orientated himself to his location. It was certainly not what he had been expecting. It was better. He was right at home.

Aside from the angled window from which Rollie could oversee the work going on below, there was a small desk and a metal filing cabinet with a fax machine propped on top. The rest was loot. An old anchor leant in one corner, a conch shell nearly as big as a man's head in another. On the walls were photos of big fish and bigger smiles, and a couple of photos from Rollie's days in the navy with a captain's hat hanging between them. Scuba finds covered every other inch. Most impressive though, on the wall beside Rollie's desk, was a bleached shark's jaw - rows upon rows of teeth forming the empty leer of a monster.

Catching Eddie admiring the specimen, Rollie said, "Ja, there's a story to tell."

"I'll bet," commented Eddie. "Not many sharks in the North Sea, where'd you catch that fella? Durban?"

"Not far off. Madagascar," replied the grey-bearded seaman, as he showed Eddie a chair and stepped over to a couple of old ammunition boxes that were stacked to form a rudimentary table, upon which there was a kettle, cups, a tin of carnation milk and a tin of chicory coffee, which he offered to Eddie.

"How do you take it?" Rollie asked.

"Navy," was all Eddie said, knowing that the old sailor would get it, making his coffee strong, milky and with two sugars. Plus condensed milk on top. Out at sea, sweetness was synonymous with survival, and a true seaman never left the water.

They backed and forthed for a spell before the poker game began in earnest.

Once Eddie had built up a rapport with the shipman, feeling like they had a genuine connection, despite the older man holding his cards close to his chest, he watched as the fellow relaxed into salvaging banter, Eddie using the opportunity to introduce his team, most of whom Rollie was familiar with, by name if not in person. It was then that Rollie pulled out his first hand, saying, with a cocked eyebrow, "It's a good team. Others have good teams too."

"Ah, that's well and good, but do they have the right *location*?" Eddie countered. "It takes more than a team to find the gold. You have to know where it is."

The two men had settled nicely across from each other at the desk, but at this statement, Rollie rolled his worn office chair closer to the table. Pressing his hands on the arms of the chair, he leant forward, his whole demeanour shifting from hanging back to keen interest, barriers dropping. An eagerness on his face to see how Eddie would back up what he was alluding to.

Standing up, Eddie selected the correct map from Rollie's impressive collection and rolled the sea chart across the table, Rollie himself clearing the way and weighing it down with brass trinkets. On the map, Eddie placed the pad with notes from Captain Faulkner's LOG. Reading out the coordinates within, he allowed Rollie to locate the point on the chart before the Dutchman slumped back down into his chair saying, "This location is not news to me."

In response, Eddie turned a sheet in his notes, all numbers on the page as usual, found the set that he was looking for and traced his hand on the chart to stop at a different location, "I have another diary account that puts the wreck here."

Rollie's face screwed up with intrigue, which was just what Eddie was aiming for.

"One of the men who loaded the gold, chap named Walkey, made an entry in his diary that puts the Edinburgh here," he said, tapping the location, and then answering the obvious question without Rollie needing to voice it, "Captain Faulkner had every reason to put down the wrong coordinates, or, in the least case, to encode the right ones, so that not just any Tom, Dick or Harry could go down and get the gold. Whereas some regular shiphand, who had no concept of the whole conspiracy, would have given no thought to putting down the correct coordinates. But, that still leaves us with a bit of a dilemma. Who do you believe? Which entry is right?"

"And also, from what I gather," quizzed Rollie, "The ship was torpedoed a long way off from where it was eventually sunk: who's to say that the gold isn't scattered all over the seabed at the site where the ship was first hit?" Another strong hand played.

Eddie countered, knowing full well that the seaman had only said this to gauge how much he knew. Known in the small and secretive community of salvors as something of a Holy Grail, any of them worth their salt had read and talked about, and even done some research on the Edinburgh.

"Right," agreed Eddie, "I did read a diary account that the ship was hit in the ammunition room where the gold was stored. So, yeah, did the gold just fall to the seafloor?" And then, using the opportunity to reel Rollie in more, Eddie asked, knowing what the answer was but giving his new friend a chance to offer some input of his own, "But you'd have to have blown a hole in the undercarriage, right?"

Rollie launched into something of a speech, his enthusiasm for the subject showing through, which was just what Eddie had wanted, "That first explosion when a torpedo hits, it makes a large gas bubble," explained Rollie, his hands ballooning to exhibit the effect. "This bubble expands so fast the shockwave strikes the ship's hull and punches the hull plates in," he punched into his cupped fist, "rupturing the hull. The force from this impact is enough to tear the surrounding plates of the hull right off. After this breach, the shockwave moves right through the ship - the sheer pressure can rupture seams, split seals, crack bulkheads, dislodge hatches…" he paused for breath. "If the torpedo hit the ammunition room and the blast managed to penetrate a magazine?" Here his hands mimed an explosion. "You've seen the photos of the ship, right?" Rollie said more than asked. "The whole backside bunched up like…" and he tore a piece of paper from his notepad and crumpled it in his fist.

"Yes," Eddie conceded, "but everyone who has scanned that photo and done their reading knows that the underside of the hull was still intact - the ship got a whole two hundred miles away before they applied the *coup de grâce*. The only trouble is that there are no reports of the gold being offloaded onto the Gossamer when the crew left the ship, so no one has been able to figure out for sure whether the gold was left on the ship or not when it went down."

"Ja, that's the problem, is it not?"

This was the point Eddie had been leading up to, purposely letting it feel like he was just as stuck as the others who would surely have approached Rollie for the use of his ship. He wanted the shipmaster to feel as though this whole sales pitch was running toward the same loose end everyone else had come to, laying his cards face down as though he was defeated.

"If I may say, it's not a problem for me, Mr Visser. The work of an accountant is to follow the money. Gold leaves a trace. And I've tracked every thread of expenditure, scanned every ledger, turned out the pockets of every weevil in the money market, put myself upon every cunning cash converter in the business and followed every trail of interchange that could lead to the exchange of gold - not just any gold, mind, but the Tzar's gold, that would raise a few eyebrows along the way, would it not? But there's not a single sign of even one bar, even one carat of one bar, of that gold making its way into the market. No doubt about it, sir, that gold is sitting right there on the Edinburgh, on the bottom of Barents, waiting. Just waiting. And the only reason I'm here, Mr Visser, is because you are the only man with the right ship that can retrieve that gold."

"Ja, and that is why your competitors have also approached me…" Rollie seemed like he was going to say more, his smile saying that he liked Eddie, but his eyes blinking with pity.

Having the shipman like him was half the job done, having him reveal, however subtly, that the others who had met with him had the upper hand helped too. This was all a build-up to pulling out his trump card, but now Eddie saw that he would need to increase his lead on the competitors first. Yet, before he raised the stakes, something was troubling him that he needed to be clear on first. "Did you say, *competitors*? Plural. I had it that we are only up against the Norwegians?"

"Them, ja, and the *Russians* too," he divulged, with obvious distaste.

"They kept that quiet, didn't they?" Eddie had not heard of any Russian team being put together

"Ja, it was all cloak and dagger. I thought I was in some Michael Caine spy movie. This guy, Kaliakov, he seemed quite driven - his father was apparently some big shot in the war - had personal dealings with Stalin himself. Gave me the shivers. And I'm an old seadog; I don't scare easily."

"Well," said Eddie jovially, "you won't have to deal with them now, will you?"
"Oh," said Rollie, "And why is that?"
"Because, not only have I got the best team, we are the only ones who can assure you that we have the correct coordinates."

◇

Eddie had been trying to get through to Anja, just to check in so that when he returned to the UK she would not need to pester him over the fact that he had not called. He had it in mind to keep the information about the Russian team to himself, for now. God knew how Anja would react when she heard, and standing in a partially open cubicle at an airport was not the time or place to have that conversation. On his third attempt, he got through to her, but as Anja picked up on the other end, the final call for Eddie's flight was announced over the tannoy.
"KLM Flight 404 from Rotterdam to London, final call."
"Anja!" Eddie half shouted over the clamour in the departures lounge. "Been trying to get through to you for *ages*. Now I've got to go, that was my final call. Anyway, just rang to say that I'm on my way back to the UK."
When Anja asked when he would get home, Eddie let her know that he had to head to London first - that there was a royal connection to the salvage that needed to be addressed, right away. When Anja began to complain about how much longer he would be away, he had to say, "Listen, Anja, stop.

I've got to go. That's my flight." And then it just came out, "Listen, there's another team. Russians…"

Anja went silent on the other side and, internally, Eddie cursed himself for not being able to hold his tongue as she began her interrogation, there and then, despite what he had just said about needing to board his plane.

Over the noise, Eddie could just about make out Anja asking, "Who? Who is leading the team?"

"What does it bloody matter, woman," he protested as he tried to pick up his satchel and briefcase and to take his ticket and passport out of his pocket while still holding the receiver, "I've got to go!"

"Don't hang up on me without telling me. I know you, Eddie, you would not have mentioned this other team if there wasn't more to tell me," Anja insisted.

"Fine…uh, hold on," another call came out for his plane, this time calling him by name, and he pulled the receiver cord as far out as it would stretch so that he could see his boarding gate, where the hostesses were still waiting, "I've got to, Anja, I'll tell you when I get back."

Anja was shouting too now, "I'm only asking for a name! Tell me!"

Eddie could see the hostesses beginning to clear up at his gate and, for one second, he shuffled back into the cubicle and focused. He breathed out, then said what he knew to be the cruellest word his wife could hear, "Kaliakov. It's Kaliakov."

Chapter 22

Gipsy

1940 Siberia, Soviet Union

Out in the distant nowhere of a Siberian gulag, Josef lay crumpled on the floor of the detention centre, having just taken another boot to the side. The NKVD guard standing over him shouted in Josef's Polish mother tongue, "How many times are you going to help our workers to escape!? I know it was you!"

As the guard leant down and pulled his arm back to strike Josef again, an easily recognisable said, very evenly, "Enough."

Having closed his eyes in readiness for the blow, Josef opened them now to see sharp, shiny shoes stubbing out a cigarette, then, craning his neck he saw from the corner of his eye, the pencil-moustached Kaliakov standing over him, hands on pot-belly, "Josef, Josef. How many times must we go through this? If you were not so good at logistics I would have done away with you, long time ago. But here we are again, *sukinsyn*. Now we must go through this tired routine once more. Why don't you make it easier on yourself and just tell me that it was you who helped another of my workers to get out?"

It was true: Josef had indeed helped a young man, and many others before him, to escape the gulag. This was no small task. The gulags were set up as high-security facilities surrounded by manned walls, themselves surrounded by barbed-wire fences, with the ground between patrolled constantly by Russian soldiers with dogs. But, as mining and manufacturing centres, putting out most of Russia's raw materials, munitions and goods, these were not the dank caves that the mind conjures up when the word gulag is mentioned. These were towns in their own right. Rows upon rows of multistoried brick-built tenements, with roads leading to fully equipped factories and mining centres. They were based right out in the far reaches of the freezing Siberian tundras, or where the raw materials could be found, and also as far from the German front as possible. Accessibility to these centres was primarily by rail, which provided the main routes in and out for both goods and supplies. And that was where Josef came in.

As protegé to the station master at Lwów's major interchange, Josef had experience managing the strict routines required for the daily mass movement of people and cargo, which had, in turn, been a vital skill required for the successful running of the gulag system of production.

In Stalin's time alone, over fourteen million people worked in these mining, manufacturing and forestry centres, churning out the bulk of Soviet output. The sheer volume of people and work being undertaken by them required a massive logistical effort, that was, for the most part, achieved by the captives themselves. The conditions were tremendously harsh, yet the prisoners still needed to be fed well enough to maximise productivity and be organised into a labour force that could comply with the demand for supplying the Soviet war machine. Men like Josef, who could take on large managerial responsibilities, were indispensable, hence, despite his reputation for using his skills to cart out escapees along with produce, he had been kept alive and, for the most part, healthy.

It had not taken Josef long to work out that as many men and women died, or, for that matter, escaped the gulags, they would be replenished. The relentless intake of prisoners created an almost constant influx of unfortunate souls who had, for any reason imaginable, found themselves either on the wrong side of the NKVD or valuable to their operations in Siberia.

There was certainly a pecking order which determined how well a prisoner would be treated within the whole system, and for the most part, where you fell within this ranking came down to one of two things: where you were from, or what skills you had.

Those selected to form the prisoner police, for instance, were predominantly from Lwów and otherwise, north-eastern Poland, where they considered themselves to be a separate people - this very nation would later break away to form what is now Ukraine. An enduring undercurrent of mistrust for their Polish compatriots - practically within their DNA - made them the ideal candidates for policing the rest of the prisoners. To add to this, they were plied, on one hand by meat on their plates, good boots, socks and blankets, and on the other hand, by the unsettling reassurance that their families would be kept safe. There was no margin for choice:

you toed the line or you and your family would be dealt with accordingly.

Administrators were generally appointed from Krakow, playing upon their general air of being better than the rest of their countrymen. This minor elevation of status within the gulag, along with placing them in dormitories that had their own ovens - large brickwork structures upon which some of the prisoners slept to stay warm - made administrative roles a position any prisoner would want to hold on to. This in turn created a pliant staff who were more inclined to keep their hands clean.

Josef, though born a Romanian, had grown up in Lwów, which would usually have put him in line for being a guard, however, his skills trumped his birthright so that he was put in charge of all import and export, both by road and by rail. His ability to manage such complex duties made him practically irreplaceable.

When escapes were traced back to him in the earlier days of his imprisonment, he was given due beatings and time in solitary confinement, only for him to be released early and nurtured in the hospital wing, because whoever took over from him simply could not manage the position. It was a momentous and unceasing task of executing decisions that entailed multiple vehicles, transport routes, various cargos and destinations and on- and off-loading of goods. Factoring in the added elements of adverse weather conditions, manufacturing delays, shortages, breakages and more - and all of this whilst living under the very acute stress of being a prisoner - it took a certain calibre of person to cope.

So here he was now, under Kaliakov's shoe, trusting once more that he was too vital to kill or even to hurt too badly. It had not taken long for the Soviets in charge of the gulag to see that there was no point in allowing Josef to be beaten to a pulp, and then out of action for weeks, when they would end up paying for it themselves.

And then there was always the fact that Josef had the savvy to put doubts in the mind of anyone interrogating him, sewing seeds of doubt that he had been responsible for any escape attempts. It was, of course, his old mentor who had suggested how this could be done. Following Mr Politowski's advice, Josef had constructed a way of carrying himself which gave out the message that he was no threat, and he also did his best to give off a humble air of subservience. Neither of these dispositions matched up with the crimes he was inevitably accused of. When one then took in his undying enthusiasm for what he did, his ability to keep good morale in his co-workers and his knack for seeing to details that others might overlook, it became difficult to see him altogether as a dissonant.

"Come on you little fox, how did you do it this time?" Kalikov asked while pressing his heel into Josef's neck.

There was a saying that the Germans would kill the body but the Russians would kill the soul. Within the gulag system they had ways to crush a person, or, in the least case, to suppress someone into subservience without having to render them physically unable to perform their duties. That is not to say that prisoners were not beaten to death or killed outright, it is to say that in cases like Josef, where he was needed alive, men like Kaliakov had ways to make life difficult.

Kaliakov fitted nicely into the sadistic position he held, using his twisted mind to keep men under control - the same skill he had used back when he was rounding up prisoners like Josef. Any boons afforded to Josef because of his important role had quickly diminished. If Josef was popular, Kaliakov would find a way to make him unpopular. If the clever Pole had accrued any luxuries for himself they would be taken away. Prisoners who were seen to get on with Josef were tortured, simply disappeared or were openly shot in front of him.

And yet, Josef being Josef, he still carried on getting people out of the gulag.

When Josef tried to speak, Kalikov took his foot away and told the guard to sit the Pole upright. Thanking the guard for doing so gave Josef the satisfaction - though he dared not show it - of seeing the soldier bunch his brows in confusion.

He looked up at Kaliakov and asked plainly, "How am I supposed to work when your men keep beating on me?"

The only time Josef let his confidence shine through was when he talked about his job. It would not serve for his captors to lose faith in his abilities. Adding just an edge of cockiness regarding his role, he had found, threw his interrogators into cognitive dissonance, making them second-guess themselves about doing him any real harm.

"Work? Is that what you call it?" asked Kaliakov with a huff of disbelief.

"Come on, boss, you know I don't have time to help idiots escape - you try managing exports and imports - there are just too many things for me to keep track of. I have enough of a headache without having to focus on making escape plans for fools who would just as likely get me killed," Josef said to Kaliakov, all earnestness and common sense, before slipping in that touch of bravado that always seemed to turn the tide. "But go ahead, shoe my ribs in, you have a major delivery coming in. Good luck organising that without me."

Kaliakov had to laugh. There was always the sense that, within his distorted mind, the Kommandant respected Josef. "Ah, what am I to do with you?"

"Let me get back to work. I have kept you on schedule for months now, that has to count for something with your gracious Premier - no doubt, if you carry on like this, you will be promoted and be able to get out of this shit hole."

There was a pause, as Kaliakov toyed with the signet ring on his finger, before he swivelled on his heels and walked out, saying to the guard as he left, "Do as he says. Clean him up. Get him back to work."

Gulags, and their 'lesser corrective labour camps,' were sited all over Siberia. This vast portion of soviet Russia could fit the whole of Europe within it four times over. The inestimable number of camps within that expansive area would make locating one particular worker nigh on impossible, the prisoners given numbers rather than names, and their numbers being assigned to new prisoners if they died.

And, from a prisoner's perspective, there was no knowing which camp they were in when they arrived, the train that brought them there being shunted from track to track and the route snaking so that any sense of direction would be lost. The pains of hunger and the indecency of having no toilets also increased the sense of worthlessness. The entire trek was filled with the sounds of discomfort and despair. Moans and groans, coughs and mumbling of men and women stacked and packed like cattle to the slaughter; all of them succumbing to the strange despair of uncertainty, of not knowing where they were going or what would become of them when they got there.

Those in open-top carriages - meant for coal transportation - would have to hunker down against the cold, and those in closed carriages would have to accept the dark. These conditions created utter disorientation. The endless echoing cadence of continual clacks over connections in the tracks and the intermittent shrieking of metal against metal, as wheels scraped on turns on the rail, was enough to drive the prisoners mad. It was an excruciating journey which, in the end, took them deep into an unfamiliar land.

So it was that Maria had no idea where she had been taken to and whether she would ever see Josef again. Wherever it was, Hell could not have been worse. Perpetually freezing, in a way that was torturous in its own right, the days and nights of menial labour blurred into a never-ending shivering nightmare. At least as she worked, the monotony of the task, screwing nuts onto bolts all day, rendered the cold into something of a bearable numbness, taking the edge off the biting cold that would otherwise have driven her insane. But at night, in the dormitories, where only so many people could huddle around the small chimney stove provided to menial workers, the cold would set in, especially when their bodies gave way to sleep.

The old gipsy woman who slept in the bunk below Maria had grown successively slower as the days went by, the occasional beatings for her lack of progress not helping in any way, so that now she lay shuddering and vacant in her cot. Maria lent over and offered the elderly woman one of the worn hessian sacks that she used for a blanket, unsure whether the gypsy registered it or not.

"It's not much, but it's an extra layer," she said apologetically.

Before Maria could climb back onto her bunk the gypsy called, "Psst, psst."

"What? What, Mamu? You need to rest," Maria said, her tone full of the harsh kindness synonymous with her people. In general, Poles conserved their energy to survive the hardness of life. They had no time in their talk for politeness: the approach was very direct. So one would have to be familiar with their ways to know when they meant well despite their curtness. Hence the crone never minded Maria's manner.

Motioning with her clawed and gnarled fingers - worn, cut and calloused from the work - for Maria to come closer, the gipsy whispered, "I'll read your fortune."

Maria was suddenly full of dread. The old lady was near her end and the dying had no time for lies. "Leave me alone, I don't want my fortune read. We know what's going to happen - we're all going to die."

"No…" the gipsy woman tried to respond but was racked with a fit of coughing, and when she came to, her strength seemed to have diminished all the more, her breath coming out in rasps. "No," she said again, "not for you."

Not wanting hope to break her defences, Maria tried to brush away the old woman's words, "Leave me alone, I want to go to sleep. I'm tired."

But the gipsy persisted, "What's your name, child?"

Maria relented and told the woman her name, realising that she had been so caught up in surviving, in holding on to whatever reserves of strength she had, that she had never even introduced herself before now.

A heartbreaking sympathy and a perplexing spark filled the fortune teller's milky eyes as she repeated, "No. Not for you, Maria." Another back-arching fit of coughing wracked the old woman, so that when she relaxed again into a quivering quietness, she breathed, "I haven't got much time, listen."

The gipsy was not the only one coughing in a room full of sick women. They lay murmuring and groaning, intermittent whispers breaking through the awful echoes of illness.

"Proszę," Maria begged, "leave me alone, old woman."

With a strength that belied her fragile state, the gipsy reached out her bandy arm and pulled on Maria's work dress, an urgency in her failing eyes demanding that Maria listen. "You are going to live a long time, and you are not going to live in Poland."

"What do you know, staruszka?" Maria said. "I don't have time for bajki," even though she had given up fighting what the woman had to say, knowing full well that this was not the time or place for fairytales. In her fragile state, the old woman would not be offering Maria false hope. And this was a gipsy, after all.

"You already have a daughter, born in the shadows," the diviner said, as Maria's eyes widened, "and she is safe. She is with your mother."

Reflexively, hearing that truth come out, and hoping desperately for any good fortune to come to the daughter she had borne out of wedlock, it was Maria's turn to cling to the gipsy. "How do you…" but the elder was not finished.

"You will bear five children in all," the gipsy said, her eyes full of motherly pride.

"What?" It was the last thing Maria was thinking of. Having more children had to do with a life beyond captivity and it was not a dream she had dared entertain since being put on the train, having seen so many others, some stronger than her, wither and die in those terrible conditions.

There was more. The old woman's crumpled hand motioned in small circles at her forehead as she found the words to fit the images and feelings that were coming through to her. Eyes closed, then she said, in little more than a whisper, "One of your children, the firstborn to freedom, will have fire in her eyes," and she smiled at this, as though remembering herself or her own daughter perhaps. "This child will have revenge…" It was more than Maria could take, but she was drawn into the telling. "…There are riches surrounding her - she brings much *gold*," the woman said, as her eyes opened again and she twisted her hand to point in small stabs for emphasis. "She is the one who will change everything," and just when Maria thought that was going to be the last of it, the gypsy added, "Your husband will be safe and well."

Maria sighed and complained, more to herself than to the woman, "He never listens."

"I know," said the gypsy, with a little smile, and Maria knew that she did.

Now the gypsy seemed to be completely spent. She curled into herself, looking more like a newborn than an old woman. "It's getting cold, cold, so cold. I'm tired. Listen to what I have told you. Remember, remember…" her whisper of a voice trailing off into a mumble.

Maria could do nothing else but take her coat off, her last shield against the pitiless cold, and place it over the poor woman.

Unexpectedly, the gipsy's hand pressed out from under the coat in a fist. "Here, take these coins, they will help you on your journey," and she dropped some money into Maria's hand. Then she turned over and hummed a stammering old Russian melody until she went quiet altogether.

The following morning, when the routine noise of the siren for the start of the workday sounded, the workers stood mechanically and filed numbly out of the dormitory, having learned to step in line without delay.

When Maria saw that the old woman had not got up, that she was still curled up on her side, she quickly shook the woman's shoulder, glancing nervously at the doorway as she did, hoping that a guard would not see that the gipsy had not complied with the alarm, as she whispered tersely, "Wake up, mother. Wake up, it's time to get up - you'll be in trouble." But with no response, Maria paused and turned to lean over, seeing the whites of the old woman's eyes and knowing even before she eased the old lady's shoulder towards her that she was gone. Her head lolled to the side, with glazed eyes open, looking at nothing, a pinched smile on her face. Reaching her hand gently over to the gipsy's eyes, Maria closed her lids and, dropping her head for a moment, said softly, "Peace be with you, Matka," but that was all she had time for, hearing the last of the workers shuffle out of the room. She stood and hurried over to join the lifeless march to the work trucks.

The spirit taken out of the prisoners, they went straight from the exit of the tenement building and automatically into lines, awaiting the trucks to pull up and take them to their workstations. As usual, a young Pole guard walked up the lines counting, and then gave his report to the Russian overseer, "Three missing, sewing detail."

In his long grey coat and grey Ushanka hat, the woollen lapels pulled over the top - the gold laurel and red star with its golden hammer and sickle shining in the early morning light - the officer looked up without expression towards the entrance to the tenements where, on cue, another soldier emerged to call out, "Three dead, sir."

Walking stiffly over to the line where Maria stood, the overseer counted off three people from the end of the row, Maria being one of them. "You three join the sewing detail." Without question, Maria and the other two went over to join the line that would take them to the sewing station. Climbing into the truck with the other women, Maria sat down and, in the time it took to be driven to her new task, pondered what the old lady had said with her last words.

Chapter 23

Under Observation

1940 Siberia, Soviet Union

Guns and uniforms. These were top of the list for items needing to be regularly delivered to the Russian front. There were just never enough of them. Guns had been in short supply since the onset of the war. Uniforms were a tally of lost souls, droves and droves of men fed to the front line to die. Today, for Josef, it was the shipment of uniforms he needed to check up on. The sewing-detail were behind and if they did not catch up with their tally, workers would pay with their lives - be made an example of - to get the assignees working faster.

Workers were not nearly in short supply as uniforms.

Stepping into the warehouse and immediately finding a high point from where he could scan the workers, Josef peered around the room. Working at the train station, he had often needed to spot a particular person in the crowds of people getting on and off trains - some businessman or other, some dignitary or politician he would need to look after especially. Now his skill for finding that one particular person was put to use for one reason only, in hope that he might see his wife. Day after day, in various factories across the gulag, in that small city of prisoners, he had searched for Maria. He remained mindful that, should he see her, he would need to be careful when and how he approached her. He had learned early on, in his new career as a people-smuggler, that any sign of him knowing someone personally could be used against him. Kaliakov had assigned guards to Josef, with the sole purpose of watching his every move. Before he was aware of this, Josef had seen his old mate, Pietrosz, and even though he had tried not to make it obvious, in his unpracticed efforts to get a message to his friend, the guards had easily picked up on it, only for Pietrosz to be executed in front of him.

Despite the polio in his leg, a disfiguration that would usually have seen him shot rather than put on a train, Pietrosz had survived all that time. Only to be killed then. Because of Josef.

It had been a breathtaking blow, at once his most unforgivable mistake and his source of determination to get as many people out of the gulag as he possibly could. He would make his friend's life count.

Since then, Josef had, along with the rest of the prisoners, come up with more subtle ways of passing messages to one another, akin to the age-old system found in any correctional facility, in any prisoner of war camp. People would find a way to communicate even under the most vigilant scrutiny, as Josef was under just then, blankly scanning the faces of the workers in the sewing detail.

As it was, there was nothing unusual in him observing the workers. The very nature of Josef's position as head of logistics meant that he had to be methodical about timetables, delivery routines, staffing and stock. But it would be foolish to wait for items to be loaded aboard trains and trucks only to find *then* that there was a shortfall. Josef had to make sure that there were no drawbacks in the run-up to stock being loaded, and that any complications along the way were addressed, including any discrepancies in the flow of work on a factory floor.

As much as Kaliakov had it in for Josef, both he and the managers at the various points of material sourcing and manufacture, had come to see that when the cockey Pole made a suggestion that could help move things along, improve efficiency - an additional few workers borrowed from another detail here to bulk up another there, an observation that the focus at a manufacturing unit shift to a lesser item - it was well worth everybody's while to pay attention to what the smart little man said. Josef simply had an aptitude that allowed him to pick up on the weakest points along the production line. Seeing the surplus of gun handles being produced at the lumber yard, for example, he would be sure to compliment the productivity of the person in charge, whilst gently hinting that some rough planks were required for new train cars, to cater for the shortage there. It was all about maintaining the fundamental balance that would lead to everything getting to the train on time. Holes plugged; factory lines tightened or reorganised; work stretched to the maximum with what tools and workers were available. An all the more difficult task considering the continual loss of workers due to cold, hunger and, of course, Soviet soldiers' proclivity for shooting people without thought!

So here he was, allowing his intelligent eyes to roam over the rows and rows of women working the sewing machines side-by-side, in the forefront of his mind the desperate hope that he might see Maria. Naturally, Josef had to simultaneously take into consideration what stock had already been sewn and gauge the speed of output, to be sure that he would meet his quota for delivery.

He had learned to pinpoint where productivity could be improved upon without implicating anyone with his report. Any potential shortage of stock he mentioned, which could have a knock-on effect on the quota being met, would ultimately boil down to workers not being productive enough and, eventually, some would be singled out and punished, or even killed. Either way, that did not help with the problem at hand: one worker less, whether incapacitated or dead, meant a further slowing of production. Hence Josef had learned to be very tactful about how he put the problem, making sure that the perceived shortage could not be construed as any particular failure on behalf of the workers but rather on their machinery, for instance, or a need for swapping workers perhaps, so that the issue could be addressed in a way that did not lead to people being hurt or killed.

With this in mind, Josef had disciplined himself to look out across any worksite with a studied detachment, not allowing his eyes to settle on anyone who could be pointed out as either someone he knew, who would then be removed, either quietly or blatantly to keep him in line - or anyone who could be seen as the weak link, to the same effect. Josef had learned to numb his responses when he did take note of a certain worker not being up to scratch or did see someone he had known in his previous life, and not to let his gaze fall upon them, but to rather continue the sweep of his head. The site managers often wondered what exactly it was that Josef had caught sight of when he scanned a room, the scrawny logistics manager not allowing the tiniest inflection in his voice or marker in his expression to indicate where he had seen a discrepancy.

Not many could pinpoint where the issues were in a room full of workers. Others would be distracted by all the individual movement, the heads turning, the hands shifting, the small cogs in a large and complex machine. But it was the whole machine that Josef saw, a fluid motion that needed to work in tempo for the engine to flow. Engineering, he would say, was within one-thousandth of a millimetre: any imprecision and the end product was not going to work at optimum level or work at all. The calibration had to be precise. Being able to see where the inconsistency arose, was to be in touch with the timing and the overall movement of the beast so that anything not keeping up to speed was registered. It was being able to catch where the pace slowed, where the chink in the chain was. It was all fine-tuning, and that required a trained eye.

With that honed sight on full alert, Josef had already seen that there were three new workers today, each of them adjusting their movement to keep pace with the rest, and one of those workers, he realised with a jolt that took all of his will to suppress, was Maria.

Chapter 24

On the Take

1940 Siberia, Soviet Union

After looking over the workforce, Josef politely nodded to the factory manager and asked, "With your permission, I would like to address your new workers. I have a shipment leaving tonight and given the right direction those new women can keep up with the rest and you will reach your quota. The boss will be pleased, yes? Two of the newcomers just need to be put next to an experienced worker and one of them has strong arms - better suited to stirring the starch." With a wave of his hands that said it was no trouble at all, Josef went on, "I will spare you the trouble of arranging this and I will come back later to check on their progress, if I may. There is a lot of pressure to get this shipment out on time, as you know."

Only a fool would argue with such a sensible request, yet there was a pause as the factory manager looked at Josef with wary eyes slit in scepticism. Internally, Josef kicked himself. He had gone through this scenario so many times in his head, contemplating what would happen if he saw Maria. As he had gone about his work, he had scoped out the various places within the factories where he could pull her aside inconspicuously, blind spots on the factory floor where he might get to speak to Maria and explain how he would help her escape. On his bunk, night after night, he had chewed over what he would say to the guards, the right words to use so as not to arouse suspicion, but now he feared it had come out sounding insincere. Too obvious, too polite.

The manager turned away from Josef and panned his eyes over the workers, but he clearly could not spot either who was new in the sea of sunken faces, or where the line was lagging.

In that terrible pause, not knowing whether the Russian would take the bait or not, Josef stood by, trying to look as calm and neutral as he could. Yet, in the end, the manager gave a nervous nod, obviously afraid that Josef's innuendo about missing the quota would come true if he did not let the astute Pole do as he suggested. It seemed that he had chosen his words well because the manager was only too obliging, allowing Josef to rally the three newcomers to the side of the factory. From there he could place the two of them next to experienced workers, who would show them the ropes whilst still keeping to their workload.

Maria was the last worker to place. To her credit, she had kept her mouth shut and her head down, with eyes to the floor, as was the way with prisoners - eye contact was not wise, you had to play dumb and servile. It was only when Josef took her right to the back of the factory, where the clothes were starched and steamed, that she dared to glance up at him. In that quick look, he saw hope instantly bloom in her eyes, before she looked down again. Then, as a billow of steam rolled out from the great starch baths, she dared to look up at him properly.

"Josef? It *is* you?" his wife grimaced, seeing the welts and bruises on his face. "My God, what have they done to you?"

"Kommandant has a soft spot for me." He gave a tell-tale sign of a smile through all the swelling.

And then it all came pouring out of Maria, "Oh Josef, how are we going to get out of here? I am cold and hungry - the cockroaches eat better than us - I hate those bastard Russians; I could kill them. It's like living in a nightmare. Why didn't you hand in that gun!? You never listen to me."

Josef made a show of calling out to one of the other workers before replying, "I shouldn't have put it in that book…"

"You should have handed it in, that's what you should have done."

"I could have hid it in the ceiling," he said, as the other worker approached and he told her to take Maria's post at the sewing station.

With the steamers blasting, the guards would not have been able to overhear what was being said, nevertheless, Josef knew that he had to stop speaking with Maria or he would arouse suspicion, but she would not let it drop.

"They would have found it."

"I've got to go," he urged. "I'll find a way to speak with you again."

He made to leave but she said, in a small voice that was barely perceptible above the noise, "I'm so afraid." How could he turn away from that?

"Don't be afraid, my wife, we will get out of here soon enough," he assured her, "there are rumours that Hitler has turned on Stalin."

"Rumours? What rumours? Yesterday they were saying that Churchill is a fascist sympathiser."
"Well, don't listen to rumours, listen to me," he said, as he took the paddle that the other worker had handed over and showed Maria how to stir. "When I come back do not ask any questions. Only listen. Can you do that?"
"What will happen to us?" asked Maria as she took the paddle from him. "How are we going to get out of here?"
"Not us: *you*."
"Me?" she replied but he had already left, disappearing into the mists.

◇

Hand-in-hand with managing logistics came the need for Josef to observe staff rotation - people coming and going and changes of shifts - in order to know not only where the workers were, but also the guards and, more importantly, how and when they could be slowed or distracted. Josef capitalised on his ability to have oversight of the full orchestration within the compound, which extended to the movements of the entire, interconnected device that was the gulag.
The way Josef saw things, it was not he who was Kaliakov's enemy, it was *routine*. Men got sloppy with routine. It would have been an omission of duty for Josef not to take advantage of the opportunities this created. Guards kept the same hours every day, with shift changes grafted into their body clocks. The brain-numbing regularity of their role gave

way to malaise which made them susceptible to making mistakes. One simply could not pay close attention every second of the day - the mind tends to wander and eyelids droop. This was what Josef kept in mind when getting people out of the camp.

And also getting goods in.

Under the circumstances, bribery could not get you very far, in terms of distance, but it could, in the least case, get someone to look the other way. Guarding a gulag was a banal position to hold, both the monotony and cruelty of the role were soul-destroying, meaning the soldiers stationed at the gulags were, in many senses, in prison too. The small luxuries that Josef could acquire for them made life that little bit more livable and helped them forget that they had drawn the short straw in being stationed at a gulag. The respect one could earn for as little as a single chocolate bar or a pack of cigarettes was not to be underestimated. For the right price, a man could turn a blind eye to anything. In this sense, if the use of routine could not be utilised, then a bribe was the next bet.

Being noted, both by regular guards and soldiers and even by Kaliakov himself, as a man who was able to acquire contraband, Josef had started something of an internal economy of trade between the soldiers' personal belongings and the goods that he could sneak in. Officials were not overly concerned with how Josef managed to get things, so long as they got their bottles of vodka, biscuits, coffee, jams, butter and other treats, as well as the regular request for photos of scantily clad women. Questions were not asked after that.

Cocky as he was, Josef had started his trade in illegal goods by skimming off Kaliakov's extravagant supply of items. Unlike the others, who thought small in terms of creature comforts, Kaliakov had expensive taste, requesting champagne and caviar, Cuban cigars and Goldwasser vodka, in quantities that allowed Josef to delicately skim off the top and use the pricey goods to bring in stockpiles of lesser items. The odd cigar here or there, to a particular delivery person, was enough to prime them for more risky requests.

Aside from the difficulty that lay in trying to communicate with one another to make arrangements for escape, an added element to smuggling people was to find all the ways that the prisoner could be hidden. It was all very well Josef getting them out of the gulag, but getting them to safety would require passing through many stop-off points and checks along the route, and there was no chance for Josef to influence inspectors out there. The hiding place had to be inventive enough. Escapees were stowed amongst detritus, factory waste, or in boxes, covered with goods. Sometimes Josef wondered whether he had killed any of them by suffocating them in the tight confines of the boxes. At least, he placated himself, they died thinking that they were on their way to freedom.

That would not do for Maria. She had to live.

One of the truck drivers, who regularly took consignments of guns and uniforms to areas along the front line that could not be reached by rail, had done well from the back-and-forth contraband trade that Josef was part of, however, Josef had never relied upon the man to take a person aboard his vehicle.

Until now.

It had been difficult to convince the driver, whilst being observed by Kaliakov's guards, that he had aboard his vehicle a secure hiding place that would not get him into trouble, and then it had taken a considerable bribe to consummate the deal.

Aboard the truck was a trunk that was used for Kaliakov's personal supply of goods. It was empty on the way out and it had a lock and key. It was well-known by now, at all the checkpoints, that this was his lifeline and that it was not to be touched. Anyone new, or anyone bold enough, who dared ask the driver to show them the inside of the trunk, could be threatened with the name for whom its contents were destined, or from whom the goods were being sent: *Kaliakov*. No one wanted to be on the wrong side of a man who had Stalin's ear, a man who could make you as good as vanish. Or worse.

Returning to the sewing factory, Josef made a display of checking on the first two workers he had placed next to experienced sewers, and then he made his way to the starching section to speak to Maria about the arrangements he had made.

Wasting no time, he went right over to where Maria was sweating away at her task and told her, "I've bribed a driver who delivers the supplies to and from the prison. You will be part of the loading party..."

"What?" Maria looked up at him, aghast. "You're not coming with me?"

"No. I told you. There's only enough room for one," he said with a heavy heart, his eyes were wet with love. It was all he could do not to reach out and hug her. "I will be distracting the guards with cigarettes when the driver slips you onto the truck. Do exactly what he says." Then he shot her a warning look. "Don't *argue* with him."

"How are you going to escape?" she asked, her voice high-pitched with desperate concern.

"Too many questions…" Joseph tried to tell Maria, but when he saw the anguish on her face he relented and answered, "I will wait 'til the water rises in the river; two others and I will build a raft, and make our escape that way." He was not in the slightest bit serious about this idea. The truth was that he had never given it much thought, his only focus had been to find Maria and get her out. As to his escape, he could not imagine a way that it would be possible with the role he was in. It would simply be too obvious if he was not there, and he was certain that Kaliakov would stop every truck and train and have them turned over, and have every possible escape route searched just to find him. No, Josef thought, not for the first time, there was no escape for him.

"How the *diabła* are you going to build a raft?" Maria was saying, not seeing that he was being sarcastic. "Even if you did, how are you going to hide it - you couldn't even hide a gun!?"

Josef laughed. Something that would have made him mad before, now made him love her all the more.

This, even though he did not have the heart to spell it out for Maria, or the time for that matter, was likely to be the last chance he would ever get to see her. There was nowhere left for him to go. He was between a rock and a hard place: stay and he would die, try to leave and he would be killed. Even though he would continue, getting as many others out as he could, for him it was just the same as being at Death's Door.

Standing there with Maria, knowing that he would never see her again, was like seeing his end. Yet instead of fearing his demise, he registered that he had already surrendered a while ago to the fact that this was how it would be, and now, having connected with this, all that was left was laughter. Hence, as he looked at his dear wife, enshrouded in the soft white steam, his heart had no room for regret or fear, it was too full of endearment to the woman who knew him better than he knew himself.

She, of course, was still caught up in what he had said, "What did you bribe the driver with?"

The laughter caught in his throat.

"I said you would fuck him."

Maria slapped him.

Josef looked around, afraid that her slap had drawn attention to them, which it had, only the guards were laughing at him - probably thinking that he had been trying to chat her up only to get a smack. Nevertheless, he knew that he did not have any more time to be with Maria. "I'm sorry. I had to offer him something. I couldn't give him twenty rubles for risking his life, he needs something that will keep him going for a bit."

"I'm your wife, not your whore!" she responded, and it looked like she was going to hit him again.

"Shh!" he pleaded. "I had to say something. I have to go, my love. I love you, wife."

Her face was suddenly ridden with shock, and he was not sure if she had heard him.

"...I said, I love you, wife." She had heard, but behind his words, she could also hear his goodbye.

"Love you, husband," she said as he turned to go, but she yanked his sleeve, pulling him right in close, and finished, "But I'm not going to fuck him!"

Chapter 25

Swan Song

1980, London, UK

Anja had told Eddie the story of her parent's woes many times over, the same story that her mother had handed down to her, and now he had discovered the uncanny connection between the salvage mission and his wife's family: Kaliakov. The same menace who had overshadowed Josef and Maria's lives was now haunting his own.

"Un-bloody-believable," he breathed to himself, for the umpteenth time, in the back of a taxi from Heathrow airport.

It made logical sense to Eddie that it would be Kaliakov *Junior* who was leading the Soviet salvaging project, but there was always the chance that his father, Josef's old enemy, was still pulling the strings. After all, on the British side, even the royals were now involved, so who was to say that on the Soviet end, it was not the communist leader himself who was interested? And, standing at the right hand of the General Secretary of the Communist Party of the Soviet Union, having worked his way up, from managing one gulag to overseeing them all, was Kaliakov. The one man who could be entrusted to win back Stalin's treasure.

On his way to agree to yet more addendums and amendments to the salvage deal on the UK side, Eddie himself could boast that they had the support of none other than Prince Philip and Prince Charles, because perhaps for them too, the gold was a prize. Though publicly, in the newspapers, they spoke only of an academic interest.

"That's highly likely," Eddie had quipped to himself when he had read one of the articles. When all was said and done, almost all of his team's share of the gold would go to the consortium Geoff had put together to locate and retrieve the gold, then the rest to the British Department of Trade and to the Russians. Eddie, Geoff and his team would get to take a cut of 45% of the value of any gold recovered. Even within the standard bounds of the 'no cure, no gain' rule, this was a hell of a finder's fee, one that would no doubt set Eddie and his colleagues up for good. A fair portion of the treasure itself, however, belonged to the Russians. No matter who won the salvage contract, the Soviets would keep just over a third of it. What was left would go to the UK's Department of Trade - which administered all the country's overseas trade and shipping - apart from a single bar of gold, which would go to the Crown. It was an interesting token, Eddie had noted. Perhaps it had been made in honour of the fact that preceding the name of the Edinburgh, of course, came the title: *His Majesty's Ship*.

The ship itself had become so much part of his thought life that everything - the dimensions, the layout, the speed, the firepower, and, after reading all the historical and diary accounts, the crew - had been grafted onto Eddie's mind. All this information affixed to his experience as an engineer and salvor. As with all the other serious treasure hunters, Eddie lived and breathed every detail of each operation, taking the time to do in-depth research, so that now there was nothing he was not versed in about the boat and even the other famous boat in its class, the HMS Belfast.

It staunched the mind to think that the Edinburgh was called a light cruiser, when it was a 10,000-ton vessel that was not lightly armed, with no less than twelve 6-inch guns. The only lightness to be found in the design was in its speed and manoeuvrability. A nimble ship which could accelerate up to a speed of 32.5 knots and was able to swiftly turn to and from attack. The larger gunships, of up to 22,000 tons, arguably had more weaponry but not the speed, theirs pushing 25 knots, and nowhere near the agility of a light cruiser like the Edinburgh. She was the fast gun of the sea.

Planned under the Hansard programme of 1936 and built for the Royal Navy in 1938 in Newcastle-on-Tyne, by Wigham Richardson and Swan Hunter, the HMS Edinburgh was completed on 6th July 1939. She was one of the last town-class vessels made in a group of 10 light cruisers, built in the three distinct sub-classes, including the *Southampton*, *Gloucester* and, finally, two *Edinburgh* class ships. Having added further weaponry to each design, to accommodate extra gun turrets, the Edinburgh was longer than its predecessors, coming in at 187 metres, to create room for the upgrade in its arsenal. Going from the two previous sub-classes with their twelve 6-inch guns in four triple turrets to *sixteen* of these guns in four quadruple turrets gave the Edinburgh far more firepower - however, manufacturing issues meant that the turrets tended to jam. In a later refit, four extra 4-inch (102 mm) "High Angle Low Angle" guns, eight extra 2-pounder (40 mm) guns and further armour protection were added, making her a formidable presence. Not unlike a British Bulldog, thought Eddie: short, stocky and built for a fight.

Serving right from the outbreak of the war, from operations in Scapa to the Middle East, from mine-laying operations in the Denmark Strait to patrolling duties between Iceland and the Faroe Islands, HMS Edinburgh was then assigned to escort duties on the Arctic convoys. Both the ship and its crew of 850 had journeyed far and been through a lot together by the time they were commissioned to be an escort to the fateful QP11 convoy. As the flagship of Vice-Admiral Stuart Bonham-Carter, they were to escort the 17-ship Allied convoy, leaving Murmansk, Russia, on 28th April 1942.

Two days later, after being spotted by the Germans, both by a Junkers Ju 88 reconnaissance plane and two U-boats, the Edinburgh had come under attack from the U-boats.

All necessary restoration and repair duties were undertaken after the first two torpedo hits, including getting the "B" turret at the ship's bow operational - freeing the barrels of the guns from the metal plating that had been plastered against them. Therefore the ship still had a good deal of firepower and used its artillery to force the U-boats back.

Having sent out a mayday signal and given the necessary commands to counter the flooding of the hull, Captain Faulkner had walked the length of the ship, boosting the morale of his men, rallying the engineers and stokers to do all they could to rejig the engine and get the ship moving again.

Under extreme pressure, aware that another torpedo could hit at any moment, the men had pulled together and worked with determination. In a truly noble effort to repair what damage they could and otherwise use whatever resources were available, the team was able to put together a workable engine. Yet the way that the undercarriage of the vessel had been torn had created a false rudder, so the ship could only manoeuvre in an arc.

In fine timing, an escort arrived and began an attempt to protect the Edinburgh and get her back to Murmansk. The escort was made up of the destroyers HMS Foresight and HMS Forester and the four Halcyon minesweepers, Gossamer, Harrier, Niger and Hussar, who took the Edinburgh into tow.

But U-boat 456 had sent out its reports to German HQ, so that by this time it was joined by Axis torpedo bombers which began an all-out assault on the rescue team. The next day, after non-stop, harrowing attacks from the bombers, the German destroyers Z.7 Hermann Schoemann, Z.24 and Z.25 joined in the attack near Bear Island, Norway. What had started as an attack on a single light cruiser now turned into an all-out battle, with men like the gunner John Napier having to be fed at their stations. There could be no rest when the enemy was coming in from all sides.

At this point, Captain Faulkner had made the radical and brilliant decision to cut the towlines. Working with the fact that the ship could only move in circles, he created a ring of fire, using the surface guns to fire upon the planes, the surrounding ships and the two submarines still involved. On her second cannonade round, the Edinburgh pounded the Schoemann heavily enough for it to retreat and have to be scuttled later. In the midst of the battle, however, a torpedo from Z.24 hit the port side of the Edinburgh. This third torpedo sadly struck the side precisely opposite where the first torpedo had hit so that, even though the extra inflow of water stopped the ship from listing, the structural integrity was now in question. She was not going to make it to shore.

Chapter 26

A Calculated Risk

1942 Bear Island, Norway

Whilst all the attempts were being made by the German forces to sink the Edinburgh and her escort, beneath the waves, Kapitänleutnant Max Martin Teichart had ordered his crew to hold the U-boat's position.

With the Schoemann badly damaged and the Allies holding fast, the three destroyers and one of the U-boats eventually left the battle scene, but Teichart remained, even though he had no torpedoes left. He considered it valuable to surveil the enemy ships and to send information to his headquarters as to the direction the convoy would now take. Having shadowed the Edinburgh up to this point, Teichart had now positioned his U-boat directly beneath her, hiding so to speak, in plain sight. He would be there when it went under. Only then would he know that his mission was complete.

The sonar operator, with both hands holding his earphones and eyes closed, suddenly opened them and craned his neck round to tell the captain with urgency, "Depth Charge, Kapitän," and then, before anyone had time to respond, he added, "Detonated."

Clarifying, the captain asked, "The depth charge was deployed and detonated at surface level?"

"Ja, Kapitän."

Teichart paused, teeth gritted as he scratched his chin, and mumbled quietly to himself, "Then it was not for us probably." Lifting his head then and looking over towards his commander, Teichart offered, "They might be scuttling their own ship."

No sooner had he said it than the sonar operator confirmed another depth charge detonated at surface level.

To his commander's questioning eyes, Teichart said, "Hold position. Silent running."

While the commander gave orders for the U-boat to run on silent, Teichart went over to his desk and made an entry, then leaned against it and waited, gauging whether the enemy was sinking their damaged ship or searching out his boat. But after two more depth charges were reported by the sonar operator to be below the surface, and then another depth charge was confirmed by the hydrophone underwater sound detector to be even lower, but only by metres, there were still no signs that the ship above was sinking.

The usual protocols for a battle scenario must have been running through the captain's mind. Where the Allied escort would have taken note of the departure of Axis ships and planes it would not be sure that the U-boats had also left the scene, in which case the dropping of depth charges at successively deeper levels might have been enough to flush out any lurking U-boat. All the Allies would need was for the U-boat to move for them to pick it up on their sonar or radar and to deploy appropriate measures.

One more depth charge at yet a lower level and the commander said what the rest of the crew must have been thinking, "They can't know that we're here?" and looked to his captain, asking, "Should we take evasive action, Herr Kapitän?"

All eyes were on Teichart.

The captain bowed his head, his brow furrowing with concern. He removed his hat, rubbed at his right eye with his forefinger, and then ran his fingers through his blonde hair before replacing his hat. Head still down, he let out an exasperated grunt, saying a slow quiet, "Nein." Then he lifted his head and looked up to the left for a second, before looking back to his men. His eyebrow cocked, in the way it always did when the right action dawned on him, and, looking up again, this time to the right, his mind did a quick search for confirmation from memories of previous encounters. In his time at sea, there had been many confrontations in which he had been required to make a decision either way. In the end, it always came down to him. He was the captain. There was no one else to look to. He would turn then, to a combination of his training, his experience, his logic and, of course, his intuition, and make that decision.

He stood squarely and let out a firmer, "Nein," offering, as he always did, an explanation, "Moving will only confirm our whereabouts." Stay where they were and they might be sitting ducks. Move and they might be found.

Catch-22.

He stood to attention, and addressed the commander, "Stand by, all stations. All systems silent. Not a breath."

Up and down the U-boat the command was relayed for the crew to man every station, along with the command for silence. Long minutes of waiting ensued, all ears and devices attuned to what might be happening on the surface. In the cramped space, with little room to move for valves upon valves and tubes upon tubes, the apprehension of each man could be felt by every other crew member, as if they were a single entity, tensed and ready to fight or to fly. But still, the captain waited.

Finally, the sonar operator called out, this time with the dreaded words, "Torpedo, heading 0.0 at 100 metres."

Calmly, the captain ordered for the U-boat to be taken deeper, but gave no call for any further evasive action or attack procedures.

"50 metres and closing."

Teichart looked at the ceiling, rubbing the sides of his chin with forefinger and thumb.

"30 metres."

All eyes were on the captain.

"20 metres."

Teichart leant forward to place both hands against some pipework and turned his head towards the crew, his eyes scrunched nearly closed in thought.

"10 metres."

Collectively, the men on the bridge listened silently, slightly agape mouths, the whites of wide eyes showing, heads cocked to one side. Time drew out, disappeared. The eternal moment. The reckoning.

At this point, everything that could be done, to German proficiency, had been done. Now the men could only wait until the moment of impact before they could respond. Only if and when the torpedo struck would they know where it had hit and then, and only then, could they do what was required of them.

Teichart's eyes were focused on the sonar operator, whose hands were clamped to his earphones as he leant forward, forehead almost on the counter, with eyes tightly shut in absolute concentration, bearing in his taught body the apprehension of the entire crew. His head suddenly jolted back and his eyes opened and flicked from side to side and, as he turned to his captain, his brows raised and eyes stretched wide.

"Impact," he said.

Chapter 27

The Deciding Shot

1942 Bear Island, Norway

There was an instant of intense, heightened concentration, each body aboard the U-boat was primed for survival, every nerve and every sense attuned to whatever information came through. The hive mind, preparing for devastation. Waiting for the shockwave. Listening for the horrific crunch, warp, twist and tearing of metal, the screeching strain of the buckling hull, the high-pressure bursting of pipes and the ricochet of bolts and caps shooting like bullets against opposite walls, pressed from their hold in the unstoppable surge of pressure, the force of destruction working through the length of the sub, each compartment giving way as the wave of death approached.

Every man waited, preparing themselves for the sudden loss of pressure and tensing for the terrifying onrush of waters speeding their way.

But nothing came.

The sonar operator's eyes widened further still. He yanked his headphones off and leant back in his chair, turning to the captain with an expression of sheer relief.

"It's not us."

Teichart flipped his hat off his head and, with a great smile, turned to the hailer and declared to the crew, "Stand down. All clear. Stand down."

On the bridge, and no doubt throughout the U-boat, the men sighed in unison, giddy relief washing over them.

Serious once more, the captain said curtly to the sonar operator, "Report."

"Their ship is breaking apart, Kapitän."

"Ja," nodded Teichart, and said to his men, "Fangshuss." The *coup de grâce*.

The commander stood to attention and said proudly to his superior, "Victory, Herr Kapitän."

However, that declaration brought no hint of a smile to Teichart's face. It was a dreadful thing to take a ship down. Victory meant the sacrifice of lives. Yet, still, he needed to be certain that the job was done. "Okay. Gently now, take her to a safe distance, Kommandant, quarter speed, then up to periscope level," was Teichart's response, "I want to be sure she's gone under."

Minutes later, looking through the periscope viewfinder, all Teichart could see on the surface was the bubbling of oily waters, aflame here and there, the odd smattering of debris, and, in the distance, the retreat of the Allied rescue force.

He ordered the U-boat to be taken under once more, then said, "New heading, set a course for docking at base," and gave the coordinates for the return trajectory to Norway. There his men would rest, the U-boat would be restocked, and then they would be back to resume their mission to find and locate enemy ships.

Walking then to his desk, Kapitän-Leutnant Max Martin Tecihart wrote down in his log the coordinates for the sinking of the HMS Edinburgh.

◇

The odds had been heavily against the Edinburgh and her brave escort. Yet, despite facing off three German battleships, several submarines and a constant barrage from German air support, they had managed to fatally wound the Schoeman, and send the rest of them packing. In the fight though, Able Seaman Joseph Bleakley, Stoker Second Class Patrick Beattie, Crystal Radio Operator Edward Anderson, and Ordinary Seaman John Bamford, were killed, along with two officers and 56 other brave souls.

Among the 790 survivors, saved by the experienced and decisive leadership of one Captain Hugh Webb Faulkner, the tenacity and sheer courage of their fellow crew, the brilliance of the engineers and the efforts of the ships and crews who came to their rescue, was a trusty Signalman named Francis James Dawson.

Amid the battle, when the ship had taken that dreadful hit from a third and final torpedo, he had shown bravery and loyalty to his country by retrieving the ship's flag. Holding the flag tight to his chest, Dawson watched as, last of the survivors to step off the ship, Captain Faulkner climbed aboard the Gossamer. He nodded his respect to Dawson and told him to keep the flag. (Many years later he would cede it over to the Leith Museum in Edinburgh.)

The Vice-Admiral had then made it clear that the flagship had to be scuttled at all costs, calling on every vessel in the vicinity to use whatever weapons they had to do so. Several depth charges were deployed but failed to do the job. Defiant to the last, the Edinburgh just refused to go down. Yet it was crucial to dispatch the ship.

Every torpedo had been used to fend off the attackers, apart from one. Regardless of the fact that they still had over 200 miles to get the rescuers back to the safety of the Soviet dock, upon the HMS Foresight, one David Loram was ordered to fire that final torpedo. He would later become Vice Admiral Sir David Loram.

As the HMS Edinburgh sank below the water, Faulkner turned to the portly fellow, who was standing to his right and said, just loud enough for the Signalman to hear, "Vice-Admiral Bonham-Carter, there are no penguins in the Arctic."

Chapter 28

Ace Up The Sleeve

1980 Westminster, UK

Sitting in an austere waiting room within the Parliament Buildings of Westminster, about to parley with royalty, Eddie smiled and gave a little huff of satisfaction as he recalled the last part of his conversation with Rollie Visser.

"This I would like to hear," Rollie had said, with genuine interest, after Eddie had suggested that his team were the only ones who knew for sure where the Edinburgh was buried.

Eddie had reached down for his satchel then, and placed it on his lap. The air had thickened with anticipation, Rollie pressing right up to his desk, as Eddie unbuckled the straps, slowly, one at a time, but then, leaving his hand outside the bag, he had paused, as if an afterthought had struck him, "How much did you say the charge is for your boat, per day?"

At this the Dutchman had tilted his head to the side, wondering, it seemed, where Eddie was going with this. "That would be three hundred thousand Guilders a day," he answered plainly.

Withdrawing his hand from his satchel, Eddie had reached over and grabbed Rollie's notepad and pen, and begun to do sums as he spoke, "So, you are charging three hundred thousand Guilders a day, which is equivalent to..." and he scribbled away, "Sixty thousand Pounds, give or take a Guilder. We'll likely need the boat for over a month - let's say three months to be safe; so that would come out as five million, four hundred thousand Pounds, which then converts back to twenty-seven million Guilders for a full three months." He had let that figure hang in the air for a few heartbeats before saying, with easy confidence, "I'll give you *eight times* the amount it would usually cost to hire your fine vessel."

At this Rollie's eyebrows raised, but all he said was, "That's a good deal more than your competitors offered."

"I'll wager that they were nowhere near as confident about the ship's location as we are," Eddie had said with a small tilt of his chin and a wink, then put his hand inside the satchel and pulled out a folder from the German War Records Office, and placed it on the table. Opening the folder, he tapped his finger lightly on the cover of a leather-bound book.

"Herr Kapitän-Leutnant Max Martin Teichart's logbook, which no one has laid eyes on since the end of the Third Reich, except me. And now you, sir."

"Someone's going to be missing that file," said a broadly smiling Rollie.

"I'm only *borrowing* it," was Eddie's conspiratorial reply. *This* had been his trump card, the ace that he had hidden up his sleeve throughout the negotiation, waiting right until the end to pull it out.

Gingerly, he had opened the log book and carefully turned the pages to find the one he was looking for, saying, with unabashed triumph on his face, "May I draw you to this fine number, right here," as he had pointed towards what was a familiar set of coordinates. "The last man on the scene after the Edinburgh went beneath the waves was, in fact, Teichart. And the coordinates that he put down for the location of the ship are, as you might have guessed by now, the same as those put down by a lowly sea hand going by the name of Bob Walkey."

Rollie had slumped back in his chair, folding his arms across his chest and nodding in congratulatory defeat: this cunning Yorkshireman had him.

That was when Eddie moved in to consummate the deal. As he began to put the log back in its folder and into his satchel, he had added, with the air of someone who knew that matters had come to a close. "In fact, I made a phone call from my hotel this very morning and can happily report…though I'd prefer if you kept it to yourself for now - the news was given to me in code, you see - that Geoff's team has scanned those very coordinates and, as of yesterday, sighted, and *confirmed*, the location of the HMS Edinburgh. So, you see, Mr Visser," he had said, bold as a prize-winner after the fight, "we have *already* beaten our competitors to it. All we need is a ship, the *only* ship that can get the team down to the bottom of Davy Jones Locker to grab the shiny stuff. And, I do believe, now we *have* that ship."

"Ja, indeed you do," Rollie had replied, half-chuckling, "I'll have someone draw up a contract for you."

"No need," said Eddie, pulling another folder from his satchel, "I've already had one drawn up."

Rollie had to laugh out loud. He had definitely backed the right horse.

In the Dutchman's eyes was the recognition that there was a passion and commitment to this Englishman's approach that seemed to go beyond the job. And he was right.

For Eddie, getting the gold had become personal.

Chapter 29

New Recruits

1942 Gazala, Libya

Four months after having escaped from the gulag, Maria was all the way down in Libya. As stiflingly hot and arid as Siberia had been freezing and wet. Further from home than she would ever have imagined she would be, and unable to return whilst Poland was under German occupation, her great solace had been the joy of reuniting with her old friend Lusha.

"Lusha, a few months ago I was in prison, screwing nuts on bolts," Maria said, pressing her hand against a stubborn crease in her khaki trousers, "Now look at me: I'm in a Polish uniform, fighting with the British, against Hitlerowski..."

Lusha looked up from her bunk. "Yes, a lot has changed," she said with meaning, her eyes distant. She had mentioned nothing of her own journey to get out of Poland. To speak of these things was to recall what it had taken to escape and to remember those who did not get out, and the pain was still too close for words.

Maria had recounted her tale several times over, of how Josef had arranged for her to be stowed away in a trunk on the back of a truck, only to be dumped in the middle of nowhere on a dirt road somewhere in Siberia. She had refused to sleep with the driver and, as a result, he had left her by the roadside in disgust. Just before driving off, taking a last disappointed look at her, perhaps seeing Maria for what she was, a desolate and defenceless young woman, some humanity must have found its way to the surface for the driver to at least throw her a blanket and point her in the direction of the nearest village.

There, on the tundra, in the outback of Russia, where war was just a word on the wind, the folks in those parts heard rumours of what was happening but never saw anything, fearing only that the terrible tales they were told of Hitler's ruthless regime would eventually find a way to them. To the hardy farmers in the village, Maria had been simply a woman in need of help and she had been taken in without question and looked after. There Maria had learned that the Rusians were just people like her, trying to get by - people kind enough to nurse her back to health when she had nothing to offer.

As soon as she was strong enough, Maria started to help wherever she could with the workload. She had not needed to be asked, it was plain to see that life in the wilderness was hard, the families there working overtime to feed themselves and make their quota for the state, most of the adults working in a nearby mine right into the night and their older offspring running the farms.

Every day had been a prayer, desperately hoping that the war would never reach them. Months down the line, however, it was good news that came their way: Russia had changed sides and was now fighting with Britain and America against the Germans.

This is where the Lend-Lease Act came into play for the Soviet Union. With Hitler turning on Russia, Stalin was now chums with Churchill, which was to say that Russia would pay in nothing less than gold bullion for America's aid. At its heart, war was a transaction, money changing hands and lives spent for the sake of profit. Nobody won but the bank.

However, for the Poles who had no way of returning to their German-occupied homeland, news quickly spread of an army being formed to fight the Axis armies in North Africa as part of the wider Western Desert Force. For them, this was their chance to hit back at Hitler, to deplete his forces and hopefully, when all was said and done, to win back their country.

Not so for Maria. The last thing on her mind had been war. Maria's only interest in making her way to Libya had been in the hopes that she would somehow be reunited with her husband. The final part of the Lend-Lease deal was that Polish prisoners in the gulags had to be released and consigned to the 8th Army in Persia. Yet four months in there had been no sign of Josef since she got there, and after the division changed locations a few times Maria had resigned herself to the fact that she would never see him again, finding comfort in her precious friendship with Lusha. That did not stop her from repeating time and again her anguish at not knowing what had become of her other half.

"Yes, a lot has changed," she paused, her eyes going to the tent flap and the dusty light entering the barracks. "I don't know where my Josef is - he could be dead for all I know. I wish I knew where he was. What am I saying? Of course he's dead...So few of us got out."

With her usual optimism, Lusha responded as she always did when her friend was being pulled from pillar to post in her desire to be back with Josef, "He's okay; he's alive. He doesn't die that easily. He could be...he could be here for all you know."

"Oh come on, Lusha, we've been here months already and we have not seen him - no one knows if he came through here."

"Tak, we're all just numbers here," Lusha sighed.

"Little has changed..." Maria said, her voice full of melancholy. She must have been thinking about her time in the gulag but her thoughts were broken by an officer popping his head into the tent and calling out jovially, "Good afternoon, ladies. We're having a vodka or two in the tent. Come, have some fun. You don't know where you'll be tomorrow. Live a little!"

Always game for a drink, Lusha replied immediately with a wink, "Okay, we're coming," and then she looked over at Maria, eyes coaxing her with mischief.

"You go," Maria said, "I have work to do."

"Come on, what work? Driving officers around? Tell them you don't feel very well," cajoled Lusha, "Let's live a little, like he said."

The magic word had of course already been spoken. Vodka. No healthy Pole could ever turn that offer down, especially in the Middle East, on the battlefront, where life was short and liquor was hard to come by, "Okay, alright, only a couple of vodkas, yes?"

"Tak, just a couple. Come on, let's go," said Lusha, her face grinning with that same old zest for life that never failed to win Maria over. Lusha had a thousand ways of persuasion and Maria found herself happy enough to step out of the tent with her, if only for a way to forget her troubles for a spell.

Across the way, the tent flap to the men's barracks opened and out stepped none other than, a somewhat inebriated, Josef.

"Maria!" he shouted, his eyes wide with joy.

"Josef?" It seemed impossible to have only just been speaking of him to walk out and find her husband in the opposite tent.

"Maria...it *is* you! Where have you been?" Josef asked as he closed the gap between them, his arms opening wide to her.

Maria went rigid. "Josef, what are you doing here?" But before he could get a word out in answer she scolded him, "You're *drunk* - look at you!" and gave him a light shove with both her hands, before just quickly pulling him back in for a hug full of emotion, her embrace saying how much she had missed him, that she thought he had died, that she could not believe he was there and how much she longed for him, all at once.

She finally asked through her happy tears, "How long have you been here?" as she pulled away to scrutinise him with narrowed eyes, weighing him up in the way she had always done, to make sure he was in good health. And he was. Aside from a scar over his right eye, there was no sign that he had been in the gulag. He was his good old strappy little self, confident and charming as ever. But in his eyes, she saw the short-lived happiness quickly replaced with sadness.

"Listen," he said, gently, taking both of her shoulders in hand and dipping his head forward slightly to look right into her eyes, "I'm leaving for Alexandria tomorrow: I'm a sapper now - an engineer. I'm on tanks. We'll be fighting against Rommel. He wants Alexandria. We can't…we can't allow that to happen." Even for the common soldier, it was clear that taking out Rommel's headquarters near the historical Egyptian port would be a strategic win for whoever managed to hold it, allowing for control of the Suez Canal. For Josef, whose business it had become to safeguard his people, it was nothing short of a personal mission to go out there and do what he could. Something in his eyes stopped Maria from standing in the way of his decision to join the fight. Unlike the mischievousness of his youth, there was a mature and steely determination.

"What…How long are you going to be there?" was all she could ask.

His hands came away and with a quick shrug of his shoulders and a little flick of his hands, he replied, "I don't know," but then he said more heavily, "I don't know how long I'm going to be there."

Maria picked up on exactly what he was saying. "Are we ever going to be together?"

There was a lull between them, a moment in which reality crept in, the truth that they may never be together again, but then came, as it always did, hope.

"Yes, my wife, yes: I promise you…" but he trailed off, his assurance dying with the knowledge that he could make no such promises, that the likelihood of making it through alive was slim. But then his face brightened and some of his youthful enthusiasm shone through again, as he suddenly picked her up by the waist and lifted her, almost shouting, "Come on, let's go in and enjoy ourselves - let's live a little!" with a glint in his eye, a wink, and a smirk.

As he put Maria down, the sparkle entering her eyes too, she said, only half-seriously, "Don't die or I'll bloody kill you, okay?"

Pointing at his chest in a way that said, "Who me?" he beamed and said out loud, "I'm a Krupinski, don't worry."

Still smiling, his high spirits contagious, she chided, "That's what I'm afraid of."

Then he looked at her, standing there as young and full of life as ever, but somehow more so because of the fleeting time they could be with one another, and added with meaning, "You're more beautiful than I even remember."

Maria dipped her head, her cheeks burning, as she said meekly, "I didn't fuck that driver, you know."

"I know," responded Josef, and it was clear that he had known all along that she never would have. He put his hand to her chin and lifted it, looking into her eyes with passion, "Come, let's go."

Maria made towards the opposite tent but Josef grabbed her hand to pull her round the side. "No," he said playfully, motioning with his head, "This way." Maria allowed herself to trail behind, all the months of terror and worry dropping away and, for one precious evening, the only thing remaining was the two of them, young and still very much in love.

Chapter 30

Going For Gold

1980 Westminster, UK

Standing at a payphone outside London's grandiose Parliament Buildings, waiting for the operator to connect his call to Geoff, who was in India - ratifying the final deal that would make his crew the official British salvage team for the HMS Edinburgh - Eddie contemplated the fact that his job was now over.

Despite still being smartly attired after his brief liaison with Prince Charles and Prince Philip, and then a very far from brief meeting with a representative of the Department of Trade, he was weary and on edge. It had been a rather difficult meeting, never mind the thankless journey it had taken to get to this point.

This was not to put down the considerable efforts on behalf of Geoff and his team, but that was where it lay: Geoff had a team. Eddie had done a great deal of the financial footwork alone. A man on a mission, scooting around England and Europe tracking down information and funds, negotiating deals, always one step closer but not quite there.

Just one man and an attache case.

Attaining the cash it took to hire equipment and pay for hotels and flights had been a task in itself, constantly plugging holes where the money just seemed to leak out in every direction, the costs racking up by the day. Jens would have laughed to hear that Eddie had been less a project manager than a firefighter, dealing with financial constraints and loopholes at every turn. Always another permit to acquire, another licence to pay for, another deposit to lay down, another palm to grease.

No one would ever know just what he had endeavoured to come this far. Which was actually to his choosing. Eddie had made it clear to Geoff, from the very beginning, that he wanted no mention to be made of his name in any press statements, and that his name had to be stricken from any records open to the public. It was the find Eddie was after, not the fame.

Financially everything was in place now for the last leg of this project to go ahead. All that was left was to let Geoff know, without giving up the game to anyone else.

Geoff eventually picked up on the other end and Eddie gave a brief hello before getting right to it, each of them choosing an economy of words, both to cater for the one-second delay for each sentence to carry over the phone lines and also because the information they were sharing was valuable. For the latter, they both spoke in the code that had been formulated by one of Geoff's team.

Having not long ago been in that meeting at the Rotterdam docks and heard from Rollie Visser's mouth that the Russians had paid him a visit, Eddie was all too aware that others might be listening in. There was only so much one could do in terms of remaining alert. In public, there were all manner of people around you at any one time, and even here, at the payphone, both booths left and right of him were taken up with other callers. Spy, he was not. So, having scribbled down what he needed to get across in the language of their particular code, he wasted no time to convey what, in layman's terms, was, "Deal's done my end, we're good to go."

And that was it.

The line went dead and Eddie was left holding the handpiece. He took it away from his ear and looked at it with a wry snort, before replacing it and turning around to look for a taxi.

In that moment it struck him fully that, for his part, he had done all he could possibly do, the rest was in Geoff's hands now. He looked down to the right and then to the left, backtracking in his mind to be sure that he had indeed covered everything he needed to from his end, then, with a single nod of assurance, he shrugged his shoulders and walked over to a coffee stand.

There, on a metal chair, sitting amongst tourists, businessmen, government workers, and probably the odd MI6 agent, Eddie clutched onto his satchel and its precious cargo, as though it was so much gold. Inside the bag, of course, was Teichart's log, the final piece of the puzzle in locating the Edinburgh. As soon as he and Jens had left the War Records Office in Berlin he had made the phone call to Geoff to offer up those confirmatory coordinates, enabling the dive team to be sure that they had set their search in the right location. Now Geoff would be on his way to Murmansk to finalise the search and make preparations for the dive aboard Rollie's ship.

◇

In transit, sitting on the floor of a rickety old Russian Kazan helicopter, with the rest of the dive team and their gear, Geoff was indeed headed to the North Sea to continue the final leg of the operation.

Now, with absolute diligence and discipline, they would have to undertake the technical and also very physical job of reaching the wreck on the deep seabed. What Eddie had told Rollie about the location of the Edinburgh being confirmed, had been a lie. Yes, Geoff's team had been near enough there, having used deep penetrating radar to confirm a vessel on the seabed that may well have been their prize, but they were yet to get down there and get eyes on the ship.

There were, of course, other ships that went down in and around the same location. It was carnage down there. The seafloor was one giant wreck. And it had not been a small area that they had needed to cover in the search, it was 150 miles of sea. It had been a game of reduction, narrowing down the possibilities and cancelling out the wrecks that were not relevant. In the ice of the north and the unpredictable Arctic waters, this had been an arduous task, to say the least.

On a severely cold and snowy day out on the Barents Sea, on the fringes of the Arctic Circle, whilst running their own searches, the competing Russian salvage team had also been spotted at 72.09N, 34.20W.

They had been completely off the mark.

In the meantime, running on radio silence and continuing to work with strict codes to throw off Soviet surveillance, Geoff's salvage crew needed to evaluate the validity of the information that Eddie had gathered along with their findings. The first task had been to narrow down the position of the Harrier to the nearest location where it took aboard the survivors of the scuttled Edinburgh. This then authenticated the other information the team had acquired from the crew member's diary account containing the HMS Edinburgh's final coordinates and Teichart's log, because they were all within the same zone. Working with these locations, it had been a matter of sweeping the area around these coordinates and then verifying whether what they saw on the radar had definitely been the Edinburgh. One of the clues the team took into consideration was the fact that the dimensions of the Edinburgh would fall short of the standard size of a light cruiser, remembering that a great chunk had been taken off her rear end by the second torpedo.

Having located and pinned down two plausible wrecks within the search zone of the coordinates that they had been working from, a choice had needed to be made as to which one they would concentrate their energies on investigating. By the time they had reached this point, it was already August and as the winter months approached, the window in which they could operate in those waters was reducing day by day.

A call had been made and the dive team had headed down into the darkness of the deep blue sea, everyone holding their breath to find out whether their gamble would pay off.

◇

Back home, Eddie, and Anja too, had been waiting on tenterhooks for a phone call from Geoff. Instead, they were getting calls from family, friends, funders, sponsors and bankrollers, wanting to know when Eddie would make good on their investment.

The following year, on the 18th of May 1981, just short of forty years after it had sunk, Eddie got word that the wreck of the stalwart, battered and long-hidden HMS Edinburgh, had been officially located. The team got eyes on at a depth of 243 metres (800 feet), 250 miles North-Northeast of the Soviet coast at the Kola Inlet.

From that point onwards it had been a nail-biting wait to see whether Geoff's team would find the gold and be able to bring it back up to the surface.

Now, five months later, Geoff's call came, his simple message being, "We've done it, mate. We've got the gold."

On the 7th of October, the dive had been called off due to the worsening weather conditions, but not before the team had retrieved a good haul of gold. In the papers and on the telly the picture of Geoff's team was shown over and again, all of them standing behind a pyramid of solid gold bars, celebrating like anyone would after the successful completion of the mammoth task of finding and retrieving the great prize aboard the HMS Edinburgh. In the treasure-hunting world, from the freelance investigative reporter to the respected historian, from lowly salvor aboard his two-man boat to high-end investor with his fleet of ships, it was none other than finding the Holy Grail itself.

Yet, whilst up and down the country everyday people and royals alike lauded the find as a national victory, Anja, upon hearing the news, stood with her hand on her heart, looking down with a combination of closure and sadness, saying quietly, "It's finished, Dad. We beat the bastard. You can rest in peace."

Chapter 31

The Choice

1949 Brindisi, Italy

The crackling sound of a jaunty record, spilling out the sound of Italy, came from the windows of a tenement flat in Brindisi. Entering the same apartment, out on the southwestern coast, on a broad Italian peninsula that juts out into the Adriatic Sea, were the sounds of seaside ships coming and going, the odd call of a fisherman from the docks not far away, and the incessant cry of seagulls.

Sitting in an armchair, wearing only a white vest and boxers in a vain effort to stay cool in the close summer heat, Josef flicked through a newspaper, gathering all the smatterings of news that his broken Italian would allow. Three years on from the war and he was yet to return to his homeland, not sure now that he ever would, but he was still keen to find any mention of how things were going back there.

"Food, Josef! It's ready, *amore mio*," Sofia called from the adjoining kitchen.

"Okay, okay," he called back. "Where's Giovanni?"

"*Piccolino?*" she said, looking back over her shoulder from where she was dishing up a tangy pasta and sauce. "He's sleeping."

"Hmm," was all Josef responded with, his eyes looking her up and down, appreciating her beauty and finding no shame in displaying his desire for her. Softening Sofia's cutting

Italian facial features, dark wavy hair flowed down her back to where an apron was tied around curvy hips. The meal could wait.

Taking advantage of his pause, Sofia said tentatively, "Josef, I want to ask you something…"

"Yes, hmm," he responded without really taking note of what she was saying, his mind on something completely different.

"Josef!" Sofia called, but still could not break him out of his fantasy, so she threw a dish towel at him.

"What? What?" he said defensively, still wearing a naughty grin.

"Josef, you never listen!" she shouted, but not angrily. Seeing that she had his attention now and, unashamedly using the fact that he was feeling frisky, she stated, "Josef, I want to marry you."

"Okay," he acquiesced, as though it was the simplest action to take. "Whatever you want, Sofia."

At this, Sofia untied her apron and cast it aside, danced over and kissed Josef on the forehead, then stood back to plait her hair, so as not to let it get in the way of their lovemaking, all the while saying, "I want bambinos."

"Mmm," was the only response she could get out of Josef once more, now that he was entirely enraptured by her, putting his newspaper down on his lap.

She leant forward and took his cheeks in her hands and half-shouted, "Bambinos, bambinos!"

"Yes, yes," Josef caught on. "Bambinos."

Just then there was a knock at the door. Sofia spun, her floral skirt fanning out, and she skipped over to answer, taking a letter from the postman. Looking at it as she closed the door, her whole demeanour changed from jubilant to apprehensive. She stood for a few seconds, just looking down at the letter in her hands, turning it over, and then over again, her whole body tensing as she connected with what its contents would certainly mean for them.

Quietly, she looked up and said, pensively, "Josef, there's a letter for you."

"Okay, thank you, kochanie," he said, not picking up on the change in her, as she came over and placed the letter gingerly on the arm of the chair. Then she let her hair down again, stepped back into the kitchen and stoically picked up her apron, put it back on, and began placing the food into a container.

Now it was Josef's turn to stare at the letter. A part of him had been waiting to receive such correspondence ever since the war had come to an end. But the days had turned into weeks, the months into years, and no word had been sent of where Maria was, or whether she was even alive or dead. Initially, he had hounded the war office, trying to get any form of confirmation as to the last whereabouts of his wife, at least, but even there they had not been forthcoming and had eventually told him that she was likely to be dead, that thousands would never be found.

As time had gone by, life had stepped in, and what had at first been an ardent search, had been delayed by finding work and then, of course, finding love. Next came a baby and so, with new responsibilities and priorities, another mouth to feed and his continuing life with Sofia, the time had extended, drawn out, and the need to find out where Maria was had become a dull ache that surfaced from time to time, more like mourning than hope.

Daring to pick the envelope up, with its official war office stamps and return address, he accepted what he had not wanted to admit for the past years, that he had been living with Sofia on borrowed time.

His eyes went over to Sofia, standing at the sink now and washing dishes slowly, clearly trying to find something to do so that he could be left in peace to read the letter. It only made his love for her grow.

But then, with a sigh of surrender, he carefully ripped open the envelope and pulled out the letter inside, immediately recognising Maria's untidy scrawl. Before he had even read a word, the tears had begun to fall. She was alive! And then, as he read, waves of relief and joy mixing with resignation and sadness, he learned not only that Maria was alive and well and living in England, but that she had a baby.

His baby.

Anja.

His mind went back to that night in Persia and he figured that the child would be five years old now. Six years old. His baby. He had a little girl.

And a wife.

Putting his head in his hands, he tried to console himself that he had not known Maria was alive, and certainly not known that she was pregnant. He had written to her during the war but had never received any confirmation that the letters got to Maria. Whether she had done so and written back did not matter. She was alive and he had a daughter, and now he had a choice to make. It seemed like no choice at all. Maria was his wife. He still loved her. They had been through a lot together. The very thought of being with her again had kept him going through the darkest hours of the war.

Of all the letters he had ever hoped to receive from Maria, in the end, this was the only one that counted: to know that she was still alive and safe.

Yet he looked up again at Sofia.

Sensing his dilemma and the fact that he was looking at her and why, she turned around to meet his eyes, a plate still in her hands, dripping water and soap suds to the floor. She knew. What woman would not know? It was all there in his eyes full of love and pain and apology.

There was a choice to be made, for sure, a terrible choice, but Sofia was a faithful woman and would never stand in the way of the bonds of matrimony. So the decision lay with Josef, and, tough as it was to make, there was never really any question about which way he would go.

Right then Josef's vision turned inwards, to all the years he had spent with Maria, even before they had been married. Sneaking behind the shed to try some vodka. Hands touching in the same pot of cherries at harvest. Games of cards with Lusha where his only object had been to lose to Maria. Days when, after they were married, she came to him at the station to bring him lunch, her eyes full of pride in her hardworking man. Maria's defiance of Kaliakov when she came to see him at the Gulag train. Her fear and courage on the day he helped her escape. And finally, her starlit beauty, once more, on that passionate night in Persia.

He prayed to God for help then, but not in deciding.

He prayed for the courage to do what he knew was right.

Epilogue

2023 Birmingham, UK

Here I am, forty years later, the story told and retold, and all I am left with is gratitude for my grandparents, Josef and Maria. For their courage and resilience, for all that they endured when they were apart, and for sticking it out together afterwards. And now it has fallen to me to honour their legacy.

A couple of generations down the line, both the tale and the influence of the gold have remained with our family, like a shadow, everpresent, emerging from time to time. And that is how it came to me at first: bit by bit, the narrative unfolding a little more with each family interaction, the full picture always eluding me. Until, many years ago now, my uncle, Eddie, told me his side of the story and, laughing, said that it had the ingredients for a great movie. I agreed and it sat with me, resurfacing from time to time like it always did, especially when I heard what was happening in my family as a result of being involved with the money that came out of the salvage.

In the midst of it all, there are still parts of the story that amaze me, simply in terms of the trials and adventures my family faced, yet what stands out the most are those remarkable connections between my family and the gold. How my grandfather was tortured and used by the same man who, on the Soviet side of things, would go on to oversee the search for the HMS Edinburgh, with his son at the helm.

Then there is my grandfather's daughter, Anja, my aunt, marrying someone who happened to get into the salvaging game, of all things, and then ended up as part of the team that retrieved the gold on behalf of Britain. Uncanny.

In the days commencing the locating of the wreck, Geoff's dive team had proved their mettle, successfully reaching the shell of the Edinburgh and, in the end, retrieving the first bar of gold on the 15th of September 1981.

The Edinburgh had been carrying 4.5 tons of gold bullion in 93 wooden boxes, stowed neatly in the bomb room where the first torpedo had struck, and from this room, at the bottom of the Barents Sea, Geoff's team brought 431 of the 465 gold ingots to the surface.

On the 7th of October, bad weather forced the cessation of the operation, bringing the total salvage to a value of £1.5 Million at the time it was being transported during the war, and worth £45 million when it was retrieved by Geoff's team. In 2023, as I completed this book with a friend, the value of that gold came in at a clean £180 million. A few years later a second dive under controlled conditions brought up twenty-nine more bars of gold, bringing the total find to £220 million.

Five bars of gold are still unaccounted for.

Anja's brother, my father, would have nothing to do with the proceeds that came out of that project. He felt that there was a lot of bad blood there, that it was best left alone. And, true to that principle, we watched as the curse of the Tzar's Gold wreaked havoc on anyone in my family who came into contact with its wealth.

We were only ever witnesses, my dad and I, watching the story spin its thread through their lives, while we remained neutral. My only part to play has been in the telling of this tale, offering its lessons up to the world; most important of which, to me, is that, at the end of the day, all we have is family. And that is what has always been important to my father and me. You see, I was born into this story and have had it circling me all my life, and from the tale, I have drawn out only one thing. That, for all its worth, it will always be better to choose *love, over gold.*

Acknowledgements

We would also like to thank our kind and eager little army of proofreaders. Special thanks go to Michael Theobald for helping us to make sure that the readers did not get lost: his meticulous input in terms of times and dates giving bearing to each part of the story. It is worth mentioning, by way of thanks, that uboat.net was an excellent source of information. We would also like to thank Brian Pedley for reworking the original artwork and creating our awesome website. We are grateful to Gemma Young for working so hard on the design of the cover. And, finally, we would like to mention our ever-ready team of printers at Midland Business Equipment Ltd for preparing umpteen drafts of our book at the drop of a hat.

About The Authors' Journey

Back in 2014, John and Gavin met while performing in a stage production that ran for three years. During that time they developed a close friendship. John kept mentioning that his uncle had given him a unique story to tell, this very tale of how he helped a salvaging team to retrieve the largest haul of gold in history and how the gold was impossibly and indelibly linked to their family. John went on to develop a script for a play based on the story, which he took to the Edinburgh Fringe in 2017 - the 75th anniversary of the ship's sinking.

A couple of years later Gavin was free to help John rework the script and to take the play on tour. World events got in the way of those plans, however, Gavin had been urging John to work on turning the play into a novel: there were just too many great details to the story that had to be omitted to fit into a play. So, from February 2020 to December 2023, the pair worked away for two hours or so every Sunday, crafting this extraordinary tale.

Find out more about the authors at
www.loveovergold.co.uk

Printed in Great Britain
by Amazon